COLD COMFORT

Ravella Ives

RIPTIDE
PUBLISHING

Riptide Publishing
PO Box 1537
Burnsville, NC 28714
www.riptidepublishing.com

Cold Comfort

Cover art: L.C. Chase, lcchase.com
Editors: Grace Stack, Carole-ann Galloway
Layout: L.C. Chase, lcchase.com

ISBN: 978-1-62649-918-8

First edition
December, 2023

Also available in ebook:
ISBN: 978-1-62649-917-1

COLD COMFORT

Ravella Ives

RIPTIDE
PUBLISHING

If you've read these words, this one's for you.

He stepped down, trying not to look long at her, as if she were the sun, yet he saw her, like the sun, even without looking.
—Leo Tolstoy, *Anna Karenina*, 1878

Calm down, you young neurasthenic. Look—the darkness beyond the windows is at peace, the cooling fields are asleep.
—Mikhail Bulgakov, "The Towel with the Cockerel Motif" in *A Young Doctor's Notebook*, 1925-6, trans. Hugh Aplin

TABLE OF CONTENTS

CHAPTER ONE

A Siberian railway in 1919.

The lieutenant's blood was on my face still when I saw them coming.

I let the snow fall from my hand, stuck my head through the boxcar door, and called for the Captain. The few flurries that existed in October had managed to catch up with us when we'd stopped, and they had been dusting steadily ever since. Enough to cover the ground; not quite enough to freeze the engine's water. More's the miracle. I scuffed absently at what little snow had gathered around me and hissed for James Horrocks again.

He glanced at me from the smoky yellow dimness of the car. "What is it, Ransome?"

"Can I catch you for a minute, sir?"

He eyed me up—somewhere between July and October he'd managed to perfect an air of haughty exasperation that he liked to practise from time to time. Then he climbed heavily off his luggage pallet and picked his way through the debris and men between him and the door. We were a burden, always. Another task, another duty. I did sympathise, but now was not the time.

After he'd jumped down beside me, he pulled the slider to without latching it. It shouldn't have been open in the first place. That was my fault.

"What's wrong?" he asked. He barely ever addressed me as *lieutenant*.

I gestured at him to be quiet and pulled him to where I was standing; pointed carefully through the darkening forest. Men heaving delicately over the tracks behind us. Three of them.

"What do you think, sir?" I asked.

There was a beat. Between his breaths, I could hear the snow sputter in my ear. Then he said, "I don't think it's good."

We exchanged a glance. People didn't come out here alone if they weren't running from or to something else.

James's voice was low. "Has the stationmaster said anything?"

"Nothing that hasn't come from you, sir. Should I raise the alarm?"

He pursed his lips, sucking his teeth. "Not yet. Don't get everyone panicked. They're anxious enough to move off as is. What else is out there?"

"Nothing I've seen sir," I said. "Just them."

In almost twenty-four hours, just them.

James shifted his weight from one foot to the other, unknowingly picking up a bit of grave dirt as he did so. "Your eyes are better than mine—" A branch shrugged some snow off its shoulders behind us. He huffed a nervous laugh, met my eye, then frowned. "Hang on. You all right?"

I opened my mouth to reply, and he made a sudden, harsh sweep with his arm. As if he'd been about to cuff me and stopped himself. "You've got something on your face."

I touched my cheek. "I know."

"Then get it off!"

He'd been about to rub it off for me. He kept forgetting we weren't rank equals anymore.

As I took another handful of the half-frozen snow, he asked, "Can you pick out a uniform?"

I glanced back over to the empty space beyond our last flatbed. They were still there. They didn't seem to have come any closer. "No, sir, not properly."

A muscle in his cheek twitched. "Right." He started forward.

I grasped at his shoulder, anxiety dissolving protocol. "Horrocks, where are you *going*?"

He tried to shrug me off. "I'm going to see who they are, Lieutenant."

"James, don't be an idiot." I wheeled him round to face me. "Get the stationmaster—he's the only one who's going to know who's been through here."

"What's he going to do? Shoot them for us? It's the middle of the bloody night, Ransome, he'll be in bed."

"Then get the CO!"

He laughed—a startled, incredulous beat. "And leave our half the train undefended? Just to get there and back again? Christ, if this is some half-cocked Trot offensive, what's that going to solve?"

He must have seen my face, whatever it was holding—I wasn't sure myself. But he softened, visibly. He looked more like James and less like Horrocks. "Have him sent for and tell him what's going on," he said. "Send Owen. I need you here. Get ready to raise the call if we need."

Then he put a hand on his pistol and waded out through the dark. I turned gingerly back to the carriage. Inside, I could hear the clank and clatter of the dinner things being cleared away, and I grabbed the doorframe and swung myself inside. "Rifles to hand, everyone."

"Oh?" Gallehawk put his accordion down to the side. Thank Christ he wasn't stupid enough to have been playing the thing. "Trouble brewing, sir?"

"Men approaching," I said, as quietly as I could. "Captain's gone out to check. Owen, run and fetch the major, will you?"

Owen began unfolding himself as Gallehawk got a swift elbow in the ribs from the pallet next to him.

"You hear that?" Jacobs, our big West Country farm boy asked. "You've attracted them with that sodding instrument. They've finally come to shut you up."

Gallehawk flipped a catch on his case decisively, accordion packed. Had he been cleaning it, perhaps? He loved that thing, even though it wasn't his. "Laurie, man. If anything, they've come to shoot me for bringing you along."

I clenched my teeth. "Chaps."

"For Christ's sake, shut up," Jacobs snapped at Gallehawk. "You're irritating the lieutenant."

Gallehawk flashed me an ally-winning smile. "Am I, sir?"

I ground my teeth again. "Get your fucking rifle."

He glanced at me, kicked-dog startled. That summed up the dynamic within my men. There always had to be one taking it too far, and I often overcompensated with discipline in response.

"All right, sir," he said.

Owen slipped past me on his way out the cattle car and gave me a nod before disappearing into the darkness down the train.

I didn't know how I felt about Owen, then. Or he about me. We hadn't yet worked it out.

I shouldn't be liked. I shouldn't *want* to be liked. Yet however detestable it made me, it was increasingly hard not to crave their approval. When we spoke, a sort of jolly masculine bravado would grow over me, like fur over an old wound to try to make me fit in, be one of the pack. A man's man. But no one likes a teacher who panders to their students, and no one likes an officer who wants to be friends. Especially one who tries to make himself one of them.

What was the Housman quote? *"Square your shoulders, lift your pack, And leave your friends and go"?*

I wondered if my men could see through that way of thinking. Perhaps all was well and they didn't. Either way it didn't matter—after all, I might not have the same command come morning if we kept losing officers.

It had been a gut shot. What a bloody awful way to go.

When the last rifle was set, I jumped down out of the car, took out my sidearm, and rounded the side of the carriage. A hefty old Webley is well suited to rain and mud, but not the splintering cold. I didn't know how she'd fare through another winter. We'd been kitted out exclusively with what the army had had spare from the war in France without much thought as to how it might suit us out in Russia. *"Dear to friends and food for powder."* Isn't that just what we were?

I ran almost immediately into Horrocks, who was standing just behind the rear coupling and watching our strangers' approach. He held his hand out to steady me—I grasped it and hoped he couldn't feel my fingers trembling. Battle nerves, back at last.

There wasn't anything new in seeing people alongside the tracks. They'd always been there. They'd been there when the crops had started to rot, the vehicles started to rust, when the farmers were shooting all their horses. People had marched with us, against us. They had been us, for a few months, and then they hadn't been.

The land stretched on and on, away on either side; all those unknowable fathoms deep. The ripe yellow smell of crop-rot pervaded the air. Horizons were darkened by smoke or dust or mortars whichever way you looked. And the people between came to and from.

This time there were two of them. Two men. They weren't carrying belongings. They were carrying another man. A third, slung out between them and not moving his legs.

"I think they're ours," Horrocks said to me, careful not to raise his voice. "They've seen me, but they've not shouted. Don't think they want to take a chance with the trees."

"Do they know who we are?" I asked, taking another cautious step towards him. James was standing on the sleepers, gazing out across the dark at the men struggling towards him. Prospero watching Ferdinand come ashore.

"They will soon enough," he said, grimly.

From where we stood, we could see around the boxcar that followed ours, and out over the flatbed truck attached to it. All the troop trains were hemmed in with baggage like that. It was supposed to protect us if a locomotive came toward us at full steam packed with dynamite, which seemed much too like something out of *Boy's Own* to be a possibility. Instead, it meant we got through twice the amount of coal we should in half the amount of time.

The walkers were picking their way over the sleepers. Trying not to drag the third man's feet.

Horrocks put a hand on my arm absently. "Stay here, Ransome."

"James, for Christ's sake."

I barely ever called him "Captain."

And now they were close enough for their footsteps to carry, slightly wet against the snow. I holstered my pistol, not wanting to be a threat. Not wanting to be an accelerant. But I wouldn't tell my men to lower their rifles, if they asked.

The arrivals still hadn't spoken, but James had evidently had enough of the suspense. He called across to them in his wicket-keeper voice, trying to keep it as low as possible. "This is a troop train. Please state your identity before you come any farther."

There was a pause. My hand tightened on my pistol.

Then a sharply accented voice called back: "Corporal Jaroslav Hayek. My men, Privates Holub and Jandáček. Please, stop standing there and help us?"

The captain shot me a glance. I looked back at him helplessly. He gestured for me to follow him.

They were about twenty feet from the end of our train now. The gravel crunched as someone fell off a sleeper, and I turned around to see Jacobs and Gallehawk following behind hesitantly, their rifles at the ready.

The captain must have caught them out the corner of his eye, because he signalled to them to come forward.

"I have two armed men behind me," he said, levelling his gaze towards the walkers. His voice sounded firmer now. "My lieutenant here will search you both and confiscate your weapons. I will check your papers."

There was another pause, during which Horrocks seemed to read the two newcomers' faces in the weak light. "My man will take your wounded to our car," he said. "We won't keep the two of you for long."

I took my cue and drew up beside the man closest to me, putting as much steel into my voice as I could muster.

"Your gun, Corporal?"

He turned toward me, the arm of his fellow still around his shoulders. He was the man who had spoken first. Gallehawk jogged up and held the injured party's waist, then guided him to the ground as he fell off the shoulders holding him.

Even up close, I couldn't see the corporal's age. He had a haggard face and a somewhat thick, unsoldierly beard.

He held my gaze the whole time as he handed over his rifle and unholstered his bayonet. I held his.

In my peripheral vision, I could see the captain disarming the second man, identity papers in one hand. Their owner didn't seem able to do anything more than hand over his belongings and try to stay on his feet.

Jacobs stood nearby, his Enfield still uncertainly primed.

I cleared my throat and gestured to the prone figure between the two new men, whose head was lying on an uncertain Gallehawk's knee. God knows how far they'd come. "And this man's belongings?" I coughed again; tried to sound stronger. "I take it he's not carrying them with him?"

"No," came an answer. "They're—"

"Here," said Gallehawk, rolling a pack to Horrocks. It stopped short, but Horrocks grabbed it just before it disappeared off the tracks.

"His," the corporal said. "Bayonet and ammunition both. His rifle we had to leave."

I nodded and performed a quick pat down of the corporal. He was so tightly upholstered into his uniform I wouldn't be able to find a weapon quickly. All those layers upon layers we wrapped between us and the snow.

James caught my eye and gestured. I followed him to the other side of the sleepers, glancing behind me as he murmured. "Czechoslovak. Looks like the remains of a patrol."

"Oh," I said, not knowing what else to say. "Where from?"

The captain shrugged. "Best ask them. Poor bastards are scattered about like ninepins." He glanced at them once. "See to the injured man, Ransome, I'm going to fetch the MO."

I opened my mouth, my anxiety over their identity in no way allayed. *How in the hell is he so willing to trust that they're telling the truth?* While we both lacked grim cynicism of the Regulars, his capacity for naiveté astounded even me sometimes. How hard would it be for someone to find a dead Czech along the railway? If they threw on a corpse's overcoat, picked up some papers, they could be anyone. I screwed my mouth shut and kept a hand on my pistol. Better not to show them we disagreed. Undermining authority and all that. James could be a decent commander, even for a brevet, when he remembered he wasn't floating down the Cam reading Clausewitz. He deserved my trust.

As Gallehawk carried the unconscious man ahead, Jacobs and I escorted the strangers to the train, where more armed and curious figures stood lit completely by the car's lantern. Behind them, a trickle of faces were visible, emerging from the sliding doors. Post-dinner tidying had been forgotten, evidently; this was the most exciting thing that had happened since Amos had thought he'd seen that wolf.

Attacking a fully armoured troop train would be suicide, if there were only three of them. Surely they wouldn't. Not now, so close to the end.

Owen—the captain's ostensible batman—was sat on his haunches beside the bloke Gallehawk had just hauled in, framed by the carriage door. He dragged the man back as we approached, making him as comfortable as possible on the open floor. Then the corporal climbed heavily aboard, using the side to lever himself, and reached out for his remaining fellow.

Jacobs and I followed, brushing sleet from our greatcoats and stamping. Our uniform really did seem to be designed to hold the water.

I looked down at the wounded man. There was no colour in his face.

Owen got to the floor with Gallehawk, and they scrambled together a makeshift pillow from the casualty's pack and part of Evans's old blanket. The corporal undid the man's coat. One side of his midriff was significantly darker than the other. His officer's mouth twisted.

"Climbed over a log this morning and stumbled," he said, sitting on his heels. "Impaled. Could not walk by himself. Became unconscious an hour ago. We stopped the bleeding as best as we could, but it's a matter of time."

I nodded sagely. This wasn't the best moment to introduce myself.

"What's his name?" I asked instead, coming down to the wounded man's level, hoping the corporal would follow the lead if I dropped my guard.

I was already trying to piece together where the Czechoslovaks could stay. This carriage wasn't full—and less so than it had been this morning—but of the beds free, two were being used for storage and one of them had been Evans's. Whatever happened, someone would be on the floor. I didn't know if it would be us or them. Us, presumably, but after all the fuss made about proper officer carriages last year, I couldn't be sure.

Not that the fuss had done us any good.

The corporal caught my eye. "Holub. Adam."

"I'm sorry," I answered, remembering my question. "Were you close?"

"No."

I wondered if I should say anything else and decided that I shouldn't. I held my hand out instead. "Lieutenant Ransome."

There was a snowy scuffle by the door, which announced the arrival of the captain followed by the medical officer: a small and direct man by the name of Bannatyne. The captain helped him up and then forcefully smiled at us.

"Sorry about that. I hope you understand. I've just talked to our major; he wants you all to report to him in the morning. Until then, make yourselves at home; you're dead on your feet. Our MO's here—he'll have a look at your man."

"He is welcome," said the big corporal, stepping aside, "but we brought him here to die."

The MO looked at the dark patch on the man's midriff and the corners of his mouth turned down. He seemed to agree. "I'll do what I can," he said tightly. "Someone boil some water."

There was a brief moment of chaos as Gallehawk and Owen both tried to take down the stove at the same time. This was the most excitement we'd had for days. I couldn't blame them for wanting to be involved. The resulting *clang* made everyone glance around, including the second Czech, who'd installed himself sleepily by the doorframe. We'd been storing the little stove on the topmost bunk of one of the beds, firstly because it was used so often and secondly because it had to be separated from the other metallics since it rattled. It had been put away after dinner and must not have been balanced well.

The corporal smiled wanly at Bannatyne. "Thank you." Then to James—"I have made my formal introductions to your lieutenant."

Decorum lit up James's well-bred face. "Ransome!" he said, as if my name were a verb. "Glad to see he's been taking care of you. Captain Horrocks, 6th Royal Light Hertfordshires." James reached over Bannatyne's hunched form and took the corporal's hand. "Sorry we had to meet in such a way."

"Captain Horrocks." He smiled, shaking James's hand, and his face thawed. "Corporal Hayek. Nice to meet you. And you, Lieutenant."

I smiled and gave him a small nod of acknowledgement. I think the corporal saw it, but then cast his eyes down at the man at his feet and the atmosphere changed.

"What do you think?" he asked the medical officer. The MO glanced back up at him and shook his head.

"I'd give him something for the pain, but if he's not conscious, he's not feeling and that's the end of that. I'm surprised he lasted as long as he did."

The corporal's eyes didn't leave his man—Adam's—face. "We wanted him to be buried somewhere."

There was a brief lull, before Bannatyne said, "And you brought him all this way?" His voice was very quiet.

Hayek looked at him, then his mouth quirked at the side. "Well. Thank you, doctor. Could you see to the next one?"

The MO raised his eyebrow. "The next one?"

The other man the corporal had come with had curled himself up incredibly small and seemed, for all intents and purposes, to be fast asleep. I tried to guess his age, but he had his face buried in a scarf, which made it hard to tell.

"Oh," said the MO, eyes catching on him. "What's wrong with this one?"

"Shoulder came out a few days ago. We managed to get it back in. May be damaged."

The medical officer stood abruptly. He was a short man of about forty, but managed to convey more in that gesture than one would think. His aptitude for kinetic expression surprised me every time.

"He . . . Jesus, didn't you strap it up?"

"Of course. But after Holub impaled, we had a more pressing use for bandage."

The MO clenched his jaw, crossed over to the other Czech, and then glanced back at the corporal. "Which one?"

The corporal blinked. "Excuse me?"

"Which *shoulder*? Christ, I don't want to shake him by the bad one if it's out of its bloody socket."

"The left."

The MO glared at him thunderously, and I decided to help with heating the water.

I offered my box of lucifers silently to Owen, who smiled at me and lit the edge of the oil-soaked rag he was holding. Coal and proper meths we could never have enough of, but I'd be smelling whale oil in my sleep for the rest of my life. It was the same provisions that had been issued to the army out in France. They'd given out oil for officers to rub down their men's feet to prevent them rotting off. It hadn't worked. Mutual unenthusiasm for the idea had seen that we had more oil than we could ever use.

It burnt well, though. Even if there was no point boiling bandages, something hot to drink seemed important.

Nevis, ferrety-faced and older than all of us, sat on one of the equipment boxes looking on. He was a miner in real life. God knows how he'd ended up with the Hertfordshires. Now his expression seemed . . . 'paternal' wasn't the right word, but something close. Avuncular, perhaps. Gently knowing. Jacobs had got back into bed with a cigarette; Gallehawk was propped up alongside him with the accordion box by his feet. The captain had closed the door and tentatively hooked it shut, and everything was bathed in the yellow light from the few overhead lanterns, creating a strangely cosy scene. The MO had the other lad awake now. He blinked at us good-naturedly.

When it was lifted out of the scarf he was wearing, his face was so angular that it cast shadows of itself under his cheekbones. It was impossible to tell how much this was his natural appearance; how much had been brought on by the hunger. His face was strong enough to look like it had been sculpted, right up to the slight fingerprint the sculptor had left on his chin. He had very wide, grey eyes.

"Bannatyne, Medical Officer," the MO introduced himself coarsely. "How's the shoulder?"

I glanced over at the corporal, expecting him to interpret, but the boy answered in cut-glass English. "It's been worse."

If Bannatyne was surprised, he managed to rein it in. "Do you mind if I have a prod around?"

"Only if I can put my coat straight back on."

The MO grinned wryly. "Of course. Let's have a peek."

The water had started to boil. Owen did his best to extinguish the flame while I rooted around for the little handle it came with. The Canadians had left us with almost the best of everything, but not a stove with a handle that didn't regularly make illicit excursions. I'd thought about fashioning some kind of chain for it.

I found the handle under a few dry packets of Huntley & Palmers. Since I was down there, I killed two birds with one stone and got the tea leaves out as well.

The MO was finishing up as I had my nose in the tea. You don't hear of it going off, but one can never be too careful.

"Staying for one?" I asked. "Smells all right."

He held up his hands and shook his head.

"Thanks all the same, Ransome, but I think I'll sit this one out. Good night, everyone."

We all wished him good night in return, and Owen started dishing water into waiting mugs. I held mine out with the intention of donating it to the man with the dislocated shoulder, but when I looked back, he'd fallen asleep again. *He must need it.* I gave the tea to the corporal instead.

Even on the floor, he was about an inch taller than me. Under his beard, the twins of sunburn and wind scouring had flaked skin into his hair and down his collar. I watched as he drank about a third of the tea and carried the rest to his young fellow, still curled up by the door. He said something to him in Czech and the man twisted into wakefulness and drank. Then he curled back around himself and went to sleep again.

"That man need a bed?" Horrocks asked.

"Needs rest. We walked since daybreak. If he sleeps, I will not disturb him."

Horrocks nodded, but asked Owen to lay a bed out anyway. The man's belongings were stowed over by the door beside him, exactly where he'd dropped them. Owen dragged them over to the foot of one of the three-person bunks and spread his greatcoat over the top one. If that second soldier's arm was still a state, he'd never be able to get up there. I could see a rent in his coat's shoulder even from here. Was this from the strike that had wounded him? A remnant from when his joint had been knocked out of its socket?

The captain clasped his hands around his mug and turned to Hayek. "Where have you come from, Corporal? Today, I mean?"

The corporal blew air out through his nose. "Don't know. Middle of this fucking forest. Still not far away enough."

He spat onto the straw, paused. In the quiet, I reached into my pocket for my cigarette case. Then he said, "We had a car from a farm. Out of fuel, almost. Left it two days ago. Never have got through the trees."

I tapped two cigarettes on the top of my case and offered him one. He lit up in silence and I followed.

"A car?" asked the captain, with a forced casual air. "Impressive. Where were you going?"

The corporal exhaled, hard. "Irkutsk. Medical officer was using the ambulance as a first-aid post. I collected the mendable and tried to bring them somewhere to recover." He spat again. There was a soft but definite silence around the carriage.

Eventually, the captain broke it. "Corporal . . . was this a *medical* evacuation?"

The corporal tipped his head and started to unlace one of his boots. "We were going south. Back to the beginning. No room for those that couldn't keep up. Nowhere to keep them. Fresh men never arrived. I can drive, speak passable English. It was for the best."

"Just these two men?"

"Five. One worse than we knew; one reopened his stitches on the way. Novak knew what was coming when we lost the car and shot himself. Left me with these two." He smiled without humour. "Holub had a fractured collarbone."

Another, longer silence fell. It started to ring.

The corporal pushed his boot off and started to unlace the other. "Novak couldn't walk. Neither can he, really." He nodded to the sleeping figure by the door. "Did a knee a few years ago and the cold gets into it. No use in the field. Shame. Not many linguists left."

"Your English is remarkable."

"No one is going to learn Czech."

The captain huffed a laugh and stood. "We'll do everything we can to accommodate you, Corporal." He stretched down his hand to shake. "There's a few things I've got to get squared away with the major in the morning, but that can wait. Our company commander is overseeing the whole show from Vlady, so Major Barclay's the acting CO for the moment. He'll keep you right." James was holding himself stiffly. He had a habit of stretching out his shoulder, but he didn't like to do it in front of the men in case it seemed unprofessional. It was clear he was fighting that urge now. We all have our little tells. "Choose a bed for now, man. More than enough room. There's nine of them and only six of us."

I cast my eye around our half of the carriage. There'd been a scramble for the bottom bunks as soon as we'd been assigned—it was easy to get tipped out when travelling by train. The only free ones were on top.

The corporal thanked James and started to take off his coat. He laid it on the top bed perpendicular to the door, above Gallehawk and Owen. Opposite him, Jacobs was already fast asleep.

The captain whispered a gentle good night to us all. "I sleep in the top carriage," he explained to the corporal. "Wake my batman if you need me. Good night. Welcome to the Hertfordshires."

"Good night, Captain." Hayek nodded good night to Owen as well. If our unorthodox method of musical beds seemed novel to him, he didn't express as much.

I watched James go, all the way up to the top carriage. Then I extinguished two of the lamps, leaving one alight for people to get to bed, and slid in under my frigid covers.

This had been my favourite time when I was younger, between going to bed and going to sleep. When I was a child, I used to lie and relive my favourite parts of the day, replay tunes I'd heard. When I was a teenager, I used to think of all the jokes and phrases I'd heard and wanted to repeat one day. Things I wished I'd said in conversation but hadn't. I'd try to coax the cats to stay on my bed through the night. And I'd think of Dickie covered in mud, marshalling his men and wielding a rifle above his head, although I had no idea if Dickie had actually done that. It seemed impractical, on afterthought. I used to think of the men, the men that followed him, the men pressed together and sharing air and space.

I'd tried not to think of the men for too long.

Now, I simply lay and I thought. I couldn't say what of. Wood. The cold. The mud, the mould. The snow and the heat. God, the heat. One might read all about the Russian winter; the Russian summer was worse. I could have torn my skin off from the heat. I could have torn my skin off from the sweat, whether I'd meant to or not. Sometimes, I thought of the unfamiliar stars. How many would we pass underneath? Sometimes I thought of the woods, the size of them, the animals in them. I would only think of Russia. I could not think about anything else, even when I wanted to.

I wasn't sure if I slept at all. I seemed to lie semiconscious in the dark, the cold stealing through me. I thought of motorbikes. Outside, gravel shifted. A sentry coughed.

What a miserable work detail. All that space around you became negative space in the dark. Stand there too long and your clothes froze to your skin.

Eventually I opened my eyes, and in the low light, the figure of the young Czech soldier and the dead man's head in his lap were barely visible.

Then he looked up and our eyes met.

CHAPTER TWO

T he man smiled at me sadly.
  I uncurled from my blanket, not knowing what to do. He looked away from me now, stroking the hair of his comrade. I couldn't let him sit like that alone.

"I'm sorry," I said, redundantly. "You must have known him well."

He glanced over at me, where I was sitting up in my bed. Like a child at midnight. I could hardly see his face in the half-light. He must have struggled to make out mine too. "Not at all." His voice was quieter than I'd expected. He'd held a comrade as they'd died, but still had a mind to those around him. "I don't think I knew his name until a few days ago. But he liked horses." He paused. "He did like horses."

"You brought him such a long way."

"He has children."

"I'm sorry."

He sighed and calmed his hands. They were still in the dead man's hair.

"Here," I said, kicking myself properly free of my blanket and sleeping bag, doing my best not to disturb Jacobs. The dead man's pack lay next to the door, where his fellow must have shifted it when he tried to make him more comfortable. To give him someone to spend his last moments with. Over it was his greatcoat, still slightly damp from the sleet. I tugged it off and brought it over, negotiating my way around the other sleeping forms.

"Here," I said again, laying it over his face.

His comrade looked at me gratefully. "I should wake up Hayek."

The corporal. I glanced towards the bunk at the top, at his sleeping form. "Not just yet," I said.

I'm still not sure why.

This still time of night used to mean talking to one another back home. With porter or port, and cheese and leftovers from the kitchen. Lounging on sofas deep with that secret, after-the-party feeling. There was a magic to it, a camaraderie. Wells's dark red ocean of shadow, thickened with the blood of the covenant, et cetera. *God, I'm glad I'm not back there.* This time alone was sending me into paroxysms of pseudo-poeticism that wouldn't even be welcome in Bloomsbury.

Perhaps it was my loneliness that pushed me, or perhaps it was his.

I took the stove down from on top of the coffee box and filled it with water from the communal tank. We were entitled to our own, being so far away from the others. My mug was there, where the corporal had left it. I lit the stove quietly. "How long ago did it happen?"

"About ten minutes. I stayed with him."

"Good."

"He shouldn't have been alone."

We were both quiet for a moment. Then I stepped over to the pack on an empty bed and unhooked Evan's mug from the side.

I poured a rough quantity of tea leaves into the bottom of both mugs. The water started to simmer. While I was standing, I pulled the young man's greatcoat down from the bunk Owen had lain it on.

So, he hadn't been able to make it up there at all. I do sometimes hate to be right.

"I don't think we've been properly introduced," the Czech said. He wasn't wearing a sling or any strapping. I remembered what Hayek had said about their comrade's accident.

The layers on layers of wet wool might provide support enough for a healing shoulder. They'd made do with worse in France, to hear

Toby talk. Anyway, I could always offer to dig a fresh piece of gauze out in the morning.

I passed the coat to him as he offered his good hand to me. His eyes were very wide in the dark. "Jandáček. Alexandr."

"Ransome," I answered, taking it. "Pleasure."

"You too."

"Your English is good."

"Yes."

I smiled a faintly embarrassed smile. "Did you learn it at school?"

"No."

"University?"

"Never went."

"Oh. Well," I stumbled as he shrugged the coat about his shoulders. "It's remarkable, regardless."

"I know. The English are always so impressed with any form of Slavic polyglottery." He let the barb hang, and then flashed me a grin.

I blushed and dipped my head, unable to tell if he was jesting or genuinely making fun of me. "Well. It's a lot better than my Czech."

"Do you have a first name, Ransome?"

"Francis," I replied, half an eye on the simmering stove. "Are you 'Alexandr' or 'Jandáček'?"

I swallowed to stop my heart beating in my tongue. It seemed so daring to ask, but he had introduced himself with both. Wasn't it only polite to ask a preference?"

"Sasha," he answered. "Are you 'Francis' or 'Ransome'?"

"Whichever you'd rather," I copped out.

The water began to bubble in earnest. We'd cleaned the tin after dinner, scrubbing all the bloody bandage residue out of the corners with a toothbrush no one had ever claimed. It suddenly struck me that there was meant to be another tin. "Is there a mess tin over there by you?"

"Oh. Yes." He pulled the tin out from under his torn greatcoat and passed it over to me. It was half full of bread. "I apologise. My corporal filled it after you went to sleep."

"Not hungry?"

His coat hung lopsided on him, the torn shoulder gaping mouthlike.

He met my eyes and flashed a humourless smile. "Not hungry."

"You ought to eat."

"I'm aware." He nodded in the direction of the stove. "This is convenient."

"This?" I went along with his transparent attempt to change the conversation and gestured to the stove. "Yes, it is rather. The Canadians left it. Marginally better than a Tommy cooker. Gave us half their clothes as well." The water was just starting to steam. "There's no milk, I'm afraid, but there is sugar. Do you take sugar?"

"Do you have jam?"

"Jam?"

"If you do, I'll have a spoonful. If not, don't worry."

"It's hardly worthy of the title," I warned him.

"I'm not a fussy jam drinker."

We kept the relatively communal aspects of our supplies with us, alongside the two spare mess kits and the stove. The captain had always done it, and it blocked some of the wind from coming through the slats sometimes. I retrieved the jam and held the jar up to the light, then scraped off the mould on the surface and put a dollop in the bottom of his mug. We'd been about a quarter of the way through jam tin number two—which I think originally belonged to Nevis—for about three weeks. None of us were particularly big jam users anymore.

For want of something else to do, I fished into the pocket of my greatcoat—we'd been sleeping in them for weeks. My cigarette case was in the same pocket as my lucifers, and I lit him one from the stove. Then did one for myself.

I started to talk, for some reason.

"Mitya does that as well," I said, exhaling. "Sometimes. He's our interpreter. Liaison officer. 'Mitya' is short for Dmitry, apparently. In a roundabout way. I don't take sugar, either," I added, in an inexpert attempt to change the flow of conversation. "I used to when I was younger. Now it just makes me thirstier."

I took the water off the boil and poured it into both mugs, trying to keep my hand steady. "I miss milk, though. I haven't got used to not having it yet. We had a cow back in Yekat. Ekaterinburg," I clarified, glancing up at him. "Jacobs got her from some farm. So we had fresh milk for a while. But there's always milk powder and sugar in the Samovar, that big vat of tea in the kitchen carriage. If you can concentrate on how much you don't like tea sweet, you can forget it tastes of petrol."

"I used to put rum in mine." He smiled, tipping his head at his mug. "The Russians got me into this. Although I don't know exactly how they make theirs."

"Mitya mentioned it, once upon a time. Vareniki they call the stuff, isn't it?"

"Varenye," he said absently, the word rolling off his tongue. "Although you can eat that with vareniki too."

"Thank you," I said, awkwardly. "Haven't quite picked up the lingo."

I handed him a mug with two hands, trying to keep the worst of the heat off with my coat. We had gloves, but they were so thick and cumbersome that it was better to just go without unless your fingers were actively turning black.

"I can only attribute that knowledge to a farm we used to stay at," he said, taking the tea from me. "Kipatok and any tea under the sun."

"There's a knack to it, isn't there? Mitya told me once. You've got to keep it in and strain it through your teeth. I don't know—I could never get the hang of it. Keeps the leaves out, I imagine."

He held the mug between his two gloved palms, clasping its heat to him. As I sat down closer, bits of his face were picked out by the lantern in starker relief than they had been. He, or his corporal, had taken off his Adrian helmet. They were so hopelessly dated. Although, here was I in my cream breeches. The army had phased them out as early as they could in France because subalterns had kept getting shot and they'd reckoned the colour made them easy targets. Plus, they were a nightmare to keep clean. That meant there had been no shortage of spares to kit us out with when it all kicked off over here. Lucky us.

Like his corporal, Jandáček was strangely ageless. Any feature that might have made me think he was older than me—the stiff way he held himself, his rough, calloused skin—was counteracted by something else that made him seem so young. His dusty freckling, his big, wide eyes. But there were things I had missed about him, at first glance. The wrinkles beginning to form by his eyelids. The slight but unmistakable hint of grey beginning at his temples. He wasn't far from my age, then. Closer to thirty than twenty.

If he noticed me watching him, he must not have read it as judgement, because he reached over to me and clinked his tin mug against mine.

"Cheers," he whispered.

And so we sat and drank hot weak tea together, side by side in the middle of the forest with a dead man between us.

CHAPTER THREE

We buried him in the morning. Jacobs and David Young from the carriage ahead dug a shallow grave by the side of the tracks and laid him in it, uncovered. I think we all wanted to wrap him in his coat—or at least his blanket—but we couldn't afford to let them go. Not with winter on its way. The ground was getting so stiff and stern that this would be one of the last times we'd be able to dig, though it probably wouldn't be the last time we'd have occasion to. As it was, our sticks and shovels scratched like fleas on the back of an elephant.

When they were finished digging the hole, we left the two to have their funeral. It didn't seem right to stand over a stranger's funeral, and they hadn't invited us. The captain had lent Hayek a Bible, although I didn't know if he planned to use it. Likely James had been trying to feel useful. I tried not to listen as Hayek spoke a heavy, gentle stream of Czech behind the closed door.

"What's going on there, sir?" Owen asked, rolling up his blanket. It had just turned six. "They staying with us?"

"Erm," said James.

It was slightly too early for him to have put on his full officer bravado. I caught him in mistakes like that because I made the same ones.

I couldn't stop feeling like I was pretending all the time, and one day my men would find out. James and I had never talked about it, but I knew he felt it too. His expression was exactly the one I felt myself wearing when I was asked questions that hadn't come up in my abbreviated training. Could the men sense it? They probably humoured us, being as relatively out of danger as we could be. At least there were competent officers a carriage away.

"I'll take it up with the major. I don't suppose they'll be too much of an issue. They can stay with us until Irkutsk, I'm sure."

Owen gave an imperceptible nod.

"Beg your pardon, sir, but when exactly will that be?" asked Jacobs, caught partway trying to stuff his blanket into a passable roll. "Only I want to put the trees behind us, like. And I'm bored out of my skull."

"He isn't used to seeing bush," said Gallehawk conversationally. "Rather get back to that lovely flat scrawny scrubland. Reminds him of the girls at home."

"Or a hill," said Nevis, surprising us all by speaking. I was so used to seeing him in the shadows. "I want to see a hill."

"What?" asked Gallehawk, clearly taken back by the non sequitur.

A grin passed over Jacobs's face so boyish it hurt. He obviously sensed some fun afoot. "You know what I'd give my right arm for?" He lay down on his bunk with his arm under his head, his blond hair catching the light. I shot him a warning glance that I usually reserved for one of my cats about to jump on a table, but he managed to neatly avoid seeing it. He often did at moments like this.

"A fried egg. A fried egg on toast. That's all I want."

It had become a ritual between the men about three thousand kilometres ago, just as we were leaving Omsk. Gallehawk had started it, as was typical. He'd suddenly started reminiscing about food back on the farm, and no one had been able to stop him. James and I didn't mind. It was good for morale. Gallehawk had been instantly reinforced by Jacobs, as was also typical.

Nevis hissed and leant back. "Jesus. I haven't had an egg for a fucking age."

I've heard it said that in the army *fuck* merely serves as a warning that a noun is coming. Whoever was responsible for that must have known soldiers very well.

"With bacon. And *tomato*. Nothing tinned, like."

"Is it the weather for eggs?" asked Owen. "Besides, you don't have egg with tomato." Since he was the one true Northerner among us, I secretly felt Owen was justified in his difficulty containing his regional loyalties. Not one of the Hertfordshires on this carriage was from Hertfordshire. "Fried bread. Fried bread is the only way to properly respect an egg. Which I maintain it's too cold for."

"And what would you have?" countered Gallehawk. "Pease bloody pudding? And the egg's got to be scrambled." He was fiddling with the latch of his accordion box. It was a habit of his. "Milk. Butter. Nothing better."

"Jesus, if milk crossed my path . . . You farmers have gone mad with abundance."

Gallehawk caught Jacobs's eye and smirked. Jacobs was a farm boy, all big and wide and rangy. Gallehawk might have been as well. They were always together, which hadn't helped me tell them apart when we'd first met. They didn't look much alike; it was all in the action. Their easy stride, the comfortable, loose movements with which they sat and talked and gestured. They were so utterly at home in themselves. I found it hard to believe anyone could be so uninhibited. Confident men were a foreign language to me. I never learned to speak like them, move like them, look like them. I'd made my peace with it.

That didn't mean I couldn't dwell.

"Sausage would be good," Owen said, a fag hanging out the corner of his mouth. "Real one, like."

"Not made of sawdust, you mean?"

"They do eat that in Middlesbrough," said Gallehawk helpfully. "Had a cousin up there once. Swear he ate better at the field kitchen."

"And here you are, swanning about in your train carriage like a king! I haven't forgotten you carrying on in Soton about that man trying to feed you a hedgehog."

Jacobs guffawed, his kit more or less manhandled into his pack. Even Nevis smiled.

"Look, mate"—Gallehawk sat back on his heels in friendly indignation—"I do know what I saw. I'm not completely stupid."

"Fuck off did that man try and make you eat a bloody hedgehog."

"Not with the spines on, obviously! He'd peeled it first."

"Peeled it?"

"Skinned it, whatever. Not really a skin though, is it? More of an armoured coating. Anyway, they were defused and all, but I could see them. They had the little hands."

"Their feet are a bit weird," said Jacobs, knowingly. Gallehawk gestured towards him in overt thanks.

"You see? Besides, they eat all sorts of odd shit down there. No wonder I got the lurgy."

"It wasn't just you, either," Jacobs backed him up, knowingly.

"And over *here*, they don't even have the decency to tell you what's what. It's all just called 'meat.'" Gallehawk pursed his lips theatrically. "I don't trust that."

"Look on the bright side, mate. Army rations— It's rarely actual meat."

"Could one of you get the stove on?" I asked.

The conversation stopped. It was like they'd just remembered I was in the carriage.

They likely thought I was reserved. Stiff. Standoffish, probably. Not a toff in the way of James and Evans and the major, but something altogether more unknowable. More untrustworthy or insidious. In a way, I was glad I had protocol to hide behind. As an officer and—nominally—a gentleman, my silence meant I didn't have anything to say to them. It couldn't mean I wanted to join in and couldn't think of how to phrase myself. Or couldn't think what to say at all. My tenuous grip on upper middle-class status gave me that, at least. It was the only bit of reprieve becoming an officer had ever given me. That, and being able to miss my father's funeral.

Nevis got up, stretched, and cracked his back. "Bacon grease. Best way to fry an egg. I'm making tea. The tea bucket or the Canadian piss pot?"

There was a bedraggled but uniform cry of "Tea bucket." As Nevis unearthed the dixie from its tarpaulin, I glanced over at

Horrocks. It was unlike him not to try to wrangle in the breakfast conversation.

He caught my eye. His face didn't move for a second. Then he waved me closer.

"Ransome," he said in a low voice, glancing over to the men. They were all focused on the dixie. Owen was still good-naturedly sparring with Gallehawk. James looked back at me, hesitantly. "Ransome. Listen, do you think . . ."

There was a funny beat of silence.

I'd just opened my mouth to tell him to get on with it when a blast of cold air hit me from the side. The boxcar door slid open, and Jandáček's face emerged. A hot wave of guilt flashed through me as I remembered that the boisterous conversation about foodstuffs was going on two feet from a funeral.

Jandáček didn't seem to have noticed. "Captain. May I have a word?"

Christ, his accent was perfect.

Horrocks glanced back at me one last time, then at him. "Of course." He got to his feet, nodding at the corporal outside. "Would either of you like breakfast?"

The corporal said something to Jandáček, but he was waved off. He shot Jandáček a glance that I was not, for the life of me, able to decode. Then he climbed back on board.

"Ah, Corporal," Gallehawk said. "Tea?"

The corporal, minutes fresh from having buried one of his own men, gave Gallehawk a bewildered glance. I was still thinking of how he'd looked at Jandáček. It had been paternal, cut with something . . . else.

Not *else* else. I know how to spot that. I know when I see it. This was a concerned, helpless frustration that put me on my guard for some reason.

The tea was brewed by the time the door swung open and Horrocks got in, seeming much brighter, which was odd. Jandáček came behind, still in his torn coat. Horrocks reached down to help him up. It was higher than it looked.

"Tea for me too, please, Nevis," said Horrocks, rubbing his gloved hands together. Early morning in October could still cut below freezing. "Owen, could you run a message up to the major? Tell him I'd like to meet with him after breakfast if he can. Provided we're not moving off."

"Sir," said Owen, extricating himself from wherever the conversation had taken them. My eyes followed him out. A crude wooden cross, lashed together with shoestrings, stood by the side of the track where it hadn't before.

"Tea, sir?" asked Nevis. Still in thought, I said something and he pressed a hot mug of tea to my hands.

It really was almost unbearable without milk.

He gave one to Jandáček too, who didn't ask for jam. I gazed at him, remembering our midnight conversation. Remembering how he'd held that man while he died.

Jandáček took a tentative sip and his face tightened. He was so wan against the frost.

Gallehawk put down his mug and turned to Hayek. "Corporal. What is your opinion on fried eggs?"

I flashed a warning glance at Gallehawk. Breakfast was not the first worry of a man whose day had started with a funeral. But the corporal met his eyes, squared up to him. "On a roll. With smoked sausage."

"Oh, we're back to sausages." Jacobs fell back onto his pack again.

"Have them with tomato too, do you?" asked Gallehawk, his guard up

"You eat sausages with fresh honey."

Horrocks hummed, and then said decisively, "Mustard."

"Mustard," Jandáček agreed, tipping his mug towards Horrocks. Hayek nodded in supplication.

I smiled wryly and joined in. "I'm with Jacobs. It's honey, I'm afraid."

In the garden we'd had bees. They'd made honey with the lavender my mother had grown leading up to the front door.

Gallehawk raised his eyebrows. "A bit of Home Counties loyalties going on here, do we think?"

"What about you both?" I asked, trying to deflect the inevitable homesickness nibbling after too much debate over provenance.

"Where's home for you? Prague?" It was the one place I knew, so I hoped it was right.

"No," said Jandáček, with an enigmatic expression. "A while away from Prague."

"North or south?"

"North. I'm from the north. The corporal's from South Bohemia."

The corporal gave a tight smile.

"Expect you're all desperate to get back, now Austria and the Fritz are out?" Horrocks asked.

I shot him a sharp, speechless glance.

"More than you know," the corporal replied darkly.

Owen's head appeared at the door, shortly followed by the rest of him. "Major wants to meet you at eleven if that suits you, sir," he said, hauling himself inside. "If all goes to plan, we'll be back on the move by twelve."

This piqued Jandáček's attention. "I meant to ask, Captain. If you don't mind. Have you been here long?"

Horrocks took a hot swallow of tea and peered at him good-naturedly. That was James's command strategy, stripped to its bare essentials. "Two days. Bolshie wrecked a post train, and it's taken all this time to get it off the rails. We've been sat here waiting for the all clear since."

"No track defences?"

"What we stand in." Horrocks smiled sadly, glancing down at himself. Overcoat, a bayonet. His pistol around his neck on a rope.

Just us, among the tins and Palmer's and caggage. In the back carriage, with all our spillover belongings.

Jandáček raised an eyebrow but didn't comment. He didn't need to.

Our train was the standard, depressing huddle of cattle carriages that exemplified the exodus out of Central Russia. Apparently when Colonel Ward arrived, hurtling up-country to the Middlesexes, he'd had a fit. An officer travelling in a cattle cart lowered the entire standard of the country one represented. Allegedly.

It was enough that we all had somewhere to sleep and were able to get out of the Urals at last. Not everyone had been so lucky.

"You don't think it's impractical, do you?" I'd asked James, back in Omsk when we'd both been lieutenants. "Badly armed train and all of us sprinting to get to the nominal CO. It wouldn't be hard to take a pot-shot."

"I don't see why anyone would." To his credit, he seemed to genuinely believe what he said next. "The naval gun will put them off."

"Errant partisans six metres from the track aren't going to be blown to kingdom come by a ship's gun attached to a railway car. And we haven't got the shells for it."

"That isn't common knowledge," he said, sharply. "And I'd suggest not mentioning it again to ensure it stays that way."

I'd snorted, scuffed my foot against a sleeper. The Russian gauges were so wide. "And where are we going to eat?"

"In our carriages, I assume."

"Which one? The officers' or the one we're billeted in?"

"I'm not sure. No one's told me."

No one told me either, so our meals became a generic muck-in. The rations were shared, the stove was set up and washed and taken down. We had a mess carriage of sorts, for dry storage and the Samovar and all the water. During the day, it was where we stored the quartermaster.

All of this disorder because of the retreat.

"If we're moving off, we best have something to eat," I said brightly. "I've got some porridge set aside."

Owen eyed me sceptically. "The buckwheat, sir?"

"I'd never do that to you. Here."

I'd been saving up my oatmeal rations, generally not being a porridge eater. The spoonfuls of Quaker Oat Pudding, which were expected to serve as lunch, came into their own once hoarded together. I didn't know how many ounces I had. It should get round us, just about. "Pass me that tin, Owen."

I emptied the small bundle I'd fashioned from parts of an unwearable shirt into the tin, alongside water from the storage tank. We'd have to top that up soon.

Owen took the tin back and arranged it to fit the stove. "Damn generous of you, sir."

I waved him off. Better put it towards four of them than one of me. Besides, if what we'd seen coming down the line continued, I'd rather they save their own.

I'd realise later that what food shortages we came across were nowhere near as bad as it would get. I only met one man who had been there at the time, after we'd gone. He told me so little about Russia, and only that the night before he walked into the sea.

By the time the porridge was done, thick and burnt at the edges, I was almost ready to eat it myself. I brought down the jam for sweetening. Owen fetched around mess tins and set them down beside me.

"Oh Christ," said Jacobs, hanging over his shoulder. "Jam's gone to hell."

I thought I'd scraped off the most offensive of the mould last night, but evidently I hadn't caught as much as I thought.

"It was close enough already. Do you want jam in yours, sir?" I asked, offering James first refusal as his position allowed.

James wrinkled his nose. "I'll pass, thank you."

"I won't." Jacobs pushed his tin towards Owen. "I think that might be my own jam."

"You donated to the communal as well as any of us," said Owen sternly, giving him an extra spoonful, anyway. I glanced up at Jandáček, unconsciously. He seemed to be asleep again. I hoped he was all right.

"Stick another spoonful in for him too," I said, clapping Owen on the shoulder. "He looks like he needs the energy."

"How is he?" Horrocks asked the corporal, evidently sharing my concern. "Didn't he sleep last night?"

I thought of what had happened in the night and kept silent.

Hayek knelt down and shook Jandáček gently by the shoulder, and then again. Jandáček came awake, groggily, and waved the tin away. Hayek said something sharply in Czech, and Jandáček took the tin off him and gave him a fierce glare. My eyes switched instantly to the corporal. If he'd noticed that little insubordination, he hadn't yet registered a response. They must have been together long enough for hierarchy breaches to become the norm. Or perhaps it was just paternalism.

I'd put the corporal in his late thirties if I had to pass judgement. Perhaps I should find for sure.

The corporal took his place back among us as if nothing were amiss. Jacobs had cleaned his tin out and was now sucking his finger absentmindedly, like a child. "Any more of that jam?"

"Probably not enough to get us to Vlady," I replied.

He shrugged. "Jam tomorrow then, sir."

Horrocks choked on a quick half laugh.

Owen got up automatically, taking the tins from me and Horrocks. He filled the dixie with the remains of the water from the tank, collected the rest of the tins, and jumped down onto the side of the tracks.

I still don't know which disconcerted me more about the landscape beyond us: the forest or the steppe. The wide bloody steppe.

Now that the sun was up proper, I should really get on with the rest of my day. I left them—Nevis in his customary corner, Jacobs and Callshawk talking absently—stepping off the carriage like swimmers. Owen was kneeling a few feet from the buried men, scrubbing with that same toothbrush I'd used the night before. He nodded at me as I went by.

I passed three cleaning, numerous brushing their teeth. One man was perched on the side of a boxcar, emptying his boots of soil or stone, a cigarette dangling from his mouth. He saw me before I clocked who he was and raised a hand. "Morning, sir!"

"Morning, Sergeant," I said, pulling level with him. "How are things at your end?"

"They're much of a muchness, sir," he said, his breath misting in the air. "Staying for breakfast?"

"I've already eaten I'm afraid. Just making sure you're all still here. Stevens all right?"

"Very much here, sir. Stevens seems up to his old tricks."

I smiled wryly at him. If you had asked a child to draw a picture of a sergeant from a story book, he would have drawn Brown: an old sweat, staid and avuncular. I liked him. And I appreciated his reassurance. Kim Stevens had started coughing and rattling as we'd left Omsk. It was nice to know he was on the mend.

Some of the chaps the army'd shipped in from Bombay had been riddled with influenza by the time they reached us in Hong Kong. A lot of them had missed the boat to Vlady, still holed up in bed while we sailed. I didn't know what happened to them after that. No scenario I imagined had much of a happy ending.

Infection had been at the back of our minds ever since.

"Well, as long as you make sure you're all still about by midday," I said. "Captain says we should be moving off again shortly."

Brown let his head loll back with a long, hissing breath to the sky. "Thank Christ for that, if you'll excuse me saying, sir. Cleared the wreck, then, have they?"

"We've heard so, but keep your wits about you, nonetheless. Make sure the men know their rifles are clean, et cetera. In case we're forced to stop again."

"I will, sir. Have done so, if you don't mind me saying. Don't like being surrounded by those trees."

A tight smile crossed my face. "Very wise. Spread the news, will you, sarnt? I'm going to do my best to do so myself, but I don't want anyone slipping through the cracks."

"Most certainly, sir."

"All right for provisions up this end?"

"Seem to be, sir. Haven't heard any complaints." He tapped off his ash.

"Good. Make sure your men have everything they need before we move off."

"Yes, sir."

"Good morning, sarnt."

"Morning, sir." He saluted and started the laborious process of lacing up his boot.

I walked slightly farther up the line. The officer carriage, the impotent guns, and the engine lay in the middle of the train between the flatbed trucks and the cattle cars, protected at both ends. The thing came to life with men in the morning. We were like ants over a megalithic corpse, or whatever other simile might fit.

First group to move was the guard detail. They usually stood for between an hour or two in the summer. In the winter, we had to shorten it to thirty minutes or less. You heard strange things about the cold: men could freeze solid, their teeth could explode. Nobody wanted to find out how much of that wasn't hyperbole. The hope was that we would be out before winter came around again, but it was getting closer and closer and we still seemed no nearer to home.

I stood, watching the morning unfold for a moment, still not believing what was in my purview. That men relied on me for information—correct information and reliable timing. To keep them fed, watered, alive. And how innately they expected me to do it all.

The cold was starting to insinuate itself from the frozen ground to my boots, so I walked down the train, giving half greetings until I saw a familiar face.

Toby Harris looked up from brushing his teeth and flashed me a grin.

After the war in France had started, Toby had turned eighteen and signed up for five years. With so many in for the duration and so many dead, I don't think the C-in-C had been sure what to do with the sudden flush of young officers on his hands. Some had been sent to outposts or administration. The majority had found their way over here.

He stepped over the couplings and called out "Hullo, Francis," as soon as he was in earshot. "Business as usual?"

"That obvious?" I answered. "Nice view this morning."

He exhaled stiffly. "Four days in a carriage. I'm going to have to go home and live in a crate to readjust."

"I've got bad news for you."

"The moving-off orders? Just been told myself. Can't say I'm happy about that, but it's better than sitting here for another bloody day."

He was so alive. I never knew what I gave his friendship in return.

I forced a huff of laughter. "Any news from number one?"

"Nothing yet. Think he's just as bored as we are. Although." He turned to me, his eyebrow raised. "I hear there was some excitement with your lot last night."

I tried to hide my grimace. James wouldn't be able to keep mum under orders from God himself, but I had still somehow expected better. "He's supposed to keep that sort of thing quiet."

"It's no trouble, Francis. We ought to know anyway. Besides they can't have been having a lot of fun. Kicking around out there on their tod."

We both looked over the forest together. I was barely aware of doing it. Was it a conscious choice on his part?

"All goes well, we'll be in Irkutsk by tomorrow evening," I said eventually.

He touched the wood of the car. "If all goes well. And we've still got that sodding lake to get around."

"Not for a while yet," I said optimistically. "And we don't know how long we'll be in Irkutsk for. May even get a pass."

He smiled but humoured me. "As long as I don't have to sleep on a plank while we're there, I'll take anything."

I liked it when people called me by my first name. The Army does try to stamp that out of you, but Toby had proven immune. Public schoolboys often seemed to be. Perhaps it was the institutionalisation from an early age. They learned to defy rules as second nature.

Toby's personality was a lifejacket to a drowning man. Whenever I was stuck for conversation, I would deploy him like a social grenade. He was blessed with the gift of knowing what to say and when to say it. I didn't know if he was aware of it. The people that have the breeding for it rarely are.

I touched his arm. "How are you all doing at the Ritz?"

"Smoky. We get the coal smell coming in through the slats. Mind you, I suppose you get that too. I'm sandwiched between Horrocks and a coldly furious quartermaster."

Indignation flashed through me, wrapped in humour. "Has old Waggers taken my space? I'm shocked."

"When you're holed up at the back guarding the virtue of our rolls of gauze. If not, he sleeps where Haddock is. And probably where I do when I'm not there." He fished into the pocket of his greatcoat and came out with his tin. He took a Woodbine, tapped it twice on the metal casing, and offered it to me. "Fag?"

"Peace offering?"

"For replacing you with Wags?" He put one in his own mouth and raised his eyebrows, smiling. "Name has never been less worthy of a man. You're more the wag he'll ever be. Here."

I smiled back, took the cigarette, and retrieved my lucifer. Keeping the thing in my pocket meant it was less likely to roam. He leant in, and I lit them both behind my cupped hand.

We stood in companionable silence for a few minutes. Then I exhaled, long and slow. The air was cold and crisp, and my nerves began to loosen.

"How is Haddock?" I asked, after a moment. He really was wonderfully named.

Our other lieutenant had also inherited a third of Evans's company days ago, and I hadn't seen him since. The major had divvied it up while Evans had been expiring messily on that bunk so close to mine.

Toby raised his eyebrows, tapped his ash. "He's all right. Wondering where you are." He paused, thoughtfully, and added, "Still has that mouth organ though, so he might not be around much longer."

Between Gallehawk's accordion and Haddock's mouth organ, we'd managed to land a part of the battalion so aurally objectionable I was convinced that was why the CO had given us our own train.

I smiled. "He's still practicing, then?"

Toby sighed. "Tries his best. Can't imagine why he brought it in the first place. There's a limit to what could be termed a 'home comfort.'"

"I'll swap him for an accordionist I know." I took a deep drag, let the smoke out through my teeth.

I could almost feel Toby thinking next to me. After a casual exhale, he said, "I hear the new guests are Czech."

"That's what they say."

"That's all right." He tapped off his ash. "I like the old Czechs."

We'd come across them before, just after we'd arrived. We'd still been trying to fight our way out of Vladivostok at the Ussurie line and over in the maritime provinces. Still at the Pacific. We were at a little junction of no peacetime consequence called Runovka. If you were fighting a war by train, there was nothing more vital than a junction. The Cossacks had been there too, that time. What a fuss over nothing that had been.

"Rare sentence to hear from someone of your background, Tobes."

Toby had that Tommy distrust of anyone east of Alsace, given that they'd spent the previous three years shooting at him.

He smiled, not taking his eyes off the forest. "You know what I mean. Our lot." He glanced back towards my carriage, taking a drag as he did so. "They've probably been holding down the fort here since we were still floundering about on the bloody Salient."

When it all kicked off five years ago, a group of Czechs had decided to hell with it and had sided with the Entente: us, France, and Russia. It meant that as a nation, we had all decided they were collectively all right. With the Expeditionary Force dug in through Belgium and France on the Western Front, they'd helped take up the baton in the east. If the Czechs and Slovaks helped us take Jerry down a peg or two, they'd reckoned they could draw on us for support to kick out the Austro-Hungarians when the time came. It could have worked, had the Bolsheviks not decided to throw a spanner in the works.

"How many?" he asked. "Just the two?"

"Had another man with them but he died in the night."

"Well," said Toby. "Bet they weren't pleased."

I hated him for making me laugh, sometimes. "Think they were expecting it. Their corporal said they brought him here to die."

"Better than out in the forest on his own."

"Yes. Better than that."

"So, a corporal and a . . . what? An enlisted man?"

"Yes." I tapped my elongating ash. "You should come down from your tower and have a fag with us. They're quite friendly."

"Speak good English, do they?"

"Both of them."

Toby eyed me, exhaling slowly. "Now there's a stroke of luck."

"I know," I said, preempting the doubts before he could vocalise them. "I think it's a bit too convenient as well. But Horrocks has taken their papers up to the major, and he seems to think they're all in order."

"Yes, well," said Toby. "That isn't really saying a great deal."

"They're with us as far as Irkutsk."

"And do you reckon we'll find somewhere to drop them off?"

I shrugged. "More so than here."

I let a beat of silence pass between us. I had meant for it to make my upcoming change of conversation more natural, but it made the implication of my last sentence hang in the air unpleasantly. "Do you know if anyone is missing a toothbrush?" I asked. "We've had one turn up in our carriage, and I don't know where it's come from."

"No one's asked me," he said. "Are you sure it isn't Evans's?"

"He had his pack on him, I think. Most of it was ruined."

"Was his toothbrush in it?"

I clenched my teeth. "I suppose I'll know if I get haunted for using my dead superior's toothbrush to clean a mess kit."

Toby clapped me lightly on the shoulder. "He's not your superior. You're rank equals."

"Predecessor, then. To my brevet status."

"It could be worse. You could be Horrocks. Man's wound so tight you could play him."

Toby had been a first lieutenant for longer than me, and for far longer than Horrocks had been a captain. But circumstance had dictated that Horrocks be promoted and Toby not. I used to think that secretly, Toby was glad. He'd probably had enough in France. This was a holiday for him.

That naivety astounds me now.

"None of us are that sure what's going on, so he blends right in." I sighed. I took another drag on my cigarette. "I should head off. Need to check that no one's done the bunk or starved."

"Francis, if someone deserted along the line, we'd be able to watch them run away for days." He inhaled, tapped. "But I suppose I should really be doing the same. Come up to our carriage for a drink sometime?"

"I'm up there the day after next. Unless we're in town by then."

"Let's set it as a date anyway. You can stand me a vodka."

"And you can show me how best to deal with a mouth organ. Morning, Toby."

"Ta-ra for now, Francis." He clapped me on the shoulder and headed back over the coupling, patrolling the other side of the train. Just in case.

I worked my way down the line, knocking on the doors of the carriages I was responsible for. It had gone seven, and the sun was almost completely up. Everyone I met was eating, shaving, or performing some other necessity. One man was darning his socks, still half-in his sleeping bag. I thought of Jandáček's wrecked coat.

Most people seemed to know our moving-off status when I told them, the army being the malignant gossip-factory that it was. By the time I'd reached the final carriage, checked everyone was set for provisions, checked all the rolls were called, the sun was up proper.

I wandered back down the length of the train, toying idly with the idea of topping up our water before we set off again. It started to get dark in the evening by about half past six, properly dark before eight. We could make it to Irkutsk in one long push, theoretically. If we had any solid information on the state of the railway, we might. Drivers had done that, in the past. Now they were so terrified of hitting a cut piece of track, or a blockade, a mine, a driverless train that often they didn't dare risk travelling by night. Which then meant standing still on a track for six hours, heavily outlined and obvious to the world. It couldn't be more of a lose-lose situation.

Although it wasn't warm, it was nowhere near as cold as we'd known it to be. Yesterday's smattering of snow was beginning to thaw. The layers of insulation I had on, the long-johns, the undershirt, the thermals, were beginning to feel superfluous by the time I got back to our car at the far end. I was acclimatising, I supposed.

Horrocks, Nevis, and Hayek were all stood around the car door, smoking as I approached. Gallehawk sat inside, swinging his legs. Evans's and Holub's crosses were an ashy black daub on the landscape.

I raised my hand to the men, took a final draught of my cigarette, and stamped it out under my boot.

"World still where it should be, sir?" Gallehawk asked.

"As far as I can tell, Gallehawk." I returned my hands to my pockets. Even with the comparative mildness, the gap of exposed wrist between my coat and gloves left something to be desired. "The captain may have told you already, but I want to see all your kit on standby these next few hours. Sector's only just gone quiet. Be prepared in case we're forced to stop suddenly."

Owen, from the depths of the carriage, waved the bayonet he was cleaning.

"Good man, Owen!" I called to him. "Start now, hope to be finished around eleven." No drill that morning, of course. Not while we were hemmed in on all sides. That was the thing about travelling by train. Your routine got blown completely to shit. There was time for everything when you were sat in a cattle car for eighteen hours, so the notion of having a set time to do it lost all meaning.

I hoisted myself back onto the carriage. My Webley was barely used, but I took it out anyway. I was lucky to have one. It was small and hardy, exceedingly basic looking. I liked to know it was near.

I worked my way methodically through my kit. My pull-through was almost solid with weeks of grime and uncleaned gun-oil. I'd have to see to that sooner rather than later. I checked my ammunition clip. Checked the trench club. There were tales of some fighting with spiked flails further north. How brutally mediaeval.

Another thing about travelling by train is that resisting the siren call of your bunk gets much harder. The stillness and the aches from a broken night's sleep urged me to curl myself up on my pallet and pull out a book. I had two with me. Helena had offered to send me more when we had still been at Yekat and getting regular post. Sometimes, I wished I'd said yes.

I thought about writing to both of them, ready for the post office at Irkutsk. *Dear Hels and Soph. Still in Russia, but hoping to be back any month now. My kit very clean. Love to Herring and Pilch.* It would probably still give me the devil's own with the Censors' Office.

The car jolted. There was a brief, tired cheer.

Owen was cleaning his rifle now, and Jacobs was lounging about with his belongings everywhere. Jandáček was curled up in the corner opposite Owen, asleep.

Jandáček. When he stood—and I wasn't sure I'd seen him standing long enough to judge—he must have almost been my height. Maybe taller. He'd got the soldier's frame, which told you he was used to both hard labour and insufficient rations. Even from here, I could see the shadow the morning sun made on his cheekbones. His hair was very dark.

Neither he nor Hayek had shaved. Sunburn and windburn will put you off it. In the winter, the sun reflected off the snow and it was twice as bad. The weather had been bad enough on our route; God knew what had been going on further south.

Hayek seemed like a man used to having a beard. Jandáček's beard was patchy, as if he'd grown it in frail defence against the shrieking cold. I wondered if it would be in my purview to ask him to shave.

I hadn't always known what I was, but I remember when it all fell into place after seeing that clear-faced blond who'd played Konstantin in a production of *The Seagull* I'd seen a few years before uni. I never met him. I'm not sure I'd have even liked him. But when I thought of him, he was mine. That had been the final confirmation, the moment the realisation had finally, finally hit me. I locked myself in the first-floor bathroom, mouthing the word over and over.

Homosexual.

Like I'd been struck by an arrow from above. A *coup de foudre*. Homosexual.

All that said, I'd been born to a mother who had never been one for convention. She'd given her children the middle names Artemis and Eurycleia, for God's sake . My own was Leander, much as I tried to hide it. She was a half-famous Classical dilettante, and one that had not been nearly as careful with her books as she should have been. Or perhaps she had. Perhaps she had wanted me to know or hadn't minded if I found out.

I had found out. And coming up to London to University College, I had found out again. And again and again. That strange little Uranian part of the world, even in those gloomy first months of the War.

I never found what myself and not-Konstantin shared, in my mind. But Jandáček reminded me so much of that first time.

I had, stupidly, in hindsight, brought a book about the Crimea with me. It was something I found interesting for so long that getting a book on the subject seemed only natural. And James Grant was hardly taxing; about seven pages in someone had already worn heather-mixture tweed and said "Egad!" Still, he was a step up from Henty, and there was never much to be had in the Mess if you've never quite understood the appeal of Kipling. I resolved to get to at least page eight by nightfall.

We'd started off almost an hour later than intended. Even if we pushed, there was no way we would be in Irkutsk by nightfall. So it goes. Horrocks hadn't even been able to get an appointment with the major, after all of that. He must have been too caught up in the logistics of where and when our next lot of food was coming from. He'd assured both Hayek and Jandáček that he would sit down with them as soon as we stopped.

When we had a few kilometres behind us, I curled up in the corner opposite Nevis's usual one, opened my book, and tried my best not to fall asleep.

An indeterminate number of hours later, we'd stopped again. Just for the night, we hoped. By the time I was fully awake—book still fervently open on page seven—Horrocks had come back from the major's carriage with a brown paper package under his arm. I sat straight up and tried to look like I hadn't been dozing. He smiled at me benevolently and turned to Hayek.

"All squared away. I've given your papers to the major. You're staying with us as long as you need. There's a couple of things we'll need to sort in Irkutsk, but it shouldn't be a problem. I assume you've got your own logistics up there? Your own people?"

"Of course." Hayek nodded. He sounded gruff. "Thank you, Captain."

"No problem. Stopped by the quartermaster as well. Got some water on its way, and . . ." He tossed the package down. It landed on the wood with a noise halfway between a dropped-stone *thud* and an organic *squelch*.

"Sir, I hate to ask—" started Jacobs, at the same time as Gallehawk said, "Is that Trotsky?"

James beamed. "It is, indeed, the last of Trotsky. She's been waiting for us in the front carriage so long she's almost frozen solid. Could have left her a bit longer but decided not to risk it."

"Perfect occasion for four-day old, half-frozen beef if ever there was one," I said, rubbing an eye lazily.

Owen still had not fully caught on. "We're eating the rest of Trotsky tonight, sir?"

James smiled again. "To celebrate our moving off."

Jacobs wasn't half as reserved. "Thank Jesus God," he said theatrically, sinking to his knees in front of the brown paper parcel. He inhaled like Trotsky was perfume.

She wasn't so frozen that she was unusable. With a lot of effort, Owen managed to pare bits off her into the dixie tin. There wasn't that much of her to begin with. She'd had to feed almost three hundred men.

"God bless," said Gallehawk, putting a hand on the empty paper that had wrapped her. "Useful even in death, old friend."

While they debated about what to have alongside her, I stood up to open the door a fraction. In an ideal world, we wouldn't have had a stove in a wooden carriage with only a groundsheet for protection. But as it was, outside we'd both freeze and run the risk of being seen, so we had to do what we could to make sure the carriage didn't smell too much like whale oil or methylated spirit.

Jacobs came and sat where I'd just been. "Stew, I vote. I've got some dried veg left over."

"So have I," I offered, bringing my thoughts back to the carriage. "I've been looking for a chance to get rid of it."

For all their talk of food, Jacobs and Gallehawk weren't particularly forthcoming when it came to culinary preparation. That duty often fell to Owen. I got a feeling that was why Horrocks made him his batman. There was a natural drive in him, either to impress or to simply do his best regardless of the circumstances. I didn't know which. He had meat frying in the last of the butter, on the edge of turning rancid, when Jandáček came awake to join us.

"Hello," said Gallehawk, glancing across at him from his bunk, where he generally watched Owen do all the hard work. "Not seen you in a while. Avoiding us?"

Jandáček smiled sheepishly. "Sorry."

"Don't apologise, mate. What else is there to do but sleep on this bloody train? Dinner's nearly ready, if you're interested."

"Is it that late?" Jandáček got to his knees and leant over to peer into the pot. A lock of hair dislodged itself from behind his ear. "Is that real meat?"

"Trotsky. The last of her."

He glanced up quickly.

"The cow," I explained. "We didn't want to get too attached."

"Major shot her before we left the Urals."

"And now he can go home and truthfully say he's the man that shot Trotsky," said Owen. "Pass the water?"

Jacobs did, and Owen added water and then the dried collection of vegetables that we'd all chipped in. They floated on the top like dead things.

"We've got kasha, if you need anything else," offered Jandáček.

Owen screwed his face up. "You lads keep that to yourself. You never know when you might need it. I think we've poisoned this enough with those carrot bits." He left it boiling down to a simmer, added salt, then covered it. "This is going to be pretty fucking watery."

"Bread?" I asked.

We were down to the last of our bread ration. I should have told them that was it; we couldn't rely on any in Irkutsk. But then, if we didn't use it, it would run to waste anyway. It was already going hard.

"We have some left," said Hayek.

"Good. There's going to be scraping."

We sat in a silence that might have been classed as companionable. If the men disliked eating with Horrocks and I when we were forced to stop like this and overnight in the carriages, it wasn't obvious. There didn't seem to have been much of an overall divide between us recently. Did they wonder why we weren't eating with the other officers? *Probably not—it's obvious, and they're not stupid.* It wasn't worth putting James out in the snow to trek uptrain any more than was strictly necessary. Still, it should be unthinkable, us breaking bread with them like this.

Owen prodded one of the floating entities in the tin with his knife. "If I'm right in thinking that's a potato," he said, "I think we're about there."

He doled everything out into mess tins, first to James and then to me and then to everyone else. In the half-light, I couldn't tell what was beef and what was meant to be a vegetable. Still, it was hot and nominally fresh.

"You think there are potatoes in this?" asked Gallehawk, his mouth full.

"What, you don't believe the packet?"

"Says there's turnips in there too. Never seen one."

"Well, yeah," said Owen, serving Nevis. "That's because they look like potatoes when they're cooked."

"They do not."

"What, a big white vegetable that grows underground? How different do you think they can be? Laurie's over there with his bloody eyes shut."

"Hello," said Gallehawk, whose attention had clearly shifted over to Jacobs. "You trying to sleep sitting up?"

Jacobs opened one eye and regarded him magisterially. "I'm trying to see if I can tell what's Trotsky and what's not."

"And why would you want to do that, Laurie?"

Jacobs shrugged. "Bit of fun. Not a lot else to do."

"Tell you what," said Owen, wrapping the tin in his balaclava to keep it from melting into the groundsheet, "how about you do the washing when we're done. That'll give you something to think of."

"Excuse me," said Jandáček, politely. He put down his mess tin, went over to the open door, and threw up neatly onto the ground below.

"Christ!" shouted Gallehawk, springing away and glancing at Hayek. "Are you sure he's all right?"

Owen raised an eyebrow. "Any other comments on dinner?"

My attention was on Hayek too. "Is he all right?" I turned to Jandáček and echoed, "Are you all right?"

Jandáček didn't seem to have heard me, but Hayek had. The corporal marched across to the door, past Gallehawk and I, took Jandáček firmly by the arm, and sat him down on a crate. With a second nature that betrayed a routine, he pressed a filled mug into Jandáček's hands with a gruff word. Then, to us: "He'll be fine."

But he wasn't, because that night he collapsed.

CHAPTER FOUR

I heard him first. I had been half-in, half-out of a dream when the noise came. A loud, heavy thump. I probably wouldn't have noticed it, had I not looked after Sophie for so long. If you've ever been responsible for a young child, responding to random and unexplained noises is a second nature you never quite lose. I'm convinced it did more for me than my training. There and then, I did my best to break through the surface of sleep, tried to confirm we weren't being attacked.

The walls were intact. The air was stagnant. There was just a strange, wooden echo.

I drew myself up, suddenly fully awake. Across the floor, there was nothing but four forms and a crate. One body splayed unnaturally. Akimbo across the floor and perfectly still. It clicked then.

"Christ!" I leapt off my pallet, half-tangled in my sleeping bag. "Oh, Jesus *Christ*!"

I'd only seen this once before, in a man dying from blood loss. He'd suddenly dropped and started trembling—had shaken himself into nothingness. Jandáček was motionless now, but that didn't mean a thing.

I pressed Jandáček into the floor, hoping to pre-empt any kicks or shakes, and then realised what a stupid idea that was and turned him onto his side. His breathing caught and he coughed. Then he wheezed again.

"Sir?" Jacobs was awake, his voice sleep-thick.

"Get the MO, Jacobs," I said, keeping my voice as level as possible.

Hayek was at my elbow now. He said something I couldn't understand.

"Jacobs, get the *fucking* MO!" I held Jandáček under my hands, sure if I took them away, he'd stop breathing.

The door burst open and Jacobs shambled out, blond and ungainly. Then Gallehawk was by my side, clearly trying his best to remain calm.

"Put this under his head, sir," he said, pressing his own blanket into my hands. I took it from him and slid it under, gently. My hands were shaking.

"I think he's coming round, sir, look."

I nodded, not looking. Watching Jandáček's breathing and trying to rein in mine. He was still loose, but he wasn't wheezing anymore. Breath wasn't crackling. I put my hand under his head to position him more comfortably. It came away damp with sweat.

There was a commotion by the door. Jacobs poured himself in, followed by Horrocks and Bannatyne. Horrocks scrambled to light another lamp at the rafters. He fumbled twice, then managed to unhook it and brought it down to Jandáček's face.

"What happened?" asked Bannatyne, kneeling the other side of Jandáček's prone form.

"I don't know, I don't know!" I said, still unable to check my voice. "I woke up and he was like this!"

"He epileptic?"

I looked urgently at Hayek.

"No."

"Has this happened before?"

"Once." Hayek bought himself closer to the light. "Only the once."

"Any head trauma, then or now?"

"No."

"Any balance or speech problems, then or now?"

"No."

"Open wounds?"

"No!"

"Had anything unusual to eat or drink?"

"He's had barely *anything* to eat or drink," I said.

The MO glanced at me. "How much do you mean?"

"I mean he's barely eaten or drank since he got here!"

The MO sat back on his haunches. Jandáček was completely still now. "That'll be it," Bannatyne said, more decisively than I would have liked. "He's weak. Tried to stand up and cut out." He stood, rubbing his hands on the greatcoat he'd donned to come to us. "Either he's dehydrated or his body is trying to run on nothing. Or both, I suppose. If it happens again, do exactly what you've done just now and then fetch me. For now . . . stay with him. He's probably going to be confused. And for God's sake, make sure the man eats something."

I thanked him with a quick, absentminded handshake, not taking my eyes off Jandáček's prone form.

"Is he all right, do you think?" Horrocks asked me, after the MO had left. He'd pulled his coat on quickly over his slept-in uniform, and his hair was stuck up on one side. Dormitory-woken. He seemed a lot younger.

"I think so. Go back to bed, sir. You too, lads," I said, turning to the men behind me. "No sense in us all having a rough night."

"You're included in that," said James. "Make sure you get some sleep, Ransome."

"Yes, sir."

"That's an order."

"*Yes*, sir."

I could see Horrocks didn't believe me, but he nodded sagely. "Night, chaps." He hopped out of the carriage and disappeared out along the same path the MO had taken.

"Is he going to be all right now, sir?" Jacobs was sat back in his nest of blankets, looking small. Something in my heart shifted.

"I hope so, Jacobs. Thank you for running all that way. And sorry for being short with you."

"Acceptable cause, sir," he mumbled, shifting back down into his bedding. Gallehawk did so too.

The keening began then.

It started gently at first, almost a sleep-noise. Then it came again, and again. I glanced up at Hayek. I could feel my men start to awaken behind me.

"Oh, fuck," I said, softly.

Hayek said nothing. Instead, he took a crate down from the pile, then another one. Old ones, probably. I couldn't attest to what was in them: most likely everything we'd been able to nick undetected from Omsk. He pushed another aside after that, and then nudged it farther down the carriage. Then he pushed it farther. There was obviously more space out there than he expected.

"What are you doing?" I asked tentatively.

"We can't leave him in the middle of the floor all night long."

I took the lamp off the floor and rounded the corner Hayek had made. He slid a crate in front of me and his arm appeared from round the side and took the lamp. The boxes he'd shifted to create a makeshift space hemmed us in and separated us from the rest of the car. Not by much, but enough to give Jandáček some room. Enough to give my men a bit of peace.

Hayek looked around his little creation, then clapped a hand to my shoulder. "Help me carry him."

He took Jandáček's legs. I took him around his chest. It was narrower than I'd anticipated, although it had probably once been filled out. Hayek asked me to lean him up against a crate, so I did. Then I went and fetched his blanket and sleeping bag.

Hayek took them. "Thank you. Get some sleep, sir. I have him."

I glanced back at Jandáček. The light by his face picked out individual beads of sweat on his face. The cold clamminess of an invalid. It had come on so suddenly and so fiercely. I was loath to leave him.

Hayek put a hand on my shoulder. "Sir."

I went.

CHAPTER FIVE

I didn't sleep. I lay on my pallet, feeling the draught come through from between the planks on all sides, from beneath me.

Jandáček's noises seemed to be stopping. I could still hear a whimper occasionally, and a blanket-soft thud of limbs hitting wood. But between these was the sound of deep, regular breathing. A body trying to return to normal. He lay there, the other side of this wall from me. He was just . . . lying there.

Forty minutes in, I wrapped my blanket around my shoulders and got up.

As soon as I rounded the corner, Hayek glanced up at me. "You can go back to bed, sir."

"You're exhausted," I answered.

"We are all exhausted, sir. Go back to sleep. You have done enough."

I crouched down beside him. "I slept this afternoon, Corporal. Believe me, I'm all right. Let me sit with him for a bit."

He eyed me reluctantly, but I didn't look away. I heard his joints snap when he got up.

He handed me down a lump of black bread from the top of the box nearest him, where he'd been keeping his belongings—we all unpacked, sooner or later, and it made packing seem like a novelty. It was the little things that you had to find a thrill in. There was a cup of water up there too, an oil lamp with its wick wound low giving out the smallest amount of light. It shadowed Jandáček's face cruelly.

I took the bread. "Thank you, Corporal. Get some rest."

He nodded, his face in a grim line. I watched him until he was out of sight, and then knelt next to Jandáček. The wood was still warm from where the corporal had been sitting. It was still warm from Jandáček's body.

I took him gently and rested his head on my shoulder. He let me do it all. He was so soft. So, so pliant.

"Alexandr?" I whispered, having no idea how to say his name as he'd said it. I hoped it would wake him up in a fit of indignation. It didn't.

"Alexandr?" I stroked his hair from his face. He was very still.

I broke off a small protrusion of the bread. Half of it crumbled away. It couldn't be all bread, with friability like that.

I held it to his mouth. "Come on, Jandáček." I couldn't get that name either. The *y* and the *ch*.

He moved weakly.

"Jandáček?" I pressed it to his mouth again.

He turned, moving his mouth to an angle where I couldn't get to it.

"Come on, mate."

"*Ne.*"

"Please, I don't know the Czech word for yes. Please do this for me."

He stirred, but in the wrong direction.

"Jandáček—" I reached up to the water.

The crumbs floating in it said that Hayek had been using it for the self-same purpose. I wondered if he'd had any luck. Maybe it should be warm.

I wetted the bread and held it to his lips. The water dripped across the floor and trickled into my sleeve. I'd done this for my mother before, once upon a time. She'd had a long illness that should have killed her but hadn't. Then she'd had a short one that shouldn't have killed her but had.

I put the thought out of my mind as I took Jandáček's face in my hands and ran my thumb over his mouth. It was still damp with water. As soon as he opened it—in surprise? To protest?—I pressed in the bread. He opened his eyes and gave me the most offended look I've seen.

"Come on, pal," I asked pathetically. "Please."

He took it tentatively. It was like feeding a half-tame animal.

I held his chin up so he wouldn't choke. "Well done. Come on, sit up."

Against my shoulder, he shifted himself gently. I felt his bones under all that wool. Still not quite close enough. I shifted him the rest of the way and folded out my blanket to include him, trying to get as much of him as possible inside. Since the floor was bruisingly cold. I put his head on my shoulder again and broke off another morsel of bread. Dipped it in water. He took it out of my hand.

"Come on, one more."

I tried again, tipping his head on my shoulder absentmindedly. He'd gone limp, but his breathing hadn't changed. Maybe he'd just relaxed. It didn't stop me having to do everything one-handed, with his chin digging uncomfortably into my shoulder.

Evidently feeling more cooperative—or perhaps just more awake—Jandáček opened his eyes and took another piece of bread, with minimal coaxing. A little thrill of victory trilled through me. He chewed thoughtfully, gazing at something across from my ear. I glanced over to see what he was looking at. Just a shadowy corner. Grey light was starting to filter through the slats.

I turned back, and he kissed me.

I thought a lot about kissing. I thought a lot about kissing other men. I tried to be objective; I thought about how a man's mouth would feel, not how it would make me feel. How stubble would feel under my hands. Wrapping my fingers in short hair. Not that Jandáček's hair was particularly short anymore. I thought about the smell, the feel of wind-weathered, weather-beaten skin. I didn't think about his hands on mine. His hands in my hair. I didn't ever think about another man kissing me.

It was gentle. It was short. By the time I'd registered what was happening, he'd pulled away. Lay against me, as if asleep. It had been so sudden that I'd stopped still, and now I didn't want to move and stir him.

The only evidence that I hadn't imagined the kiss was his arm, which lay against mine. Our skin didn't touch, padded by uniform on uniform and blanket, and I couldn't feel his body heat. And yet, surely his hand had been cupping my face?

I hoped it had been.

I shifted my arm away and his didn't follow. I moved back, drawing him in closer to my waist. I wanted him to be warm. I wanted to warm him up. His scarf had come slightly askew, so I tucked it around the back of his head. In the morning light, he was all washed-out whites and greys. He darkened into hair and fabric, into miniscule facial crevices he was too young to have. He lightened, bones and skin. He was grey and white, entirely stitched from the new day. He lay against me, breathing low and even. I rested my cheek against his hair.

When he awoke a few hours later, I'd already been given my breakfast and waved off the chance to take it outside. The roll call had been done. I'd expected to have a fight on my hands to stay at Jandáček's side, but James had been happy to let me lie.

"He seems to like you," he'd said. "No point making things complicated."

Hayek was still asleep, sprawled in a corner with two legs in front of him. I doubted I'd have any real trouble until he woke up.

Jandáček had been moving in a vague way most of the night, but this time I felt genuine resistance in his pulling away. Panic about etiquette kicked in as soon as he did.

I wouldn't mention his kiss. I would never talk about it. But should I acknowledge it, at least? Touch his hand? Try to catch his gaze, hope he remembered? He'd been the one to kiss me. The next move was mine. But I had no idea if he remembered kissing me, if he'd even known it was me. I could have been anyone. A sweetheart from home. A dream.

He shifted and came fully awake.

"How are you?" I asked neutrally. Safely.

He stretched, cracking his shoulder. "Stiff. Cold and stiff. By travelling standards, rather well."

I swallowed dryly. Pushed some bread towards him. "That's for you. When you want it."

"More bread?"

"There's porridge too, but I'll have to heat you some."

"No, thank you."

"You have to eat."

"I don't have to be fed."

I couldn't think of a reply, so I nudged the bread further towards him. He picked it up, his hands emerging from the huddle he'd built himself so close to me. I suspected he was complying to make me happy, so was pleasantly surprised when he nibbled the end.

"Wish there was cheese."

I tried to smile. "Cheese?"

He swallowed. "Yellow, made of milk. I've been craving it."

"You'd be hard pressed out here, I'm afraid."

He shrugged. "I could get by with cake."

"I can stretch to biscuits, maybe. Or jam. Eat your bread and use your imagination."

"Was there a song about plum and apple jam?" His hands were still sat outside his blanket-nest, knuckles stark. "On your side of France. Something about it and eggs and ham."

"No idea." I felt the corner of my lip quirk. "Probably. The jam's so damn ubiquitous. We've been singing about where the lance-jack is and where bonnies lie for months."

"You don't have to look as hard to find the jam, I suppose."

"True," I conceded. "Meat's all gone, half the ammunition's rusted, but thank Christ we don't have to look over the ocean for the fucking jam."

"It's no bad thing. There's plenty for tea."

I smiled at him, quickly, wondering if he was hinting at what I thought. He smiled in return. It was a round, boyish sort of grin. But unreadable.

CHAPTER SIX

After we had packed up, battened down the hatches, and heaved off once more, I remembered that I had a repair kit at the bottom of my pack. I'd kept it with my spare socks, until the socks I'd been wearing had become too foul to be redeemed and I'd left them quietly alone in Krasnoyarsk.

I remembered it while looking at Jandáček, who was draped in his dead comrade's coat. His own, the one he arrived wearing, was folded over his bunk beside me. The rent in it probably let the warmth out; let the cold in. The bodies, the heat of the engine, and the insulation of the ash packed into the wall cavities could make the carriage weirdly, wetly hot during the day. As such, the double layering that we had adopted over the harsher winter months wasn't necessary, yet.

His hands were clasped around another steaming mug, one leg crossed and one straight out in front of him. He was laughing at something Jacobs was saying as he and Gallehawk theatrically dismantled the cooking stove. The shoulder of his discarded coat on his bunk was wide open, a mouth-sized rent that laughed grotesquely along with him.

How much stock could one put in repairing a coat? It was hardly a love note. But at least I'd be doing something. There was so much time to fill today, since we were behind schedule, as always. I wasn't sure how much more of Caradoc and Gwynne waltzing around north Wales I could handle.

It would be a very anaemic social exchange. But I had nothing else to give, and he had a hole in his coat.

I pulled it down with the confidence of a man doing something he should be doing, and seemingly disturbed no one. Jandáček was facing away, speaking to his corporal. He didn't see me take it, sit down on my bed, put a hand through the gash.

It was nearly fist-sized. What had done it?

Luckily for me the army hadn't been my first introduction to sewing, like it had been for many. It had been Helena who'd taught me, in a sudden fit of sisterly concern. As a child, I probably could have sat and happily cross-stitched away until my father, never usually one for traditional displays of masculinity, had fixed me with a silent and pleading look that said *Can you at least do something to help yourself?*

Helena'd taught Dickie and Hugo too. I didn't know if they'd ever done it since. Hugo I doubted—and not that I can ask him— but Dickie, perhaps. It must have been useful in France. Strange to think of him darning his socks just like I'd had to, on the other side of the world. How little things had changed between him putting away his khaki and me putting mine on. Six years, and only the view we had above the parapet was different.

Initially, I thought I'd overestimated my resilience. Every time I came to an unexpected lump, the top of the needle punctured the pad of my finger through my gloves. There was no traction between my gloved hand and the needle itself, but I held fast. It became relaxing, after a fashion. Therapeutic, with sudden bursts of sartorial misbehaviour.

The coat had been through a lot. Presumably as much as Jandáček himself. There were solid, darkened patches of his blood that I had to skate around or sew through. The whole canvas was stained with all manner of things; pine resin, catkin fragments, bark, stone, dust, snowmelt. Oil. Petrol. My little thread broke once against its fullness. I had to do battle with the thing. Sometimes it felt as though the needle got through to my bone.

Just off the shoulder, there was a raised ragged ridge. Not a cut in the material. It looked like something had frayed off or come away. I brushed at it.

It could have been balled wool, residue from a tight squeeze around a rough surface. But it was in a regular pattern. Distinct.

Just where an insignia might have been.

I rubbed at it again. It stayed.

Inside me, something plummeted.

We stopped for water in the middle of the day. We were still running late, still only hours from where we'd picked up the Czechs. As exposed as we ever were.

I still hadn't thought of what to do.

There were two reasons why he might have torn off his rank insignia.

The first was if the coat wasn't his. If he'd picked it up off a dead comrade and sheared off any symbols of status to avoid being accused of impersonation. It would have been insubordinate to take a superior's coat, even if he was dead. Bold.

Was this why he had been sent off with Hayek? Surely they would have taken the coat.

If there had ever been a medical evacuation. If he was a deserter—and Hayek too . . .

Insubordination is a court martial offence. Deserting gets you shot.

"Sir?"

I looked up. Jacobs had stuck his head round the door, all blond and benevolent. "Captain Horrocks has asked me to run on up to the head carriage to let them know we're ready to go. Just finishing up with the water. Take about twenty minutes. Anything you want me to pass on?"

I was briefly blank but managed to find my voice in time to say, "No, thanks, Jacobs. Go and check if the other lads need some help, would you?" Then: "Take Hayek too, if you would."

Hayek swung round at me, obviously surprised and probably not pleasantly. I didn't bother to meet his gaze. Jacobs jogged off, the corporal following in his enthusiastic wake.

With Hayek out of the way, I glanced towards Jandáček's back. He had his eyes closed and his face to the sun.

I had no idea what to say. No idea what words could get the truth out of him. Not without giving him the chance to get defensive. Dangerous.

"Jandáček," I asked. "Would you come for a walk with me?"

His eyes opened lazily. "A walk?"

I remembered with an unpleasant flush that he had trouble with his knee.

"Travelling in one of these," I carried on regardless. "It's not as easy as you might think." That was true. I had been still for so long before that I'd thought my muscles were going to liquidate. "I'm going to stretch myself out for a time. Come, keep me company."

"What about your sewing?"

"It'll still be there when we get back."

I counted my heartbeats in my throat. Eventually, after what couldn't have measured more than a few seconds, he unfolded those long, delicate limbs of his. He drew his coat around him— the dead man's. I shivered, and he pulled his scarf up.

With a hand to his shoulder, I helped him down. There was a tang of stale sweat as he came to rest beside me, and I bit my tongue.

Around us the trees folded out innumerably, an impenetrable nighttime gloom among them. It was the same forest we'd found them in. *God, I hate this place.*

I led him to the back of the train. Took him away from the car, not far enough to raise suspicion. Then I let him ahead of me slightly and put my hand on my pistol. "Sir?"

To his credit, he didn't turn. But he twitched.

"Turn around," I said. "And hands by your sides, please."

He turned to face me. There was nothing in his eyes to suggest he'd just given himself away. Instead, he looked at me. Perfectly level.

He knows I know. He's known since the moment he saw me take down that coat.

That was why he hadn't collected it off the bed. Why he still wore his dead comrade's. Even though he'd passed as a private well enough, a piece of the real uniform was better. Look too closely at his own and it was obvious that he'd torn off his rank insignia.

I cleared my throat. "What is your name?"

"Jandáček. You know that."

I swallowed. "But you're not a private."

"I never actually said I was."

Now that it was out there, that I knew for sure, I had no idea how to progress.

I took a step towards him. "Then, may I ask . . ."

He faced back to the forest. "I'm not a deserter, Lieutenant. Nor was I cashiered."

Cashiering. When an officer was ritually dismissed, in front of the regiment, for maximum degradation. That hadn't even occurred to me. "I'm—"

"I am not a *deserter*, Lieutenant."

There was a stony silence. I came towards him, knowing he could hear me the whole short way. He didn't ask me to stop, so I stood carefully next to him and began as I'd always felt. "When we were first sent here, it was because making peace in Russia was essential to the end of the war. Then the war ended, and it was essential to sign that bloody treaty. Now it's for 'peace and trade.' It's not ending. And it seems we're losing more men here than we ever did in France. No one would blame you if—"

His voice was quick and sharp. "I'm not here for peace and trade."

I tried to inject a smile into my voice. "Neither am I."

"I may be a lot of things, *Lieutenant*," he said, his voice low and even. "But don't you *ever* question my loyalty to my men again, do you understand?"

I thought of the way he'd held Holub's head in his hands while the man died. There was a little flutter below my breastbone, working into my throat. "Yes. I'm sorry, I—I apologise."

He glanced at his feet and then back up. "Good."

I swung back around towards the train, looking for something to do. I had no anxiety about turning my back to him. It would be worse to face him. And even if I had misread him, what could he do? Shoot me and abscond? To where?

I cleared my throat. "So. You had a command."

"Yes."

"And you outranked me, I imagine." His haughtiness had led me to that eventuality.

"Yes."

So I'd kissed a superior officer. That was new. Or been kissed by one, I supposed. Could he feel that kiss hanging between us? The one I'd been so desperate to remind him about by means of a repaired coat. Look where that had got us.

I pushed on through. "Why are you here, Jandáček?"

"Because I have a kneecap that means I can't run, a shoulder that means I can't shoot." He trotted them out in a neat little litany.

"You know that's not what I mean."

His voice carried a defeated tone. "I'm just trying to get to Irkutsk. We both are."

This was not the right time to ask what was there for him. If he was looking for treatment for his shoddy joints, he'd more than fucked them by trekking halfway across the country. And if he got there, would they stick him in an office and be done with it? And what about his corporal?

His corporal.

"Was Hayek your corporal before?"

"I barely knew him until they put me on his evacuation. Luck of the draw we both speak English. We left two Russian speakers behind us."

I swallowed the throbbing in my tongue. "Your English—"

"School. Stonyhurst, if you're wondering whether we were at school together."

Stonyhurst was a Jesuit school in the north that seemed excessively focused on Latin, even for a public school.

"Christ," I said. "My apologies."

He was silent for a few beats, and then: "Am I dismissed?" The sarcasm in those words was almost fatal.

"I'm sure you don't have to ask my permission. Sir."

He snorted and I schooled my face as he brushed past me, our coats making a soft wool-on-wool *thwack* as they met.

Shame threatened to force its way up to my face, but I fought it down.

I was a good soldier in that regard.

What would he say when he realised I was only an acting first lieutenant? And even then, barely. Some last-minute battlefield promotion that had been.

I watched him catch his hand on the side of the carriage and heave himself back into the train. In the middle of our mismatched line of cars, a squat little locomotive was steaming. We were moving off, at last. I forced down the last of my hot pride and followed him inside.

We were leaving from Taishet, which was barely more than a dollop of supply buildings. Moving off took a shorter time than I expected. I should have known better, after all this time, but you could never tell who would have unpacked what in a fit of madness knowing they had a three-hour delay for water.

And the train set off again. The sluggish chugging was somewhat relaxing. Like the roll of the sea.

When I was at home, I'd keep my windows open at night and listen for the sea. I could hear it, sometimes, if the wind was blowing inland. Usually that meant the wind was blowing into my bedroom, so I'd have to close it again. It had been nice knowing it was there.

When we'd first arrived, I'd tried to substitute the huge, open space of the steppe with the sea in my head. Anything to get rid of the nightmarish bigness. But all that land won out, in the end. I couldn't imagine anywhere else. The soporific rock of the train was the closest thing I had to the waves.

Thanks to the initial delay—caused by the train wreck we'd still not come across—we'd lost a day and a half of travel time. Five hundred and thirty kilometres. We were meant to be the other side of Zima by now—just inside the oblast that housed Irkutsk and pulling into Cheremkhovo.

I barely remembered Cheremkhovo from our first time along this line, when we'd stopped there for coal. From there, the track would take us out onto the steppe proper.

I would be glad not to be in sight of trees.

At the rate we were pushing, Horrocks told me, the hope was to be in Cheremkhovo by nightfall tomorrow. Six hundred and seventy kilometres (give or take) by forty-five kilometres per hour (give or take) rounded us off at just under fifteen hours, or two days of travelling. We'd set off sometime after two. Our short-lived start this morning had been just before nine.

Horrocks had told me that the driver wasn't happy risking another overnight stay this far from the city and so comparatively close to a recent derailment. He'd overnighted in worse positions, I'd countered. But us being so "close" to the wrecked post train three nights in a row apparently meant he had to watch himself for any deliberately mislaid tracks. Any missing lines. Any mines underneath the sleepers. And then the major had said we couldn't stop because our supplies were too low. We were to compromise and push on through the dark to try to get to Tulun.

I tried to straighten this all out in my head while propped up on the floor. Jandáček's half-repaired coat hung off the end of my bed like a corpse. I ignored it.

James wasted no time breaking our seven-and-a-half-hour journey into a series of futile watches. Nevis was on first; his strong, quiet presence installed itself by the viewing hatch and sat there like a pencil drawing.

James delegated me the final watch, which should start just as we came into Tulun. We'd overnight at the station, take on any new food or fuel we needed. After telling me this, he proceeded to spend the next half an hour trying to engage me in further conversation. I pretended to lose myself further and further into my book. Intimate astute knowledge of officer blustering told me that whatever he wanted to liaise about had no way of making him look professional.

I glanced once, very quickly, over at Jandáček. He was asleep. Why had I looked? I clenched my teeth in a hot, skin-tightening fit of self-loathing.

Christ man. Have some dignity. He'd always be asleep. Hit a speed over ten kilometres an hour and the man went into hibernation.

There was something comforting about the gentle pitch and toss of railway travel. It was something I'd been missing without realising it, like a young sailor home from the sea.

In our heads, Irkutsk was almost home. When we got there, we would detrain to take on food and water. Be debriefed and stay for the night. Maybe two. The prospect of two nights ashore made the thought of spending tonight on the train more bearable.

I hated nights on the train. Not because of the discomfort but because not a stop went by without a sordid tale of what might have happened before our arrival there. Kulaks or Cossacks or stalwart peasant rebels who had last come through and tried to seize food. A woman had been restrained and finally shot for having three mud-logged rat tails. A man had invited a kulak partisan to his table and begun to cut him sections of something bare and bipedal.

It didn't matter who came through; there was always conflict. Many of the Bolsheviks didn't care about the peasantry, and the peasantry resented them. Often the latter were unified against the "food-grabbing urbanites" who'd come to "liberate" them. The food they had grown—the grain, the barley, the potatoes—it was theirs. What right did these strangers have to it?

But the agricultural infrastructure had fallen apart—what else was there to eat? The uniformed arm of a Red soldier, the head of a White soldier, the leg of a child. I once sat and talked for a long time to a man who had described the way they'd made friends with a stray dog. It had been a pet, he'd explained. It was starved for human contact. It didn't know what it had done wrong or why it had stopped being loved. It had taken five minutes of coaxing, just the smallest possible promise of human affection. The dog had come snuffling up to his face and he'd kissed it and stabbed it clean through the ear.

"Nothin' on it," he'd told me, taking in a heavy draft of pale ale water. "Fucking nothin'. Boiled the bones with snow water to thicken it up. Head almost boiled dry."

He'd broken his eye contact with me then and taken a big, theatrical sniff without seeming to notice what he was doing. Rubbed his nose with his free hand. "Smell's still up there, you know. Boiling dog head. It's when the eyeballs start to go it gets you. The hair scorch is all right. It's when those eyeballs go."

He'd been a broad-looking man with an honest-looking face. The kind you'd see on a navvy or an ostler. Until then, I'd entertained the idea of taking him upstairs and letting him fuck me. Then he'd gone to get another drink and melted into the crowd, and suddenly I hadn't cared enough to find him.

I shook off the memory. We had enough food. "Enough" could get us anywhere. It could and would, I told myself, prevent us having to stop unscheduled.

We bumped and bundled forward for a few more hours. Guns came out. Guns were stowed, then came back out again. Boots came off, revealing patches of red raw skin rubbed right to the flesh. Jacobs, usually the overeager rank entertainer, held himself so still while trying to get his sock off. Brave while no one was looking.

Gallehawk got the accordion out, stowed it again. He hadn't had the chance to sing or play since Omsk, and I hadn't seen him much then. I'd been told he had a gorgeous voice, though.

I lay back and let myself be carried. The cart's familiar smell, which we pretended not to notice, was back: sweat, stale farts, and wood mould. The slightly acrid and omnipresent undertone of urine. I had never been one to feel nauseated while travelling, but the steady frowst of the carriage could do even me in sometimes.

I thought about taking Jandáček's jacket up again, to focus my mind on something else. Handing it back would give me an excuse to talk to him about what he'd said.

I was so tied up with trying not to look at him that I didn't realise James'd come to sit on the end of my bed.

I started, and he pushed down on my knee.

"Don't worry," he said. "I just wanted to tell you that I heard about you being up late last night. I wanted to let you know that it's all right to get some rest if you need it. I'm here. The sector's been quiet."

His tone said he had no idea whether he was allowed to do this but he was going to make the most of his command and do it anyway. "You know you're not on until last watch. Gallehawk has only just taken his post. You've got at least two hours."

I nodded and pretended to be grateful, having absolutely no desire to go to sleep or to "get some rest." He smiled at me and then went back to his letters. I sat up, stretched down to my pack, pulled my book out, and lay back down on my side, skimming paragraphs restlessly. My eyes itched. Jandáček lay just outside of my field of vision like the sun.

By some long-ago decision, we never talked when the train was moving. Last October, when we had first embarked at Bombay, no one had managed to be quiet for more than a minute. But there had been a lot of death since, and we'd all needed the time to ourselves. Even Jacobs and Gallehawk liked to maintain their distance now. Jacobs was curled up on his side today—asleep for all intents and purposes—and Gallehawk was sat blank-faced on the crate by the watch hatch, the view scrolling past him through the slats in the wood.

We might be in Irkutsk tomorrow. I might have a real bed— my tight, triple-decker cot would not be missed. Perhaps I could get a glass of fresh milk there. Probably not, though I might be able to send a letter home to my sister. I could tell her I was hoping to be back soon, to keep a live cow tied up in the garden.

It had been over three years since I'd been home. I knew how much had changed but couldn't visualise it happening. Couldn't imagine being there and it having changed. There'd been enough already. In my last months there, Hugo had died, and afterwards— just as everyone had been starting to get back to normal—my father had gone to his study and shot himself.

The older I got, the easier it was to sympathise with him.

My book listed lazily to one side. Behind me, I felt a warm and gentle pressure.

I turned, smiling. "Thought you were angry with me?"

He smiled back. "Not at you."

I didn't know why I cared so little for discretion. The better part of valour and all that. But instead of worrying, I cupped his rough cheek. He needed to shave, still. I'd have to talk to him about that later. His skin was so soft, though. He brought his hand up to meet my own and held on to my wrist. It was comforting.

"Why did you kiss me last night?" I murmured.

"Because you were there, and I wanted to." He squeezed my wrist. "Do you wish I hadn't?"

I rubbed his cheekbone with my thumb. "May I kiss you?"

His mouth met mine. It was a warm, dry kiss. A gentle and homey one. His lips and my lips were both ruins, all crags and broken skin. I ran my hand down his face, through his hair, and kissed him back. It felt like walking in the front door, throwing your bags down. Warmth and comfort and completion. He huffed air out through his nose. I kissed him deeper.

When I pulled away, his eyes were big and grey. I wanted to keep kissing him, so much. A soft line of freckles lay across his nose and made him look young. I still had no idea how old he was.

"Did you come through Irkutsk last time?" he asked me, still holding my wrist.

I nodded, rubbing my thumb over his knuckle. The last time we had been there, the dregs of its population had only just begun recollecting themselves from months of anarchic occupation. The town's little muscle fibres had begun to twitch again. We'd approached it via a quaint wooden bridge that hadn't looked like it had any business holding up a train. All I could remember about the city itself was a cathedral, big and domed.

I kept rubbing my thumb around the joint of his middle finger, down to and circling the knuckle and back up again.

"Yes," I answered. "But we didn't stay long."

"No," he agreed. His eyes had fluttered shut while I'd been thinking. "It's never for long."

His dark eyelashes were fanned out over his skin like the Madonna's. The weeks, months he had spent out in the sun or the wind had scoured his cheeks red, rendered them visibly painful. And up close to his lips, a sore was beginning to form. But those delicate eyelashes—they were so incongruous with the roughness of his face.

Out of nowhere, he grabbed my hand and squeezed it. Had my stroking begun to annoy him? I tried to tug away, but he held on.

The movement had disturbed a lock of hair, and it had fallen over his face. The gentle tide of his breathing lifted it up, then down again. I wanted desperately to push it back behind his ear and thought about moving our joined hands, but he seemed so peaceful.

After insurmountable minutes, when I, too, felt myself beginning to drift, he suddenly propped himself up on an elbow, taut as a bowstring, and glanced over my shoulder. His hair was so dark I expected it to leave smudges on the pillow.

I didn't want him to sit up. I didn't want him to leave me.

"Look at that," said a voice from behind.

I started up, forcing my eyes open and breaking the filmy membrane of sleep that had grown over me. I was alone in the bed. I'd been asleep. A swoop in my gut. And then something else, a voice in my head said, *Of course it wasn't real. Why would you think it was?*

James was standing beside Jacobs, who'd stepped up to take his turn on the watch. He was standing with an arm braced against the hatch, gazing down at me with barely concealed good humour. Evidently congratulating himself for having noticed my tiredness.

"Ransome, come and see this."

I swung my still dozing legs off my bed and stretched, rubbing my knee to get the feeling back into it. Then I stood and heaved myself over to stand where Horrocks had been. I deliberately didn't glance over at Jandáček, who hadn't moved from his own bed. Of course he hadn't been lying with me. Of course.

It was the post train.

It had been lifted off the tracks, but it hadn't gone much farther than that. It lay on the grass like a leviathan, wrecked out and unsalvageable. The black and burnt hollow that the locomotive disappeared into told us how she'd ended her life. Already, her engine was gone. Probably the first thing they took. Even now as we watched, there were two men on top of one of her cars, knapping away at the wood. They either hadn't noticed us or didn't care. Had anyone been able to get to the post in time? There wouldn't be much left in there now. In a couple of days she'd be completely stripped, like a huge soft whale at the bottom of the sea.

"It's the one that held us up, sir," said Jacobs from behind me. When I took my face away from the hatch, he was grinning, almost glowing with pride. He was the one who had drawn everyone's attention to it, then. Quite the find. "Took bloody long enough to sort, didn't it?"

I made a noncommittal hum.

Gallehawk strung out his accordion.

Jacobs snapped his gaze round to him. "Oh no you bloody don't."

Gallehawk flicked him a quick V-sign, which I pretended not to notice.

We'd passed the train already. I had to look backwards to see it now. It seemed like the country was so starved it was sucking her down through the soil.

That could be us. That could so easily be us. It's the trains the Trots go for, after all. Why would they need a tank if they had an armoured train and a twelve-pounder naval gun?

A shiver ran through me. I couldn't wait to get out of Russia. We'd be following the Canadians across the ocean to Vancouver, across Canada to Toronto and then across the Atlantic to home. Or to Southampton. And then . . . train to Southend, I suppose. Christ.

I imagined ringing my sister from the station. *Hels, it's Francis. I'm home. Send a trap to meet the 17:15?*

Be a long walk to Hadleigh otherwise.

And then what? Jesus. I didn't know what would be worse: the uncertainty of what came next or the domesticity I'd signed up to escape. The fixed-termers like Toby might well have orders when they got back—after a period of leave, one hoped. Yet there would be a future beyond the cliff-edge for them. But I'd have to go home to all that loneliness, the disconnect between myself and the past. That vacuum. No job, no friends, and the tacit expectation of marriage—for the family's sake, if nothing else. I was hardly going to keep up appearances with a respectable job alone.

Should I manage to cadge a respectable job. Even my brief stint in the Army wasn't furnishing me with much of the nuts-and-bolts knowledge of life. And the Service would hate me. I was a duration territorial who'd managed to get around conscription by spending three years kicking about nowhere in particular. *"Come you home a hero, or come not home at all."*

Although, in all fairness, the Hertfordshires had been part of the East Africa campaign. It was just that no one had bothered to send us there.

Someone squeezed my shoulder, and I turned to see James. He smiled at me sympathetically.

"Your turn, Ransome."

I grinned wanly at him and met Jacobs's eye as he raised his eyebrows in greeting, getting up off the crates he'd made his home on for the past hour. I sat.

"Jacobs, you've left this lovely and warm."

"That's 'cause our arses have been sat on it all day, sir," interjected Gallehawk, who'd never had a thought he could keep to himself.

He carried on, seeming to hold separate conversations with Owen and Jacobs, both at once. I half listened as the train slid through increasingly desolate arable farmland.

We'd passed Nizhneudinsk, a largish administrative town, while still on Jacobs's watch. The railway'd been joined by a road that snaked along it like a quiet loyal dog. This was how both we and the Bolsheviks had advanced before. The rail had acted as our heavy guns, and we'd travelled flanked by marching soldiers, by cars. *We* being used in its widest possible meaning—the Hertfordshires hadn't travelled that way, for reasons I couldn't tell you. I didn't know how many armies did in other parts of the world. The Trots did. That was probably why we in particular were running from them.

We'd had more railway than the world has space at our disposal. And we still lost to the factory workers.

Sometimes I wondered if I quite admired the Trots.

The road gradually gave way to a river that veered erratically between hugging the line and retreating into the forest and half-finished scrubland, before bisecting the track completely. The flatlands to the side of the embankment opened out into a depleted, brown reservoir that passed sludgily by.

It was getting on for half past nine when we finally began to slow. After the first three days out of Omsk, all the railside townlets had begun to look the same. Tulun was no different. The only sign we were arriving was that the brakes went on.

As we heaved into the station, the stationmaster on the platform raised an arm in solemn salute to the middle carriage.

Time to eat, more or less.

James unrolled the door and raised his eyebrows at me. I swung off after him and then turned back to the carriage. "Shan't be long. Start cooking, if you want to."

"Any chance of a fire, sir?" asked Owen, unfurling himself from where our onward motion had sent him to sleep.

"I can ask."

"Thank you, sir."

I followed James along the waist of the train and up the steady rise of the platform. A congregation of other officers had knotted a healthy distance away from the major, beside a bench that no one was daring to sit on. Toby winked at me as I joined them and manoeuvred myself up next to him.

Major Barclay, our ersatz commanding officer, was doing his best to finish off a conversation with a dried-up stationmaster who seemed to possess the same face as every stationmaster I'd seen so far. He was flanked by Mitya, who watched them both with his customary cool collectedness.

Mitya had reminded me of a little boy playing soldier, before I'd seen him in action. I'd never seen anyone so accurate with a pistol though. He could hit a sparrow in the eye blindfolded. I treated him with a wary respect now. Not everyone did. He was by far one of the most divisive characters travelling with us.

He turned to the major and translated the stationmaster's repeated phrases and mimery into what was likely a heavily abridged account of events. Barclay smiled genially.

There was a lot of nodding, and after an enthusiastic *Spasiba bolshoie*! from the major—which carried right the way over to where we stood waiting—and what would probably be a curt *Spasiba* from Mitya. Money had likely changed hands at some point. After a minute or two, the major came up to us, a beatific look on his face. I'd heard accounts from Flanders of COs leading their men over the top with a sword in hand—half a league, half a league, half a league onward. Since I'd met Barclay, I had no trouble imagining him in that scenario.

I shouldn't really have trusted a man my father's age who was still a major.

"Sorry to keep you waiting, chaps," he said. "We're down for the night here and moving off first light. Irkutsk is about two hundred and fifty away. Drivers are going to push her as fast as she can go. Should pull in before four, provided it's all plain sailing."

"Did the SM have any news on the current climate, sir?" asked Toby from my side.

"Not heard nor seen a thing for almost a month. Hadn't even got wind of that post train. Most of the action has gone west, I reckon. Between you and me, it looks like we're in for a quiet night. Officially, we're expecting anything."

"No campfires, sir?" I asked.

"Keep it to the station side of the train, Ransome. No one's to go wandering."

"Understood, sir."

"Good. I need to talk to the driver. Dismissed."

We fell out of file, and I'd turned to follow James back to our car when Toby grabbed my elbow and pulled me to face him.

"I hear you've had more fun with our Czech friends."

"Oh! How much do you know?"

"Ransome, I know nothing because you have told me nothing and I get the impression Horrocks rather wishes I wasn't around. I had to find out from eavesdropping on him in our car last night."

When talking to Toby, you often felt you'd be better off sitting down. I'd had one too many run-ins with him where a quick good morning had turned into a half an hour listening session, and by the end of it my knees always ached. So I sat heavily on the bench by the wall and gestured for him to do the same.

"Your man Jacobs gave me a hell of a bloody shock hammering on the door at the crack of Christ. I thought James was about to drop dead of fright." He took out a cigarette, then offered one to me. "Which is the bloke keeping you up all hours?"

"The private." I took the proffered fag and inhaled. "Bannatyne says he's nothing to worry about."

"Does he," said Toby laconically.

"Thinks it's hunger. Or dehydration. Maybe both."

"Well, loath as I am to agree with Bannatyne, that does sound plausible. The Trots have it in for them more than the rest of us. They've never forgiven Masaryk."

"Good pronunciation."

"Thanks." He smiled. "I practiced it so I didn't sound like a prat."

"Is that while you were reading up on what you were getting yourself into?"

"Actually, no. One of the lads I was with—Bailey, out in France—he was a bit of a socialist. Hell of a shock for him when they shot the tsar."

"Hell of a shock for all of us," I said, tapping off. "Most of all the tsar."

"Anyway," he said, ignoring me. "After Masaryk decided he was bringing his lads to us in France, we all suddenly got very interested in what was going on over here. Especially after Lenin freed up the Bosche. Bloody Masaryk's lot couldn't go back home the way they came. They were on the wrong side of the line. So they had to go all the way through Russia and round the Pacific."

"Sounds familiar," I said.

"Doesn't it just? Anyway, after *Fauschlag*, the Czechs were all still stuck in the Ukraine and had to get pretty sharpish."

"Diction a bit off on that one," I remarked, tapping my ash.

"No, it wasn't."

"You said '*foul slag*.'"

"Shut up, Francis, I said *Fauschlag*." He took a drag of his cigarette, eyes gleaming. "Anyway, that's about all I know. You should bring your chaps along to that drink you're buying me. Sounds like they could use a stiff one more than the rest of us."

"You going to keep them entertained by discussing foul slag?"

"I got 'Masaryk' right. I get marks for effort." He dropped his cigarette and trod on it. "Feel like I'm swinging the lead a bit here. Ought to get some real work done. Abbot might be burning my dinner." He winked at me. "Until we get shore leave, Francis."

I returned his wink. "See you there, Tobes."

"I'll give Haddock your regards."

"Oh, please don't."

On my way back to the car, it occurred to me that I should probably check on my sergeant. Brown kept himself in the car next to us, with the bulk of my other men that weren't making up numbers elsewhere, or in the overspill with me. I found him sat out the side of the boxcar door, one hand braced on the frame and another wrapped around a cup of tea.

"Evening, Sergeant!" I waved from about twenty feet off.

He waved back at me. "Evening, sir! I've been looking for you."

"Oh? Anything to report?"

"Stevens is dead, sir."

"Dead?" I bit the inside of my cheek. "Wasn't he getting better?"

Brown shrugged. "Happens, sir. Wrapped him in his bag. Thought we might as well wait until town to bury him."

I shifted my weight uneasily. "Very well. Anyway, just so you know, Major says the sector's more or less quiet. Hope for the best, et cetera."

"Of course, sir."

"He wants to be in Irkutsk by late afternoon tomorrow." His news about Stevens had opened a strange pit inside me that I had to throw all my words over. It took more effort than speaking normally, but he had to hear. "Hasn't told us any more about what his plans are when we get there. Daresay we'll find out by morning though."

"Not a de-lousing station in Irkutsk, is there sir?" he asked, half-joking. We all liked to cover our optimism.

"Couldn't say."

"I did ask, sir," he said, with a smart sip of his tea. Then he nodded over my shoulder. "Looks like you've got a visitor."

I turned around, fully expecting it to be Toby back again with a forgotten conversation piece. After so long of being aware of Jandáček's movement around me, I was disturbed to realise he'd appeared undetected. I managed to compose myself and ask, "Everything all right, Jandáček?"

"Yes, sir." His voice was like cream over cut glass. "May I have a word with you? If you have a moment?" He nodded at Brown. "Sergeant."

Brown tipped his mug to him. "Evening."

I untied my tongue. "Of course. Excuse me, Sergeant."

Jandáček smiled, turned on his heel, and immediately walked off without me. I half jogged to fall into step with him, which did nothing to prevent almost choking on my own pulse.

"Everything all right?" I repeated, keeping my voice low.

"Not here" was his sharp reply.

I opened my mouth to speak again, but he beat me to it.

"Captain Horrocks?"

James, who was halfway through washing his hands with water from his bottle, did not quite manage to hide his bemusement before he glanced up. "Hullo," he said, regarding us both good-naturedly. "Can I help?"

"Your lieutenant took me for a walk last night to loosen up my leg," said Jandáček. "After so long in the same position, I fear I've undone all his good work. If it's not too much trouble, could I ask to borrow him?"

Horrocks's baffled expression didn't change. He looked from Jandáček to me—and I doubted I'd concealed my reaction well—and back to Jandáček again.

"Yes, certainly . . ." he began. "If it would help. I'll get them to put some dinner aside for you, Ransome?"

"Thank you, sir," I said, not really sure what to make of the situation.

"Thank you. His background is most beneficial."

I registered James's surprised little glance towards me. No doubt wondering, as I was, what on earth this "background" could be. "Stay around the train, just to make certain," he said.

"Of course, sir," said Jandáček.

"Does your corporal know?"

"He does, sir. I cleared it with him before you," Jandáček said, with a well-punctuated smile.

James returned it. "Then I don't see a problem. Have him back in one piece."

"I will, sir."

Jandáček walked on, and after the shock had worn off, I took my cue to follow him. I had to break into a light jog.

As soon as I caught him up, I tried to clarify. "My background?"

He glanced behind us without breaking stride. "Yes. Didn't you say your brother's practice specialised in joints?"

"My brother's a land lawyer," I said, bemused.

"Must've misheard."

I followed his long-legged walk out of earshot, to the back of the last flatbed truck. Behind us, the rail extended all the way to Omsk.

As soon as we'd rounded the car, Jandáček dropped so quickly I thought he'd been shot. He sat leaning up against the rim of one of the wheels and looked up, as if expecting me to do the same. So I did.

"Sit opposite me," he said. As soon as I complied, he put his foot in my lap. "If anyone sees, we're trying stretches."

I, not knowing what else to do, rested one hand on his ankle lightly. He probably couldn't feel it through all his layers.

The packed railway dirt was dusty and solid beneath my other hand. Christ, it was cold.

"I should tell you that if you *are* expecting me to help you stretch out, I'm going to let you down," I said pointedly.

His gaze was fixed on his shoe, and he smiled without humour, almost to himself. "I fear I have a lot to apologise for."

"What was all that about my brother?"

He glanced up. "Sorry?"

"When did I tell you about Dickie?"

"Oh." He smiled, really smiled this time. "You didn't. But my voice carries and I wanted to make sure your men didn't hear me. Honestly, I didn't even know you had a brother."

"I've got some of both, if you were wondering. Why are we here, sir?"

A fibre in his face twitched. "Don't call me that."

I couldn't help jabbing slightly more. "You seemed rather adamant about rank last night."

"That's what I'm here to apologise for. And for Christ's sake, never call me *sir*. Not when we're here, not when we're around other people. I'm still a private to you."

I toyed with his bootlaces. He didn't stop me, so I didn't stop myself. "Does anyone else know?"

"Your captain. He checked my papers. I assume that he's told your major by now." He drew his knee up towards him, keeping one foot in my lap. "It won't matter so much when we get to Irkutsk."

"Are you still going to travel as rank and file afterwards?" I thought of Toby, how much he seemed to know already. If he knew, all the other subalterns did.

"I don't know if I'm going to travel at all," he said. "They might want me to bunker down in Irkutsk. Wait for my CO to get back."

"But you're injured?"

He shrugged. "Yes."

"And—"

He looked at me sharply. "Yes?"

"It's not going to be helped much by two days on a train, is it?" I nearly, so very nearly, had mentioned the other thing. His other thing. I was keeping a lot of secrets for him, it seemed.

He shrugged again. "I can walk. It's the cold. When the cold gets in. There's no reason they can't put me on administration when we get there."

"So you're here for service, and not your men?" It was a low blow, but I resented his tone from yesterday. The subtext had sneered *I'm better than you.*

He took it with a tired smile. I could almost see it written across his face: *I deserved that.* "It's whatever I can get."

If I said anything regarding the cryptic nature of that comment, he'd likely either dig in or walk off, or both. I decided to leave it, possibly to push at later. When I had a cleaner slate with him.

But instead of angling for the more pedestrian opening he'd first given me—family, home life—I decided to pull the conversation in a more taboo direction. "We'll be sorry to see you go."

"I'll be sorry if I have to leave you."

The statement hit without warning. By the time I'd tried to catch his body language, he was still again. In the absence of something else to do, I gave him one of my wan smiles. "We're not going anywhere exciting."

"Nowhere you haven't been before."

"Exactly."

A silence passed between us.

Sasha was one of those social creatures who I'd half envied at school. I'd half idolised them too, until sometimes that admiration had become bitterness. Their ease of conversation had made me hyperaware of the lack of my own. I'd both coveted and desired it—them. I'd never grown out of those feelings.

The silence thickened.

"What about yours?"

He looked up and made a sleepy hum. "Hmm?"

"Family. I mean. What about yours?" I bit the inside of my cheek hard.

He shrugged, the gesture oddly young on him. "I have one." He made another noncommittal noise and was quiet for long enough that I almost decided to give up, before he said, "No brothers, no sisters. My father is a shoemaker and a Communist, and I went to boarding school in another country."

"Is that a particularly communist thing to do?"

His mouth twitched. "No."

I couldn't think of what else to say. There wasn't much I could talk to him about. I wanted to ask more about his father, what his father thought of independence. And his own opinion. Why he seemed in no great hurry to get home. Why he wanted to be in service, but didn't want the camaraderie that came with it. All that seemed a bit on the nose for the current situation though. So I held off while he sat opposite me, gazing at the track between us.

Did he still think of his command? I thought of my own men. I was no closer to believing they were mine than the day I found out their names; thirty living, breathing, farting, snoring, heaving men, each with their own interpretation of himself and myself and the world. Thirty of them.

I wondered what my men thought about me.

Sasha was still quiet, and quiet doesn't like quiet.

I made another futile stab at conversation. "Do you think we'll be missed?"

He seemed to consider the question and then shrugged again. "You will, especially."

I must have made a sound at that. He gave me a startled frown and I thought I'd offended him.

"You look surprised," I said.

"The opposite." He moved his ankle under my hand. "I might have just realised something about you."

"The same thing you realised the other night?"

I heard the words almost before I'd said them. So I schooled my face quickly to make it seem deliberate. I didn't miss him drop my gaze, and I certainly didn't miss the fact he'd glanced over his shoulder.

"You know I can see," I reassured him. "There's nothing behind you but a wheel. We'd have heard anyone coming."

He quirked his eyebrows and twitched his mouth without humour. "I know."

The silence hung between us. I tried to think of a reply to him, but then he said, "Shall we head back? I'm freezing to the ground."

It was cold. I'd forgotten. So I got to my feet, brushing hard-packed steppe mud off my uniform. He was half-raised now, one hand still on the wheel. Was there some residual warmth in it? I took his outstretched hand, pulling him up and towards me softly.

He gave me a weak smile. "Thank you."

I smiled back. I almost asked him something then, but closed my mouth instead.

"No," he said. "I mean it. Thank you."

"What for?" I asked, expecting him to drop my hand.

He didn't though. "You know. Being there."

My smile widened, softened. "I'm still here."

I wasn't sure quite what I meant by that. But he squeezed my hand tightly before he dropped it, and my heart fluttered as we made our way back to the awakening train.

CHAPTER SEVEN

I n the morning, after we had entrained once again, I lay my back to the boards and tried to get Sasha straight in my head. Sometimes he blew hot, sometimes cold. Sometimes he was open, sometimes hard like a carapace.

He hadn't slept in his bunk again last night, preferring to stow himself away in a corner. I could understand his motives—warmth, security—but surely it couldn't be conducive to sleep. Surely it must hurt.

There was an element of him that I couldn't quite grasp. Whether it was a failing on my part or whether he was deliberately holding himself back—or both—wasn't clear. The way he'd conducted himself so far made me suspect the latter.

Thinking about Sasha made a pleasant change from thinking about home. I missed it in strange, sharp jags that made me want to pull the covers up to my head and have a hard cry. That childish wish to indulge in your misery until someone came and took it away.

No one ever would again. Just under a year ago, I got a telegram telling me my mother had dropped dead. I don't know if you can be counted an orphan at twenty-four, but alone on the central Eurasian steppe is a bad place to find out that you are one.

Irkutsk is entered and exited by bridges. It isn't on a peninsula, but it's surrounded by so many bodies of water it's easy to assume otherwise. We came from the other side this time, and the

Orthodox cathedral that so dominated my memory of the place wasn't visible from there.

I hoped nothing had happened to it.

It didn't strike me, as I stepped down onto the platform, that I'd been waiting to arrive here for so long. Now that I was here, I didn't know what else to look forward to. China, probably. Maybe Vladivostok. Going home.

The station at Irkutsk was big and shadowy in the gloaming. There was a smell in the air: dark, damp, and rot. Like an old root cellar, a vegetable field. In the station lights, quick golds and greens hinted at the Christmas-cake cheeriness of the buildings. Beneath them was a scuffed platform and worn benches. Wrought iron station clocks. Little had changed since I'd been here last. That surprised me.

After our customary debriefing, we received our billet.

"The cadet school," Toby said disdainfully, after we'd been dismissed and given the marching orders. "That's bloody miles away. They could at least have sent a trap."

"Don't be contrary. You've been on a train for weeks."

"It's the luggage," he clarified, shifting one of the straps on his pack. "I've got so much bloody caggage on me—I feel like a mule."

"You've gone soft," I said. Although my pack was a strangely alien, tumour-like weight on me. I felt like I'd been submerged in water and had only just emerged onto dry land. My limbs all felt too heavy, walking a distance suddenly too much for them. The cadet school was a fair to moderate walk from the station. It was a common billet, so all the trappings of barracks had sprung up round it; the RAP, the barber, the dentist. The post office.

Most of the lights were still on, which made a difference. Always a pleasure to see where one was going down an unfamiliar street. There wasn't enough lamplight to drown out the stars, though. I looked up at the sky. The night was beginning to draw in around us.

"Rain?" Toby asked, following my gaze.

"Snow. Hope it holds off."

"It better. God knows what'll happen if it buries the track." He then surprised me by spitting on the ground at our feet.

I glanced around, checking the major wasn't lurking. "I thought you said that was a filthy habit?"

He shrugged, wiping his mouth. "Filthy place."

"Cheer up, Tobes. My word's not Gospel."

"You're the closest thing to a meteorologist we have out here, Ransome. I put a great deal of stock in what you say."

"You have *never* taken a great deal of stock in what I say as long as you've lived." How best to get him out of this defeatist thinking? Time for a new subject. "Barclay's told me he's filling my carriage with gauze."

"The Fairy Godmother department has kicked into action, has it?" Toby asked, with an air of genuine surprise. He was of the opinion that much of High Command could be neatly sorted into the Fairy Godmother Department and Department of Practical Jokes. I was of the opinion he suffered from a rather overdeveloped sense of humour. "When did he bestow that knowledge on you?"

"Just now. Stuck his oar in as I was getting my pack."

"You sound like you don't trust the logistics corps much."

"I don't."

He didn't reply. As he was never one to pass up an opportunity to say something short, sharp, and cynical, I glanced to my side. His jaw was tight.

"Christ," I said. "I am going to have to buy you that drink after all."

His mouth quirked. "Sorry. Out of sorts."

"You don't say."

"Give me an evening in a bed. I'll recover."

"Whose bed?"

"Ha ha," he replied sardonically. "As long as Haddock isn't there, I won't complain about where I am."

"I'm sure the dulcet tones of a mouth organ will find you and help you feel right at home."

I let the silence take over. He appeared to want it. Logically, I knew Toby couldn't be cheery all the time. But he was one of those whose mood was usually improved by the presence of others.

It seemed to be how he showed people he liked them. I didn't like the callous man he seemed to be becoming.

I wondered if this was where it had started to go wrong for Toby: during that time in Irkutsk. In another life, we'd walked from the station in the lamplight to another billet. And here we were, back again. What did he have to show for all that time? The same uniform, another billet.

The cadet school hove into view, just outside the town centre. *No need for a map or a sign, then.* Not that the street signs meant much to any of us, since half were missing and half unreadable. The only one who could navigate by them was Mitya, and even then I don't think he found them much use. But there were only so many places we could go and you didn't need names to keep three streets straight in your head. We had taken to calling them by what we saw, for our own sanity: the cadet street, the street with the station, the one with the two looted hat shops. Of course, the topography had changed since we were last here, almost a year ago for three days. This side of the river had taken it harder than the side with the station. That happened sometimes, with cities. They were seismic, multi-lithic beings. Tectonic. Whole districts seemed to shift, all those chthonic streets with a mind of their own.

The cadet school was big. There had been a lot of cadets. The major had told us there was a billeting of Japanese soldiers sharing with us, but even so it was doubtful the place would be half full.

There was the best stab at an RAP here for a few thousand miles. When the concentration of troops is always on the move, it's hard for the chaos of the Regimental Aid Posts and the Advanced Dressings and the Clearing Stations to keep up. And the Graves Registration Units.

I thought of Evans and I thought of Kim Stevens. It didn't seem fair, in that moment, that Stevens had been kept with us while Evans lay in a shallow grave by the side of the tracks. Lucky Stevens, to die so close to town. I thought of Holub, the man Jandáček and Hayek had buried. How they'd brought him all the way through the forest so he didn't have to die alone. How counterintuitive that had been, to waste so much time and energy.

How pointless it was to try to apply logic to a decision that was so rooted in emotion.

I thought of Stevens's friends, sharing their carriage with his corpse. What would I have done, if it had been me? Would I have been able to summon any emotion at all if I'd had to live next to the corpse of Jacobs or Owen or Gallehawk? If I'd seen their bodies, uncapped and uncorked like Evans's, would I have been plunged into horror that they'd gone or relief that they hadn't suffered? I could honestly say I didn't know.

Would it matter? If I were in that situation, I'd never get them out of my head anyway.

"Bad luck if you fancy a room of your own" was the sentence that greeted me as we came into the entrance hall. I looked at the speaker—Haddock, unhatted and in a muffler. "You especially, Ransome. They've put you with that Czech chap."

"Sharing?" asked Toby, with a trace of indignation. "Surely not."

"I'm just the messenger," said Haddock. "But some of us more lowly subalterns have to double up, given the space."

"I don't mind," I said. "I've seen enough of you two."

Haddock quirked a lip, seeming to take that in the spirit it was meant. "Captain seems to think you and the new arrival are friends."

"I suppose we are," I said, but he was already turning to leave.

"Still cheeky to get you to share," scoffed Toby, when Haddock had gone. He shrugged his pack off and it thudded on the parquet floor.

"Look on the bright side," I said, eager to keep his mood from darkening again. "Subalterns are a dying breed. You might be alone after all."

He huffed a laugh. "Very true. Heard about Stevens, by the way. Tough bit of luck."

"It was." There wasn't much else to say. "I'll register that tonight."

"There's no great hurry; the man's not going anywhere. Do it tomorrow, after you've had a rest. Does the Czech lad snore?"

"Not that I've heard."

"That's an upside. I didn't realise he'd taken to you so much."

"I'm helping him with some of his joint pain," I said, lie rolling off my tongue. "His knees get stiff in the cold."

"You know how to ease joints now? You've kept that quiet," he said, an eyebrow sceptical.

"I value my own time and energy, Tobes. If everyone knew, I'd never have a moment's peace."

"That how they're teaching Physics at UCL now? Particles and joint flexion?"

I dipped my head, trying to hide my flush. "My brother taught me one or two things. Nothing major."

"I thought your brother was a land lawyer?"

"Not Dickie." I shifted my weight to the other foot.

"Ah," he said, the penny suddenly dropping. Nothing like a bereavement to stop people probing. "Right. That makes a lot of sense. Listen, I'm going to see where they've stuck me. I want to unpack before whatever's going to pass as dinner. Would you— Oh, hello. Your friend's here."

I glanced over my shoulder. Jandáček was coming out of a corridor that led deeper into the building.

"Evening," I said, as soon as he was in earshot.

"Evening. Mitya sent me to find you."

"I'll see you at dinner, Francis," said Toby. He offered Jandáček a quick nod of recognition. Jandáček returned it.

He waited until Toby had left before saying, "It appears we're sharing a room."

"Yes." Anticipation fizzed under my skin. "I heard that too."

A little silence hung between us. Whatever his thoughts were, he kept them close to his chest. But his eyes seemed to burn on me, his pupils wider in the dark.

I bit my lip.

"Has he given us any indication as to where?" I asked. It was safer to stay on topic.

"Yes. Ground floor." He wetted his lips with his tongue. "Follow me."

The doors were heavy, pockmarked with those black marks that wooden doors develop after a certain age. The school itself was built to impose in the performative way you'd expect a cadet to. *Welcome, little man*, it said. *Look upon my work, and despair.*

Jandáček held a door open for me. "Are you coming?"

The corridor he took me down was only intermittently lit by a flickering electrical light. I didn't trust that. The electric never lasted. I hoped the room had candles.

"How do you know the way?"

"Mitya showed me," Jandáček said. "We walked up together?"

"Mitya?" I said, trying not to let the surprise show in my face. "That's brave of you. Not many would want to be alone with him."

"Yourself included?"

"No," I answered honestly. "He's all right. Just abrupt."

"'Stark' is the word I'd use."

"That works too."

It did. Stark: a bleached bone on a dark, craggy hillside. Dry and hard. Lying dropped and alone. That was Mitya all over.

We passed a man so leathered and brown that he could have been any age, including several beyond the grave. He nodded and said something to us in quick Russian, then smiled. I smiled back.

"Here," said Jandáček, opening a door the other side of a supply cupboard. "It isn't a lot."

The room had been half-readied for use. There were mattresses on the beds and pillows without cases. There were two heavy crates on the other side, and a broken shelf that looked like it had been moved there for storage.

"Overnight room for chefs," said Jandáček from the door. "Apparently."

"Which one do you want?" I asked, looking at the two beds. "This one, you'll get the sunlight in the morning. The one by the window might be cold."

"I don't care," he said. "As long as it's flat and stationary."

I let my pack fall off my shoulder and onto the cold stone floor. The place smelt like wet rock, like a cave or a castle ruin. I felt suddenly adrift in a bed large and unwelcoming. There seemed to be too much air in the room. I wanted the light. I wanted the city.

"I'm going for a walk before I unpack," I said tentatively. "Coming?"

"No," he answered, sitting on the bed closest to the window. "If that's all right. I'm going to get myself set up, have a shave, et cetera."

"I'll see you back here?"

"Yes," he smiled.

I returned it, and then I left.

My watch battery had run out, I realised after I left the billet. It was quite possibly the worst place to realise this, for two reasons: The first was that the rouble had gone through the floor. Not that I'd ever had much on me to begin with, but what I'd had in my pocket when we'd embarked back in Omsk had been worth roughly two shillings then. Now, it was worth about sixpence. The second was that the few shops that had been open were shutting up for the night. The streets were half in, half out of darkness. We'd come in just approaching five. It must have been after six now.

I'd hoped more stars would come out, but they hadn't. The same three bright ones still hung there.

I hadn't thought that stars could hang before I came here. *It's like they're on picture hooks.*

Shapes came and went around me. It was an extraordinarily bad idea to walk the streets in uniform, but we all did it anyway. Everyone knew we were army, even in mufti. I paid no attention to anyone until one of the shapes came and stood at my elbow.

"Harris says you think it'll snow."

"I said it might," I told James, stopping. "Now I'm less sure. The sky looks remarkably clear."

"It's different without smoke."

"It is," I said, suddenly aware of the reason for all this clarity. It was like a switch had tripped. "Where are the cars?"

"Most of them requisitioned, I imagine. The major was telling us about some song and dance to do with the old government's bookkeeping around this area. Apparently the tsarist officials managed to misrecord a load of typewriters."

"Misrecord them?"

"They turned out to be light bulbs."

"Christ. Logistics is the same the world over."

"The problem is," he continued, "what that means for the rest of the storage records we've got. Logistics is trying to sort that out now. I'm waiting for the major to finish off cross-referencing with our divisional HQ before you and I head back and assess the damage."

"I'm positive there's a story from the Crimea about a ship carrying only left boots. It seems horribly apt."

"Oh, let's not," said Horrocks. "We all know how that turned out."

He stood up straight suddenly, looking behind my shoulder.

I turned. The major had just emerged from the building to our left.

I'd taken my cap off when I looked up at the sky. Now I put it back on hurriedly and saluted as well.

"Evening, Ransome. Mind if I borrow Captain Horrocks?"

"Good evening, sir. Of course."

James spared me a quick glance that seemed to say, *I'll get this over with as soon as I can.*

They moved a few feet away and continued to talk in low voices. I studied the faux Doric column of a doorframe, which was probably nothing but cheap plasterwork split in half. My mother would not have been pleased. She had a lot to say about neo-Classicism in general. I think it was part of the reason she'd been unhappy that I chose to go to University College. If the fake pillars at Cambridge were bad, the ones on Gower Street must have been positively hellish to her.

The sky had begun to darken more meaningfully when Horrocks finally came back over to me, while the major disappeared down the street. "Apologies. Although something exciting may be afoot in the next few days."

"Do you mean that?" I asked flatly.

"If you dislike lice. Keep that under your hat, however, it's not confirmed. Find your room all right?"

"Yes, sir. Thank you."

"Listen, I'm sorry about putting you with the Czech chap. I know we don't know much about him. But he seems to trust you, and you've got on all right so far. And— Well. We need someone we trust in with him. I can try and find a more familiar face, if you like. I can't promise anything, of course."

Sasha did seem to trust me. I wasn't sure how much I believed Horrocks's ostensible justification, however.

The two likelier suspects were:

Number one, they wanted Sasha separated from the corporal to make assurance double sure that they weren't hostile. Wouldn't make off with supplies; sell us out for some meagre gratefulness or safe passage.

Extremely unlikely, but the army was nothing if not paranoid. The only thing it valued more than its own victim complex was standing on ceremony.

Leading to the second possibility. He knew Sasha was a junior officer. And even if it wasn't supposed to be widely known, it wouldn't be the done thing to treat him like a private.

"It's not a problem, sir," I reassured him. "Like you say, we get on."

"He seems like a nice enough stick."

"He seems fine," I said mildly. "The major seems busy."

"He could be worse. Lots to catch up on in divisional HQ by the sound of it. Someone disembowelled a priest last week."

I winced.

"The Japanese don't seem to have had any problems," he said placatingly. "And we should be out of here soon. Navvies are trying to load whatever they can onto the train tonight before the daylight fails, but they haven't left themselves much time." He put a hand on my shoulder, friendly, like we had been back in the old days. Last time we'd been here and we'd both been lieutenants.

"Horrocks," I said. "Kim Stevens."

"It's taken care of."

I opened my mouth, not quite able to force any meaning out of his sentence. "James, I—"

"It's been taken care of," he said. "You shouldn't be worrying about that. Take this time off, Ransome. You look as though you need it."

I blinked. "Do I?"

"You're overworked. Overcommitted. It's part of what makes you a good man, but you can't be a good officer if you're not firing on all cylinders."

Where had all this had come from? "Do you think I'm in danger of that, sir?"

"Listen." He took me by the arm and led me further into the doorway.

No chance this encounter would end the way being pushed into doorways usually did, but my mind still partially blanked out in shock.

"I have concerns about you," he said, still holding on to my arm and talking like you might talk to a child, or how a teacher might to a disruptive but likeable student. "And I'm not the only one. Someone's approached me in confidence about how withdrawn you're becoming. I know you're all right," he said, pre-empting what he clearly thought I'd been about to say. "But you ought to be aware. I told him I would look into it. So this is me, looking into it."

"I'm all right, sir," I said, bemused.

"Yes?"

"Yes."

His voice, somehow, dropped lower. "You had some bad news from home a few months ago. You've not had anything else, have you?"

"Sir, I daresay you'd know if I had."

"You see, I'm not sure you'd tell me, Ransome. You keep yourself to yourself." He glanced down, pointedly, at my thumb. I withdrew an embedded nail from it quickly. "I'm not criticising your stoicism, but if something has happened which you want to share, I'd rather that you did before it became a problem. Either with me or with . . . the source."

"It's Toby, isn't it?"

His schooled expression held out for a few moments before caving. "I was asked to keep an eye on you. Asked how you were. I took them to mean the same thing."

"Well," I said, lost for words. "Thank you, sir?"

He seemed reluctant to let me go but nodded sagely all the same. "Take this time as a break. I want you back on form as soon as we move off on Wednesday."

"It's Monday today, I take it?"

He gave me a funny look. "Yes, Ransome, it's a Monday. Are you joining us for dinner tonight?"

"I am. In fact," I said, hit with a sudden thought. "Do you know who I could talk to about a watch battery? In the interest of me attending on time."

He blinked. "A watch battery?"

"Mine has run out."

"I'll . . . see what I can do," he said. "Walk back with me? I don't want you walking alone."

I nodded mutely and fell into step alongside him, worrying at a hangnail on my thumb. Then I stopped self-consciously, not wanting to worry him.

Luckily, he didn't seem inclined to chat. We walked back in near silence, the sky falling greyer around us. The ribbing of clouds underneath had already darkened to a nondescript slate black. Horrocks caught me glancing up.

"Still have your doubts about the snow?"

"No idea. I'm not a meteorologist."

"Natural sciences, wasn't it?"

My mouth quirked. "Physics."

"Ah. Yes," he said, clearly realising the faux pas a moment too late. They called it Natural Sciences at Cambridge, and only at Cambridge. James and the rest of its alumni couldn't work outside their own framework sometimes. Dickie was the same.

The cadet building loomed back into sight. Horrocks walked me to the door, then stopped. "If you don't have a watch battery, you can't tell the time."

"That's right, sir."

"Know anyone with a watch who won't mind you sticking to them?"

"I can always ask about."

"Good man. See you at dinner, Ransome."

"See you then, sir."

I watched him retreat up the stairs. Had his new existence on the upper strata given him a room to himself? If so, I wondered what he'd do alone, after he'd unpacked.

Inside the entrance hall of the cadet building, Mitya was standing on the stairs, shouting at men with a box, hand in his hair, looking the polar opposite to his usual composed self.

I did my best to stay out of the way on my journey back to the little scullery room.

To my surprise, the door closed out most of the noise. Leaving just me and the smell of old dust. And Jandáček, who did not seem to have moved since I left him.

I sat down heavily on my bed. The one closest to the door. I'd get the sunlight, but not the worst of the cold.

Jandáček seemed to be asleep when I looked over. One arm dangled, his head on the pillow. Then I noticed a glint from his face. His eyes were open and he was staring at the ceiling listlessly.

"You all right?" I asked.

He stayed silent.

"Don't know how fortuitous this room is," I continued. "There's a lot of commotion out there."

He still didn't stir.

If anything was to come of this, of our time alone, I'd have to work for it.

Time to be brave.

CHAPTER EIGHT

"Come to dinner with me."

"I won't, if that's all right."

I let that little beat of rejection pass before doubling down. "It won't be ready until half seven. At least. They haven't thrown anything together yet."

He was still quiet. Had he just got into the habit of living off nothing, or was something more at work?

Sometimes I wondered if it would be preferable to quietly forgo the eating, the sleeping, and just to slip away.

Cupio dissolvi they called it in one of Paul's epistles. *I wish to be dissolved.*

"Who's 'they'?" he asked after a moment.

I cleared my throat, grounding myself back into the room. "The kitchen staff. Didn't want it going to waste if we didn't arrive in time." I tried to smile at him. "Apparently."

"And you weren't tempted by any restaurants on your wander?"

Restaurants. Imagine. They'd be back, one day, but for now—I thought of that half-grey city, hemmed in by the void outside it. I couldn't imagine something as normal as a restaurant on those streets. Too pedestrian for all that sucking blackness.

"Wouldn't that be something." I sat on my bed and heard him turn on the other side of the room.

"What about the game?"

". . . Sorry?"

"The game you play." He was sat up now, facing me. "Gallehawk was telling me. If you could eat anything in the world."

"Now there's a question." I smiled. For all I engaged when the men played, I didn't know if I'd ever answered in earnest. The right answer should have a memory attached—filching bread or cheese from the kitchen. Hanging over Hestia's shoulder with a spoon as she stirred a hotpot.

I wanted to be back there, but the place itself didn't call me. It was what it represented. It was the time it represented.

But my mother would never see me coming down the road and come down the garden path to greet me again. I'd never shin up the horse chestnut tree and onto the kitchen roof. My family would never sit down around the table, all of us together. It would just be me, Hels and Sophie. Existing our lives away in those four walls.

Last time my sisters and I were together was to put a rug down to cover my father's blood in the study. "A bottle of Talisker," I answered, and I tried to flash him a grin. "Do you want to go back?"

He looked up, seeming startled. "'Back' where? School?"

Home, I almost said. But then—"Where are you going back to?"

His silence answered me well.

I bit my lip. Suddenly, I felt a real need for conversation. Anything to get me out of my head. I tried another tack. "Where were you most happy?" I asked. "*Was* it school?"

He laughed. It seemed half dismissive, half like very real amusement. "No, it was not."

"Where, then?"

"I don't know."

"You must. Everyone's trying to get back to somewhere."

"Not me," he said. "I'm just here." The words hung there, in the thick silence like flypaper. I opened my mouth to clear them, and then I realised I didn't have anything helpful to say. What could I add? My hopelessness? The sense of having nothing to hold on to?

Well, he'd trusted me enough to say that. I decided to vocalise the thought taking up space at the back of my mind. "I think suicide runs in my family."

"Why?" his voice said again, with exactly the same inflection, from the other side of the room. A flat, empty question for the universe. *Why. Why, why.*

"My father walked himself into his study and shot himself three years ago. He drank half a bottle of Talisker first." I laughed humourlessly. "He actually used his left hand. Can only assume he didn't want to hit the whisky."

Jandáček remained silent, so I carried on, with a note of envy.

"He still managed it half cut and using the wrong hand. My brother managed it by bloody accident."

What a pointless tendency to inherit. Most families pass down property.

There was a shuffle at the other end of the room as he crossed one leg over the other. "Your brother?"

"Yes."

"I'm sorry."

"It's all right." I smiled wanly. "I didn't like him much. He was a bit of a bastard."

"I wouldn't have brought him up if I'd known."

I was, for the moment, stumped at this left-field comment. Then I remembered that story about his leg. He thought I only had the one, and that he was a land lawyer.

"Dickie is. I had two. One, now. Hugo was the one who died."

There was another beat. "Flanders?"

"Oh, god no," I said, huffing a laugh. I didn't mean to, but I couldn't imagine Hugo doing anything that might take the focus off himself. "Wrapped his motorcycle around a tree. Killed the girl he was with too."

"I'm sorry."

"Don't be. I hated him. He couldn't even be considerate about dying."

"Is there ever a good way to do that?"

"He managed to find the worst way. My mother had pneumonia and was knocking at death's door herself. She tried to summon enough energy to see us every day, and then one of us upped and died."

"Christ. Did she recover, at least?"

"She did, you know," I said, turning to him. "Maybe it was the shock. Then she got the flu and died anyway."

He smiled bitterly. "I feel the same way about my mother if it helps."

"Did she also have the worst luck in the world?"

"It's complicated—I'll get to it. But I can empathise with how you feel about your mother."

Before I could open my mouth to enquire, he clarified, "She's not dead." He met my eyes with a sad smile. "I don't think. I just couldn't see her after I finished school. I barely saw her then." He drew his other leg up to his chest, hugging them both close. He seemed so utterly, utterly dejected that I was about to stand up and hold him, until he stood up himself.

"Come on."

"Where are we going?"

"I can't have this conversation without a drink. Neither can you."

I gave the room a cursory once-over. In the corner above his bed was a net of spider web, so grey with dust it looked like an animal. Like mouse fur. I could barely see it in the failing light.

"On your feet. Don't forget your pack." He took my hand in his and tugged me off the bed gently. His hand was calloused, half rough skin and half broken, dry knots. There were scabs on nearly all of his knuckles. I ran my finger over them, just like I had dreamt of doing on the train. If he kissed me then, I wouldn't make it outside.

He didn't. Instead, he led me to the door and dropped my hand as soon as he opened it.

I shouldered my pack, as per his somewhat bizarre request.

"Do you know where you're going?" I didn't fancy roaming about pointlessly in the dark.

"More or less."

"Have you been here before?"

"Once. Trust me."

I did trust him. That was a problem. Even after all he'd said, all the ways he'd acted, all the different facets of himself he'd shown me, I still trusted him implicitly. A deep trust that led me from my bones and tugged me in whichever direction he wanted me to go.

I followed him out like a shadow. The main hall was deserted, the street outside in almost total blackness. More stars were out. I loved stars. My reason for all things.

"Wait here," he said roughly in my ear.

He disappeared back inside. I waited with my shoulders to the doorway, leaning on the disintegrating wall and gazing at the building opposite. Blue stucco. Bigger, taller than anything you'd find in a city back home. Neo-Classical again. All the roads were wider here, the buildings so much larger than I was used to. Then, why wouldn't they be? There was all this space.

Something cold pressed into my hand, and I recoiled, a muffled exclamation in my throat.

"Shhh," I felt in my ear. "It's me."

"Jandáček?"

"Sasha, please. Hold this."

He pushed the thing at me again. It was a bottle, still slightly damp from condensation.

"Where did you get this?"

"The kitchen?"

"*How?*"

"I asked."

The glass bottle was unmarked, stopped up with what looked like two different pieces of cork and some candlewax.

"Jandáček, who the hell did you ask?"

"Mitya," he said, flashing me a smile. "Told you we'd be friends."

I decided to leave that statement well alone and glanced back down at the bottle. The liquid inside was ominously clear. "Vodka, is it?"

"No. Wine. Come with me."

He didn't quite take my hand again, but he did tug at my sleeve, and that was almost as good. I followed him into the dark, my other hand clasped around the bottle he'd given me, and tried desperately to make skin contact. The warmth of his body on mine was something I was almost unable to think of. What he'd do to me in the dark.

There was a laugh behind us, then a muffled plea to be quiet. Some of our boys lying doggo. Waiting to sneak off just as we were. As we turned away, I heard the groan of an accordion being warmed up.

Jandáček led us down cadet street, away from the station. I followed uselessly, leaning on him when I stumbled sometimes. His hand tightened on my coat sleeve.

We crossed another road and took a curve to the left. I wasn't sure about the direction he was taking, or exactly how far my trust should stretch on a dark night alone. I trusted *him*, but not necessarily his sense of direction. But he pre-empted me before I worked up the courage to speak.

"We're nearly there."

Irkutsk was a city of bridges. Spanning the road we'd turned on to was a long, low road bridge that led further into the outskirts. He led me to the edge.

"Take off your pack?" he asked.

"Why?"

"To sit on. I've got mine, too."

Then he sat, his back to the barrier, clearly expecting me to join him.

I did.

"Why here?" I asked, setting the bottle down between us.

He drew me close and kissed me.

It was so fast I didn't have time to react. Then, before I could lean in to kiss him back, he'd taken the bottle off the side of the road where I'd left it and begun working the wax with his thumbnail. It wasn't productive, so he started worrying the cork with his teeth.

"Do you want me to try?" I asked dimly, still reeling.

"Think you could do better?"

"No. What if it gets cork in it?"

"Could only improve the taste." Jandáček spat out a mouthful of something into the darkness beyond. "Christ."

"You all right?"

"Wax. Here." He took a long draught from the bottle and handed it to me. "Tastes like engine oil."

"Thanks," I said, dubious. The wax rim caught in my teeth, and whatever was inside stuck to my tongue bittily, and caught the back of my throat. I spluttered. "Jesus!"

"You get used to it."

I wiped my mouth on my sleeve and gave the bottle back to him. He took another swig. God alone knew how.

Despite the burn of the alcohol, I shivered. Although it still got above zero during the day, the temperatures were definitely dipping below at night.

"At least it can still break freezing," I remarked to Sasha. "Not looking forward to going back into the minuses."

"Shouldn't be for a while yet, surely."

"I think we're already there," I said, watching my breath mist. "Pardon?"

I wrapped my coat around myself further. "Oh, fuck. Habit. I'm in centigrade. That's where training in the sciences gets you."

"And in layman's terms?

"Low thirties? Anyway. Wish you'd told me to bring my blanket."

"Oh, right." He got to his knees, untangling his from the pack webbing and throwing it over us both. "That should help."

"Thanks." I chin-pointed to the wine. "Why the hell did you pick that stuff up?"

"It's what Mitya gave me. I don't think there was anything else. It'll numb your tongue soon. Just drink enough that you lose the flavour." He wiped the rim and handed it to me once again. "Bannatyne wrote me out a chit for the RAP tomorrow, so I'm all right to be out of action"

So Bannatyne had referred him to the Regimental Aid Post. God knew what they could do for him, but at least it might be something.

"And they treat hangovers, do they?"

"Forms about half of what they do treat," Sasha answered wryly.

I winced into my mouthful of wine, which was dry and acrid. "Red or white?"

"It's birch wine."

It felt like all the moisture was being sucked out of my mouth. "What if I go blind?"

"Avoid doing that. You might beat me home."

I relaxed slowly, so that my shoulder was touching his. It had been ages since breakfast, which had been barely worthy of the title. At the corner of my eye, the world was already beginning to rotate slightly. "If you give me any more of that, I won't be able to make it back to the billet."

"I'll carry you."

I let myself get a bit looser beside him, unsure whether he was joking. He didn't pull away.

"Could you manage?"

"You?" he scoffed. "Easily."

"I'm about your height."

"I'm strong. I could manage."

"Even with your joints?"

"Yes," he said shortly.

I let my hand rest on his knee. "Why?"

Slowly, like he was waiting to think better of it, his hand came to rest on mine. "Why what?"

"Why me." *Why are you like this?* I wanted to ask. *Why are you so contrary?*

His hand began to circle one of my knuckles, where all the scabbing was on his. "Why would it not be you?"

"How many words have we spoken? How long have we spent together?"

His finger rubbed along the bones of my thumb. "That's the point. I want to be with you longer. More."

His finger caught on something—scabbing of my own, probably—and I felt momentarily sick. But he carried on, just like I had done that time on the train in my dream.

"Why are you here?" I asked.

"Hmm?" The vibrations of that one sound echoed right through my shoulder, to a quick, electrical spasm in my crotch.

"You. Why are you here?"

"Similar reason to you, I'd imagine."

"I'm not sure I could tell you my reasons myself."

His body, so stiff against mine, began to give. He leant into me, slightly heavy against my side. "You don't know?"

"No. I don't."

"What else could you have done?"

"Sorry?"

"What else could you have done? If you'd wanted to?" he asked. "List your ideas for me."

I sighed. "I don't know. Followed my brother into law? Worked for the Home Office? Got a job in engineering?"

"Couldn't you have taught?"

"I suppose, but it never appealed. I could retrain if I get struck with the desire to. There's always time."

"Is there?" he said dryly. Then, "I thought you were a Classicist, but your way of measuring temperature suggests against it.".."

I stroked his thumb too. "Why would you think I'm a Classicist?"

He licked one of his chapped lips. "I thought all of you were."

"All of us repressed Brits?"

He flashed me a grin. "If that's how you want to couch it."

"All of us repressed homosexuals?"

He didn't say anything.

"Are you one?" I asked gently.

I felt him huff a breath. A laugh of forced humour. "What do you think?"

"You're not a Classicist either?"

His mouth twisted sardonically.

"Then what?" I pressed.

I was so keen to get to know him, this strange, dark-haired man. Tugging as he was on a door in my soul that had long been locked. The forgotten entrance to a nursery playroom, the corner of a garden that had once held adventure.

He took another drink and seemed to hold on to that question for a long time. "Aside from a repressed, public-schooled homosexual?"

"Aside from that."

He snuffed and looked at his feet. He took another pull from the bottle. "Some bastard exports commissar. I suppose."

I encouraged him, lightly. "And what else? If you wanted to."

He gazed at me.

"I told you what I want to do. It's only fair."

"You didn't tell me," he protested.

"I told you what I know."

He lay back against the hard stone wrought of the ruined bridge. "Would you believe me?"

"If you told me what?"

"If I told you I don't know? That I only set out here because I couldn't bear to look at another contract?"

I frowned. "Is that why you're here?"

"What else could I do?" He was picking at the last of the sealing wax on the bottle's neck. "I translated contracts. For exports. Proofread them, stamped them. All of those bureaucratic things."

"What for?"

"The contracts? This and that. Shipping for materials, mainly."

"Sounds like enormous fun."

"Oh trust me, it isn't."

"You aren't a fan of the finer points of contract law, then."

He took another swig. "Is anybody?"

"Dickie seems to be."

"That's just him."

I huffed a laugh. "Yes."

There was silence again. Then he said, "I was lonely."

I turned to him. "Hmm?"

His head hit the wall at the back of the bridge. "I was lonely. That's why. That's why I came out here. I didn't want to be lonely anymore."

Why were you lonely? It was a selfish thing to want to ask. Did he really have no one? Could I be there for him, if there was room? But it came out as, "I'm sorry."

"I am too."

There was another silence; the space between giving and receiving. He had told me something about who he was. I wanted— I should give him a little part of me in exchange. Was I lonely? Probably. In the same way? I had my family. Depleted, but still there. I had friends who I could travel down to see. Some had stayed in London. Others had left and gone to France.

Not many anywhere now, I thought to myself from the poem, *save under France.*

"If it helps," I began, "a lot of my friends' good feeling towards me is only preserved by the virtue of distance. I'm not really good company."

His eyes left me. I tried to think of something else to say, though I knew nothing of the heart-struck loneliness that must force someone halfway across the world. I was here because I had nowhere else to be. Only a house, which death had the postcode of and that I had tried to avoid lest I get spirited away as well. It had seemed I might, once. It may still.

"You're sad," he said.

"I'm not."

"You're sad."

"I could feel worse."

He smiled a wry smile and passed the bottle over to me. As I raised it, I was struck unbidden by some adolescent muscle-memory I had long since buried. Three of us, shoulder to shoulder, under Founders' Bridge at school. Huddled round two stolen bottles of dark porter and its rich, burnt-toast taste. The memory stunned me so much that the taste of wine took me by surprise.

The three. I remembered the one who'd sat on my left, the boy who'd always got the train home just before me. He seemed too well-liked to be concerned with who I was. A few weeks later, I'd started avoiding him. I'd been fairly unpleasant about him to those who'd tolerate me. He'd written me a letter about a year after we left, asking how I was. It had come with an Oxford postmark. I hadn't answered, out of fear that any contact with him would disturb the captive singularity of our tenuous friendship. I hadn't wanted anything to come between me and that moment with him. Not even him in person.

The other had followed his father into archaeology.

I turned back to Sasha, who wasn't either of them. "That stuff really is dreadful."

"I know." He took it off me for another swig. "You could use it to stop the water freezing."

I nodded, then gave a shiver. The stone we were leant against had seeped through my coat and tunic into my undershirt. I adjusted my position, glancing at him as I did. His profile looked very pale in the moonlight. And he was so still. Statuesque, save for the gentle huffs of breath that hung in front of him.

Awkwardly, I tried to explain my silence. "I was thinking about school."

"Memories of illicit drinking?"

"What else? Who would I have been to let school get in the way of an education?"

"The first time I got drunk was on gin in my third year." He smiled, looking down at the end of his boots. "One of the first eleven had been sent it as a present for a job well done. Or it was his birthday. Anyway, I fagged for him and I ended up being swept along. No one caught us, but I think the house staff had a pretty good clue about what was going on." He took another swig. "Can't touch gin, now."

"Interesting substitution you've made," I said, holding up the bottle. Fagging—using a younger boy half as a servant, half as a dogsbody—hadn't particularly taken off at Alfred's, so I had no comparison. "That wasn't bad treatment for a fag, though. I can't imagine Horrocks inviting Owen out on the lash."

"Different situation," said Sasha. "Owen's never going to get his own batman, is he? He's not going to end up on top. That stratification will always *be* there."

I had to acquiesce that point. The idea at school is that any treatment someone puts their fag through is justified, because they'll get their own to mistreat a few years down the line. So the misery passes on. God, I'm glad I hadn't been in that position. Social dynamics are slightly easier to navigate when you go home every night.

"He got expelled later that year," continued Sasha, smiling. "Rawlins. Not for the gin. He tied another lad's mattress to one of the coxless quads and floated him off down the river."

"Did the gin have a say in that decision?"

"Difficult to say." Sasha scuffed at some freezing dust with the toe of his boot. "It's the sort of thing he'd do anyway."

"The more I hear about boarding schools," I said, as he pressed the bottle back to me, "the more the army makes sense."

"You weren't a boarder?" he said, with an air of surprise. Turning to me to get into his pocket, he took out his cigarette tin and offered me one. Lit them both and passed mine over to me, still damp from his mouth.

"My mother wouldn't let us," I said, leaving off the second half of that sentence. She could not—as she'd told my father—for the life of her understand why people would have children and then not spend time with them. It didn't seem fair to share that with Sasha, though. "Dickie, Hugo, and I were all packed off to day school in Hampstead."

"Where?"

"King Alfred?" I answered. His expression remained one of polite enquiry. I laughed. "No, you wouldn't know it. And there aren't really a plethora of Old Alfredians about."

My father might have been able to compromise with her on Bedales, which had appealed to my mother's general ethos of creativity and secularism. He hadn't pushed that hard, though. Perhaps he'd shared her opinion.

I took a drag. "My sister, however. Helena, the older one. She decided that she wanted to go to Roedean at eleven. There wasn't much my mother could do once she'd passed the entrance exams."

"Your father could always not have paid," Sasha pointed out. "If your mother had insisted she didn't want her away."

"He could've," I agreed. "But I think they were both secretly quite proud. My mother wanted to be an archaeologist, but she didn't have the background. She got to give that to Helena without forcing her." I wondered if my mother had rather admired Helena's decisiveness. Wished she could have done the same. "My mid-Victorian grandparents had very mid-Victorian views."

"Did your sister get to be an archaeologist?" asked Sasha.

I thought of Hels, last time I'd seen her. Hair undone and housecoat still on at one in the afternoon. Not an archaeologist. Not anything. "I don't know. I haven't seen her in a long time."

Given that had happened in my family, I wondered what it would have been like to have not seen them at all. For months at a time. To have been in a different country. A different culture.

"Is it worth it?" I asked finally, pathetically, at last. "Boarding?"

His answer was short and smart. "No."

"No," I echoed. "I don't think I would have liked it either."

He drew his knees up and huddled himself further into his long, dark scarf. This close, I could see that the wool was uneven: knotted in some places and holey in others. He told me he thought his mother had made it, but he wasn't sure.

His mother, I learned, was flighty in the way that *flighty* is used as a euphemism for something different and far darker. She'd had an affair with his father when they had been eighteen and nineteen (I don't recall which was which), resulting in Sasha, and in his mother being promptly recalled home on the understanding that the child would be schooled by her family and then cut off. He hadn't seen her since he was sixteen. He'd been expecting her on his last day at school, but she hadn't arrived. He hadn't expected since and, assured me, was happier for it.

"Mothers are always a source of excitement, Sasha," I told him. "No two are what you'd hope."

But I'd got a dilettante who'd died and he'd got an absentee who might as well have. At least I knew who it was I missed.

Russia stretched out, into the beginning of its night, around us.

There was so much I wanted to tell him, all mixed up in my mind. *You're not like your mother. You're not the same. I think you might be the most beautiful man I've ever seen. I think I was the disappointment as well. I'm the only person I know who didn't get into that sparkling Oxbridge social circle. I had to leave that house I now so desperately want to get back to, before I killed myself there like my father. We don't have to be them. We aren't.*

"This is why," he said.

"Sorry?" My cigarette, barely smoked, had burnt its way back to my fingers. I dropped it onto the pavement and let it extinguish itself. It would probably ice over soon.

"You asked me earlier why it was you." He glanced away, tapping his ash and tossing the butt away. "Because of this. Conversations like this."

"This is the first conversation we've had, Sasha."

His mouth moved quickly. It might have been a smile, to anyone else who had seen it, but I knew it for what it was. A nervous movement while working up the courage to speak.

"On the train," he said. "You make tea. You give out your rations. No one asks you to, but you do. And I don't talk much. Can't. Who to? But you seemed like you'd listen." He met my eyes. "And I think you have a lot of love to give."

I kept our eyes locked, overwhelmed, until he glanced down. "And that made you want to get me drunk on a bridge?"

He grinned wryly. "It made me want to have you to myself."

"What will you do," I asked, "now you have me?"

His gaze caught, snagging on my face like he hadn't expected me to say anything. Perhaps he hadn't. Perhaps he'd thought we'd just pack up and go home once there was nothing left to talk about, or when the weird bottle of sack ran out.

Perhaps he was right and I did have a lot of love to give—love I couldn't give. That I wanted someone to receive it, someone to talk to and sit with and warm up.

If so, then like sought out like.

His eyes were very wide. In that moment, I couldn't imagine looking away.

And yet.

I stood, stretching myself out. A joint in my knee clicked.

"Come on," I said, reaching down a hand. "I think we ought to go."

He pulled himself up, towards me, and chanced one last, fleeting mouth-kiss on that empty street. I leant in, briefly, then came away.

I felt drunk. I was drunk.

"No," I said. Then, "Not here." Glancing around once more, I squeezed his hand and turned back. He fell into step beside me and lit another cigarette. He passed one to me without being asked. A kiss by other means. It burned.

CHAPTER NINE

That evening I ended up in my favourite place in the world. On my knees with my head between a gorgeous man's thighs—and truly, I had never, in all my life, seen a man so beautiful.

Sasha had gasped so freshly when I'd pushed him down that it seemed like no one had ever done this to him before. Now, as he lay on his back on his tiny bed while I licked the crevice between his legs and the sensitive beginning of his ball-skin, my suspicions were as well as confirmed.

Elation filled me, and I was born again.

As I licked deeper, his breathing jack-knifed. He sat up suddenly, as if his stomach muscles had spasmed beyond his control, letting out a high, jagged gasp.

"I've got you," I murmured into his skin. "I've got you."

The vibrations seemed to soothe him, and he lay down again, his breathing still fast. I moved slowly left, from his leg down towards one of his testes and took it into my mouth.

He heaved in a heavy breath. "Oh *God*, Francis."

I hummed, half in satisfaction and half to see what it would do to him. The musky, dusky smell of male virility filled me as I nuzzled closer into his coarse hair, sucking deeply. His breathing hitched, and I shifted my attention to the other.

I licked, long and determined, up the heavily ridged skin beneath his balls, up to the root of his cock. He tasted of heavy, brackish water and the pathetic, mould-ridden towel he'd used to dry himself after showering. I licked again, trying to wash that taste away. Underneath it all was that salty, indescribable man-taste.

I licked up the length of his cock, right to the top, and something under my skin fizzed and warmed. Leaving my hand where it was, I rubbed the twitching muscles of his inner thigh lecherously, dipping my tongue in, tasting salt and tang. I went deeper this time, trying to take him in as far as my mouth would let me. I loved this. I used to be so good at this. Those months as a shut-away in my family home meant I had lost practice, and I was determined to be good again. Make this as good as I possibly could for him.

I pushed deeper still, and he hit the back of my throat bluntly. He cried out, making all these noises and little movements. Things you'd never see unless you were this close to him—had anyone been this close before? Was I the first? What I did to him, wanted to do—would it be new to him?

"Francis—" His breathing cut out as he fisted a hand through my hair. I sucked again, dragging my mouth up and over, circling his tip and the fluid that had beaded there, like a prize. A sweet-salt tang burst on my tongue. He swallowed, and I glanced up and watched the stark column of his neck. I wanted to lick it, to feel its progress all the way. It was still hard to believe I was here now. All those moments of privately coveting him, and here he was.

Something warm unravelled in my heart, heating me. I took him down as far as my tight, malpracticed throat could manage. He mewled, and I stiffened my hand at the base of his cock, rubbing it up to meet my lips, following his bulging veins and arteries. His masculine texture felt both hard and soft, under me—tough and pliant. His hands tightened in my hair again, and his voice fractured. "Francis, I can't—*Francis* . . ."

I kneaded the taut muscle of his thigh—*It's all right.*

He cracked out a sob and came, just as I was drawing to the top to take him deeper. I stuttered and his breathing hitched.

"Sorry, *sorry*," he murmured, sounding genuinely apologetic.

I gave him one last, long suck in answer before pulling off. Some of his release had gone down my throat, over my lips. An escaped strand trailed from the soft, tight skin of his abdomen, dribbling down the sensitive crease where his legs met. I licked it off, slowly and deliberately.

"Francis—" His voice was low. I did it again.

"Francis . . ."

I devolved into light, dry kisses trailing up his taut body and to his neck. It was strange how I missed him when I was between his legs, and couldn't see his face. When I couldn't meet his eyes or stroke his hair.

And I loved looking at him. Of course, his time on the front had taken its toll on him: he was bony and slim, malnutrition starting to open some of the old wounds on his skin, or refusing to let them close. But underneath, I could see the skeleton of a runner's physique, all long and rangy muscle. His skin was lightly covered in cocoa-freckles—it seemed like I could lick them all off.

I ended my kisses at the branch of his neck, stroking my rough thumb over his collarbone, the bony protrusion at its end. His warm legs came up and bracketed my hips and held me to him, in place.

I felt, rather than heard, him sigh.

"Was that all right?" I asked into his hair.

"Hmm?"

"That." I continued my stroking. "How was it?"

He huffed a breath of laughter. "No one's ever done that to me before."

I circled my thumb around his Adam's apple and hid my smile in his soft skin. No one. I was the first; where no one else had been. "No one?"

He wrapped an arm around my waist instead of answering.

"I thought you public schoolboys were notorious."

"I was never quite the type. To receive," he said into my hair. I nuzzled into his in return. "Didn't want to get the reputation for giving, either. It was all very *Gerald Eversley*."

Even after his shower, the old, comforting smell of cigarette smoke still clung to him. I breathed in deeply.

"Don't, I smell awful."

"You don't!"

He wriggled away from me, smiling. "I don't want you to think any worse of me after doing . . . that."

"What do you mean?"

Even beside him, out of contact on the pillow, I could feel his blush.

"I like it," I assured him, nuzzling close again.

He didn't speak.

"Sash," I pushed myself off to look him in the eye. "If I didn't want to do it, I wouldn't have done."

Sash. I allowed myself to bask in the mind-numbing pleasure of shortening his name. *Sasha. Sash.* Better to pull too close than push away.

He avoided my eyes and ran a finger down my chest. A lot of my scars had healed, but some of the deeper dig-marks from my old habit of putting my nails through my skin were still scattered about. I tried to pull away subtly and didn't manage.

"What're they from?"

I stopped his hand with mine. "Don't worry about them."

"They're on your hands too."

"They're mostly old. Don't worry."

I gave a futile twitch, inside the warm bracket of his legs. He must have felt it too, since he pushed in closer to me.

"You've very handsome."

I was not very handsome, but I thanked him with a small kiss to the sensitive skin beneath his ear. I'd long ago given up hoping I'd be handsome. The natural curse of the red-headed man.

As if he'd known, he ran a finger through my too-long hair. I'd have to see someone about getting it cut. I fantasised about letting it grow when I got home, though. At least to my chin. It didn't curl but had a sort of half-wave caught in the middle of Helena's unworkable frizz and Sophie's arrow-straight yard of pumpwater hair. I preferred it long.

Sasha fingered it gently. "I like the colour. Like a fox."

I liked that. I let him know with another kiss.

He was so much more beautiful.

Despite myself, my cock began to fill. He rolled his hips a little against mine.

"Don't. You know what you're getting yourself into," I warned.

He smiled and met my mouth in what was perhaps our first real, private kiss. A kiss with nothing behind it but the want to kiss. Nothing but the desire to kiss. No worry, no fear. No urgent lust.

I pressed my lips against his, enjoying the closeness, the warmth of his skin. Then his hand travelled lazily up my spine and into my hair, not quite pulling me closer, but making itself felt. I pushed against him and he opened his mouth, the ghost of his tongue brushing across my lips. It was so unbearably erotic. A vein throbbed, deep and close, in my neck.

I manoeuvred my hand up to his face, covered his shower-soft skin and stroked it in wonder. His eyelashes feathered against my hand. I ran my thumb up across his eyebrow, the smooth run of skin until his hair. Then I did it again. He moaned softly at the back of his throat and invited me deeper. I accepted, willingly and warmly, anticipation fizzing under my skin.

I pressed my hips against his, enjoying the rough friction and the heavy pressure of his cock just beginning to stir again. I loved being so close to him when he was still warm and sleepy and half-formed. My jacket and trousers removed, I was still clad in my underwear and mostly-undone shirt. God, I wanted to push my way through my skin to him. His hand, the one that wasn't in my hair, came around to undo the two remaining buttons. He had to jack-knife it up between our bodies, bending his elbow sharply. Everything about him seemed sharp. I covered his hand with mine, not wanting to be away from him for too long. Not wanting him too far from me. I was at sea without him.

I helped him undo the buttons and sat up to shuck the shirt off as his hands came to my hips and dipped below my waistband.

"You don't have to," I told him quickly. He answered me by pushing further in. His thumbs came to rest in the hollows of my pelvis. A nerve jolted, all the way down, warming me utterly.

His warm, crisp voice in my ear. "I want to." His hot breath tickling against my skin, dampening my neck.

I leant onto him again, my elbows pinned by him to either side of his body as his hands came up to greet me again. He grinned. I grinned back. I loved this playful back and forth. I loved it in partners anyway, but it felt even better with him. Sweeter for having to work for it. I'd dug underneath the spikiness, and here he was. Really him. I kicked out my leg, trying to get rid of the underwear knotted around my knees, and he burst out laughing.

"Oh, be quiet," I said, then kissed him.

He hooked one leg around the back of my knee and pulled me closer to him, our hips aligning. My legs around his. An orgasm began to creep up my spine, but in the last moment I was able to tear myself away. I brought the meagre, institution-issued blankets over us to keep out the worst of the night's chill. Then I kissed him, more thoroughly than I could ever have hoped.

His cock was beginning to fill out, and I could feel its hot pressure in the nerves around my thighs. His cock was lovely, and I already seemed to know it so well: sweet and tentative like the rest of him, well-defined and well-proportioned. I wanted to get my mouth on it again, but I didn't want to leave his mouth alone. I pressed my hips against him instead, and he came up to meet me desperately. He was so responsive. So attuned to himself and what he wanted.

My hands were either side of his face, stroking the lovely skin around his lovely eyes. Begrudgingly, I took one away, covered his hand with my own, and then dipped it lower.

"Where are you going?" he muttered. He was barely audible through the thunder in my ears. I quieted him with a kiss, then answered him by wrapping my hand around his semi-hard cock and giving it a long, leisurely squeeze.

He huffed a quick laugh. "Your hands are cold."

"Warm them up?" I asked, burying my face in the side of his neck. Feeling the little subvocal sounds he was making. Usually, I loved a vocal partner. But the knowledge of where we were never left me, humming constantly at the back of my mind. Still, if we had to be quiet, I wanted to make it worth it. Make him feel everything against his skin instead.

He gave into it, melting into the pillow and grasping at the back of my head his other hand balling into the coarse bedsheet beside us. I worked my way up to his earlobe and nipped lightly, startling a yelp from him. He bit down against his lip. I squeezed him, my legs around his hips as he groaned again, longer, slower.

"Is this all right?" I asked, between kisses to his ear. He pulled my hair as an answer, dragging my mouth back to his and kissing me with such force that I took it as an order to move further.

I pushed myself up, leaving the inviting canvas of his skin ever so briefly in order to fit my hand around my own cock as well. Then I lowered back to the soft wonderground of his neck. I'd have to moderate myself, stay on watch, having been far too fond in the past of marking a partner. I rationed myself to kisses as I gave a long, slow drag up his length and mine. He stuttered out a high gasp that I felt under my tongue. I did it again, and then again until he was gasping and grasping under the covers to do the same thing as me.

His warm, rough hand covered mine, urging me on faster. His grip was slightly tighter around the top than mine would have been; he added a twist where I wouldn't have. It crossed my mind, fleetingly, that this would be better with some lubrication, some barrier. Not that I was getting up to fetch anything now.

The thud of flesh on flesh, snatched gasps, and bedsprings filled the room. The bedframe's cheap metal railings knocked against the plaster wall once, maybe twice in half a minute. Was it enough to attract attention? I always worried it might. But I stopped thinking after he kissed me again.

After a minute, his lips broke away from mine to mouth breathlessly. I, in an astonishing show of restraint, squeezed my teeth into his neck in the ghost of a bite. His muscles tightened beneath me as he released, slow and kettle-hot all over my hand. Almost wordlessly.

I kissed his seizing throat and continued working myself, trying to take in as much of him as I could. Wanted to keep him to me forever, breathe him in. Feel him under me: Far and near and low and louder. His gorgeous face. His sweet, contented bonelessness.

He suddenly sat half-up, kissed me hard, and said, "On me."

"Really?" My voice was tight with holding myself at bay, and he looked so inviting all sprawled out. He nodded, and that was almost all it took. I bit the inside of my cheek, hard, and tried to supress what moans I could when I came, streaking him all over.

I held my position, each spasm deeper than the last. But then I felt his hands come up into my hair and pull me gently back down into a kiss, so soft and tender that it almost broke my heart.

We lay there, loose-limbed and satiated, me trailing my fingers over the tempting skin of his shoulders while he cuddled into my neck, breathing heavily.

The blanket I'd been so thoughtful as to supply was lying mostly kicked off to the side, spilling over onto the floor. After a minute, I reluctantly broke the embrace to drag it back, stopping to kiss him as I did. I wiped the worst of our spillage off both of us, leaving the blanket to drape and protect us from the cold. It was very warm, snuggled in next to him.

"Do you think anyone heard?" he asked at last.

"No," I answered truthfully. "And if they did, this isn't what they'd think." There must be plenty of desperate women here, first trying for money, then for food, for a knife, for a journey out. I nuzzled the side of his head. "This isn't where their mind would go first."

He seemed to take that as an answer and stirred lethargically against me. Sasha was more relaxed postcoital than I'd seen him before. I had designs to keep him like that.

I had designs on him, full stop.

Throughout the time I'd known him, I'd had trouble keeping images of him out of my head. Not images like this, not all the time. But of him, at my house. Him, filled out with good food and exercise, his thighs in a pair of jodhpurs, smiling at me from horseback. Him stirring in the morning light, just-woken and still smelling of sleep. Him at my kitchen table, feeding scraps to my cats.

Jumping the gun had always been a problem of mine.

Of course, I didn't tell him any of that. Instead, I resumed stroking his back, a warm little gesture both of us seemed to enjoy, given that he quickly stretched out and leant against me.

I had been lucky—insofar as I could be—with my prior experience. In my circle, I knew enough men like me to know myself. To know my preferences, to have tried—more or less— what I had wanted to try. There was, for example, no chance of me being one of those fabled, lucky creatures who'd be as happy with a woman as I was with a man. Once I had held out hope, but as the years passed and I'd still refused to "grow out of it," I had slowly but surely given up.

Propriety and the law hadn't been as much of a hindrance on me as they could have been. I'd been so unrepentantly lucky, so relatively safe in my little Bloomsbury bubble. What about Sasha? Who had he had? What did he want, and how did he know he wanted it? Could I help him? Would he let me?

Sasha's breathing got steadily deeper and deeper, and I began to lose him to sleep.

I lay there for a moment longer, reluctant to leave the warm haven of his body and our sheets. To return to the bruising cold of the floor and my bed by the door. Maybe I'd take a wild chance on staying, claiming we were huddling for warmth—it was encouraged, as the nights got colder.

The fact we were both naked would probably be questioned, though. I didn't want to push our luck.

I tried my best not to disturb him as I sat up but managed to anyway. A hand came to rest on my arm, accompanied by a sleepy hum of protest. I kissed his mouth, then his forehead, then his nose, and whispered, "It's for the best," before trailing on over to my bed and a dreamless, uncomfortable sleep.

CHAPTER TEN

Waking up without him felt strangely hollow. I spent the better part of ten minutes gazing at him, wanting to slip over and keep him, soft and safe, in my arms. I loved mornings after: that warm, sleepy stirring and coming awake. Being robbed of having that with him hurt.

I got up, hoping to take my mind off the loss. I used the room's addendum chefs' shower as I hadn't managed to yesterday, dressed, fixed my puttees, laced my boots, and left in the direction of the parade ground.

There was a service for Stevens this morning.

It had been a toss-up whether to have it this morning or last night. I, for one, thought that a third option of tomorrow before we moved off was a far more salient choice. Apparently not enough people had shared that opinion.

A chaplain said a few words on the parade ground. Nothing spectacular, but better than Evans had got. We'd left our chaplain in Omsk with the other two-thirds of the battalion—I had no idea where this one had been dug up from. There were faces I hadn't expected to see, and some more obviously the worse for the night before than others. But they'd come.

The morning was still cold enough for my breath to crystallise in the air. The weather outside was comparatively mild, though, in comparison to the lung-scorching cold from last February. Those temperatures couldn't be far away now.

We peeled off as the brief service drew to an end, and I made my way to the mess hall, snagging a cup of what looked like tea and a burnt piece of toast, and then sat heavily next to a familiar figure.

"Morning." Toby wheeled around, beaming uncertainly. "What happened to you last night?"

He hadn't been at the service. Stevens hadn't been his man. He might not even have been told about it.

I took a long draught of tea. Then I smiled and shrugged. "Sat on the bed and next I opened my eyes, it was about half an hour ago. Did I miss anything?"

He launched into a tale of the night, which seemed to involve not much but the eating of hot potatoes and more of that same mysterious wine Sasha had procured. And vodka, of course.

"The captain wants to talk to us before lunch, by the way," he said conversationally. "Think it has something to do with active sectors and rather a lot to do with delousing."

I scratched an itch in the crease of my knee. He grinned.

"My reaction too." He nodded at a group of Japanese soldiers sitting at the other end of the table. "They're up first. Been here longer. Get the luck of the draw. The blokes on the ground here only got the bloody machine up and running because the major kicked up such a fuss. Barclay's good for something, it appears. And James had an opinion about it in a telegram a month or so ago." He shrugged and drank more of his ersatz tea.

I drank mine. Although the alcohol had mostly worn off by the time I went to sleep, it was making itself known this morning as a deep, solid headache. Tea usually helped. Over the room I saw Mitya was busy with his as well. He quirked his eyebrow at me in greeting.

There was an uproar from a nearby table. Then Jacobs's voice—he had undoubtedly been left out of something "hilarious."

"What's your agenda for the day?" Toby asked conversationally, before draining his cup.

I shrugged. For all that I looked forward to time off, I never seemed to do anything with it. Not that there would be a huge amount to do in Irkutsk. "Read, maybe."

"Francis!" He gave me a hurt glance, a parody of a scold. "I'm going to have a wander. See the town. Don't know when I'll next be in central Siberia. There's rivers and bridges. And parks, I imagine. It will be like Paris."

"Are you inviting me on a Parisian stroll?"

"Are you considering it?" His face humorously alight.

I was so glad Sasha had arrived when he had. If not, sheer proximity alone might have run me the risk of being head over heels with Toby.

"Can I bring a book?"

"You can bring one and talk to me. You can do a dramatic reading."

"With James Grant? Not bloody likely."

"Still soldiering on with the *Six Hundred*, are you?"

"Hardly. I'm just out of chapter two."

He gave me a deadpan stare. "Of all the books in the world, you choose the one about the prequel war. Francis, I'm shocked."

"I'm not convinced it's about the Crimea at all, you know. So far they've gone from Wales to Fife."

"They've not got on a ship yet?"

"Their logistics must be worse than ours. You should read it. It might make you feel better about things"

"It might make me feel a whole lot damn worse."

"Always someone having less fun than you are. At least you aren't Willie Pitblado."

"That can't be a name."

"There's another called Newton Norcliffe."

"You really can put pen to paper and write whatever you fancy, can't you? Tell you what," he said, popping a crust into his mouth decisively. "Bring Grant along and let me know if they ever get round to anything worthwhile. Ten points to you if it involves Willie Pitblado."

All's said, I passed a relatively pleasant day with Toby wandering about by the banks of the Angara. We did find a park, one of the strange manicured fields that marketed itself as a "Municipal Garden" in the shadow of a closed museum, with the undulating hills that seemed particular to this region. It was almost opposite the sugary-looking station we'd pulled in to. If we watched for long enough, I half-fancied we'd be able to see our train. All ugly and blunt-nosed like some blind troglodyte, belching smoke. A monument to Alexander III stood like a sentinel beside the river, and we sat by it on a frost-infected bench. It warmed ostensibly as the sun got higher, but it was never able to quite pierce the clouds. A pretension of cavalry officers shivered nearby, sharing the park with us from a distance far enough that we didn't have to converse.

It was barely warm enough to sit, even with our greatcoats. I remarked as much to Toby, who gave me a strange look.

"It's almost November, mate."

"I know," I said, suddenly floundering. "I remember. I just—"

"I know," he said soothingly. Had he meant to echo me, or had it just happened automatically?

It had seemed so warm when I'd sat with Sasha yesterday, out on the other side of town. Perhaps there were pipes close to the pavement on that bridge. Perhaps it had been being above the water. Or perhaps it had been the alcohol and we'd both almost frozen to death without realising.

The cold in my fingers had frozen my muscles. I wiggled to get them working, imagined the blood flowing up like engine oil to my joints.

"Over a year now," Toby said, his breath fogging the air slightly. "Had you ever been here before?"

"No." It had never crossed my mind that Russia had previously been a place one could visit. "You?"

"Once. To Moscow and St Pete's. Years ago."

I nodded and thought of that phrase: *Na Moskvuu*. Or *Na Moskvuu!* as you were meant to say it, clinking glasses and cheering it on. Holidays to Moscow. I sometimes forgot what a child of privilege Toby was.

We spent some hours in companionable silence, intermitted by companionable chatter. When he rose and offered his hand to me, I was almost sad to take it and leave. It was late afternoon, and the hassocky ground was just starting to become gooey with thawing ice. It would surely close again, harden up, and refreeze in less than two hours.

I followed Toby, wending our way through the wide boulevard streets, until he came to a stop and unexpectedly pulled me close. I wrapped my arms around him, more in startlement than anything else.

"What's brought this on?" I asked, trying my best not to appear stiff or wooden. It wouldn't do for me to jokingly reciprocate though, even with someone as tactile as Toby. Not if word got out. Holding another man by the lapels was generally frowned upon, unless he owed you money.

"Your Czech's on his way."

"Yes?" I asked. Toby often exaggerated for humour, but this was dramatic even for him.

He hissed something in my ear that sounded very like "Be careful."

I pulled away, stunned, but he didn't meet my eye. Acting as if nothing had happened, he held that heavy door to the cadet school open for me. And through it, I came face-to-face with the very object of that warning. The sight that must have prompted it.

Jandáček was tired; I could see from the set of his shoulders and the way he held himself. All the tension that had seemed to ease out of him last night sat on him heavily. But he gave me a smile and stood up as I came into the lobby.

Back, from wherever he had wandered to. *The sailor, home from the sea.*

Toby had gone. He hadn't said whether I should be careful of Sasha or with him. Either way—surely it would have been something worth mentioning in all those hours alone together?

I took a cautious step forward. "Where have you been all day?" Then, "Did you sleep all right?"

"Yes." He took me by my elbow into the doorway that led off into our corridor, then pulled his other hand from his pocket and uncurled it. Inside, small and glinting off the sparse artificial light, was my watch, ticking. It told quarter past five.

I gazed at him.

"I got it a new battery. I hope you don't mind."

"I—"The words for stuck in my throat. "I don't. How did you manage it?"

"You left it in the room. I managed to pick a battery up."

I had left it. There had been no point taking it out with me to find a battery, not working—the shops were a gamble with limited payoff.

"Did you have to go far?" I asked.

One of our battalion's hard and fast rules was that one should always, without fail, stay away from any shop outside the dead centre of town. Anything further afield would be guarded to the teeth, and if it wasn't, there would guaranteed to be a suspicious back room somewhere with a horrifyingly inevitable conclusion waiting to be drawn. Two weeks ago, barely out of Omsk, three men from A Company had chanced across what had appeared to be a normal enough blacksmithy and had spent half an hour trying to converse with his wife before discovering the blacksmith's body hanging from the rafters in the workroom.

I didn't think she was eating it. I wasn't sure if that was worse.

Such things were almost always horror stories, but no one wanted to be the first through a shop's door in case they aren't.

"Francis?" Sasha asked, tapping my knuckles with his. We were stood outside our bedroom now, thresholded.

"Sorry." I drew my attention back to him. "You were telling me where you went?"

"Nowhere far," he said, smiling. "Bought a watch battery off a fishmonger. Thought he could do with the business.

It was such a tiny action, and it stung in the way only tiny things can. I offered him a quick smile.

"Thank you."

He smiled back. "You're welcome."

Although it was—unofficially—a leave day, there was a meal at barracks for those who requested one. I'd put my name down earlier this morning, unable to find it in me to care about the logistics of food. Despite my hesitation, I hadn't put down Sasha's.

"Are you eating tonight?" I asked.

"No. I want to talk to Barclay. Can't do both." His face rearranged, setting stiffly. "He talked with our detachment today. I'd like to make sure they told me the same things they told him."

In our state of semipermanence, I had forgotten things such as detachments. All the armies that had been here long enough to grow vessels and nerves across the landscape.

"I'll keep you back some food," I said, not wanting to let him go that easily. "Will you be . . . staying?"

He gave me another one of his smiles: a sad one, impossible to read as yes or no.

I followed him into the bedroom to put my book away and kiss him quickly, smiling. Kissing him always made me want to smile. He laughed and squeezed my hand. I felt my heartbeat in my tongue. What would I do if he wasn't here anymore? If I had to wake up without him?

I donned my leather gloves over my poor woollen knit and walked smartly into the mess hall, trying not to think about whether Sasha would follow me, in the semi-immediate and long-term sense. If he were to stay, I could wrap myself around him at night—it really was practical.

Especially with the question of his health.

I'd been trying, as surreptitiously as I could, to snag a word with the MO. If I could find him, which I had no chance in hell of doing if he didn't want to be found. Bannatyne was the type of doctor who made a great point of not unlocking his surgery doors until a minute after nine. In the hours where he was as nominally off-duty as we could get, he seemed to wink out of existence.

I sat down alone in the empty mess hall, staring blankly at the place the tea urn had been this morning. The hatch to the kitchen was firmly shut.

The door opened a minute later and I glanced up, hopefully. It wasn't Sasha. It wasn't even a member of the kitchen staff, who I might have been just as glad to see. It was Warren, the platoon commander who wasn't me, Toby, or Haddock. He gave me a noncommittal smile and sat close enough to let me know I could talk to him, and far enough away to let me know it wasn't encouraged. He and Evans had been pals, and I didn't think he'd quite forgiven me for taking his place.

The hatch cracked open and some bread appeared, followed by a trolley trundling through the wide double doors. A laden vat of soup hove into view, tea urn accompanying it. I half rose, but the staffer beside it came bustling toward us, a steaming cup in each hand and said something like, "*Dlya vas?*"

I floundered, my tenuous grip on my little Russian deserting me. By the look of him, Warren felt the same. The staffer asked us again, barely waiting for a reply before placing the cups down in front of me and turning his back to us. I edged one cup down towards my fellow, who glanced at me, startled. We sat there in the middle-class awkwardness specific to being served.

There wasn't any milk in the tea. Of course.

Barclay came majoring in as more tea was being decanted. His own mug was pressed urgently to his chest by the staffer, almost pouring tea down his uniform. Had he seen Sasha, already? Or had Sasha merely used him as a pretext?

It was true that commanding officers were never where you expected them to be, and that you could walk for days round the halls of the cadet school before realising you were lost. I'd tell myself that Sasha was still looking for him, that that was why he wasn't with me.

Barclay seemed to have lanced a boil of officers, as one came at least every ten seconds thereafter. A group of Cossacks also wandered in to take up residence towards the back of the room. Barclay presided over us, unsmiling and unacknowledging until we were apparently legion enough—me, Warren, Haddock, Toby and James—for him to feel like it was worth speaking.

"Compulsory delousing tomorrow" were the first words out of his mouth.

I tried to exchange a glance with Toby, who avoided my eye.

Barclay announced that we'd be reverting to our "usual schedule," a mythical thing that hadn't existed for months, which meant being up at six for drill, standing down for breakfast at seven and reporting for delousing at eight. He wanted to get officers processed first, so he could tell us how he expected us to move off, and so that we could feed it down and supervise the entraining. Both the logistics officers and the quartermasters had been punishingly attentive in muscling the poor Japanese to second in line, it seemed.

Supplies taken on, coal replenished, and louse-free, we'd move on tomorrow, start to round the lake by the end of the day, wouldn't stop for any remarkable length of time until Chita.

I kept glancing over my shoulder in case Sasha had come in quietly. After the third time, Toby gave me a strange look.

The major rounded off by filling us in on some "minor disruption by partisans" on the area of track we were meant to be following tomorrow. Whether it was "minor partisan activity" of the half-clothed, three-men-to-a-rifle sort or of the surreptitious digging parties and track-mining sort, he left out. I didn't like to dwell too much on the thought. We were in retreat, after all. We'd left the five-in-the-morning stand-tos behind us, this far from the fighting. If things carried on the way they seemed to be though, those drills would make an unwelcome return.

The door swung open and shut, and I turned around out of habit and hope. It wasn't Sasha, but the next best thing— Bannatyne had just walked in and was poking around the kitchen hatch with the air of a man who didn't want to get noticed. My heart leapt.

Barclay finished up, warning us to be examples and not to indulge in any reckless unnecessary drunkenness or frivolity during our last night, and then bade us farewell. Though we had all known the shape of tomorrow from our first disembarkation, I could count on a few to be absent from their beds for a good few hours into the night.

Toby kicked my ankle, but I nodded towards Bannatyne and hoped my message came across clear. If needs be, I could always scare off Tobes with tales of horrific venereal disease.

I trotted up behind Bannatyne's stolid form and tapped him on the shoulder. He seemed surprised, turning around as if he expected a ghost. When he saw me, his face relaxed somewhat, but didn't lose the edge of forced politeness.

"Ransome," he said. "What can I do for you?"

"Hello, sir," I began. "I was . . . wondering what you could tell me about Jandáček? The Czech man?"

"Still travelling with him, I suppose?" He gave a single sage nod. "I did hear he was coming with us."

Travelling with us? I thought, silently thrilled. I kept my emotions buttoned though. "Yes, sir. I wanted to know if there was anything I could do to help him. Anything we could do to . . . manage."

He twisted his mouth. "It's good of you to ask, Ransome, but I'll be as honest with you as I can and tell you there isn't a lot I know about this sort of thing. I've never studied the brain and never will," he said, with a shade of haughtiness. "This area of study is . . . very new. There was a lot that came out about it during the war. Edinburgh in particular. And University College. Your alma mater, is it not?"

I nodded.

"William Rivers," he said as if the name should hold any meaning. "Lots of work on mental theory. Myself . . . not so much. I'm a practical man, Ransome. I deal with matters of the body. Symptoms I can see. Facts I can—if you'll excuse the literal phrasing—put my hands on. This sort of thing . . ." He sucked air in through his teeth. "Not that I don't think there's merit in it, of course . . . Anyway. To answer your question, if there were anything you or others of you could do to help him, I wouldn't know what it was. And even if I did, these conditions are very much a case-by-case basis. Some poor bastard up at Craiglockhart would be able to do what your lad can't and vice versa. Sensible to take each day as it comes and hope for the best."

"Physical symptoms, sir—that's what he *has*."

"It can manifest that way, Ransome. So I've heard."

"Old injuries?" I pressed "Healing joints? The cold gets in them. That's why they were sending him away."

I felt suddenly skittish under his intensified gaze, as if I were a ball of string he was trying to unravel. Finally, he said, "I don't doubt they get stiff from time to time, Ransome, but I haven't found anything . . . *wrong* with him physically. Certainly nothing discharge-worthy. I rather think they're proxies."

A strange chill came over me. "Proxies for what, sir?"

He gave me an abbreviated version of that earlier expression. "The wider problem."

"Wider problem?"

"Ransome." His voice was rather shocked, as if I'd hit him. "Whatever's wrong with him, it's not physical."

"He—" I began. "He isn't— That night on the train . . ."

"A combination of hunger, exhaustion, and dehydration. Plus, I daresay, a good deal of stress. You hear of it sometimes. Someone develops an inability to swallow, someone else can't stop scratching the skin off their arms . . . some take to muscular spasms, I assume."

"That can't be right," I told him flatly.

He shrugged. "Perhaps not. But I can tell you that's all part of the reason they sent him back."

"They sent him back because he can't—"

The MO's tone took on a paternal air that I instantly disliked. "They sent him back because he had some sort of nervous break in the middle of the tundra and threatened to shoot himself if anyone came near. He's a liability. Not allowed near weapons. I think . . ." He gave another one of his hissing sighs. "To be completely honest with you, I'm sure his languages were the only reason they didn't leave him behind. And he was quite popular, I hear. His men liked him before. I daresay their views might have changed afterward."

"What do you mean?" I asked, the words rolling off me.

"I *mean* that if they hadn't had a medical evacuation they could palm him off on that needed an English and a German speaker, I think they'd just have left him to die. I would have. You would have too if you'd been in that position." He shifted his weight from one foot to the other. "The Czechs are prepared to send him home, but they're not about to spend more money or resources on a man who's not going to be in fighting shape anytime soon. Not when they're this close to pulling out. So he's coming with us and making his own way back from Southampton."

I looked at him blankly. "Are you sure that—"

"Think about it, Ransome," he said, sounding a touch more impatient. "Why would the army take someone with the level of physical distress he is allegedly under? On that same note, why would that person want to *go*? He went completely in the head. I grant you, it bodes well for him that you haven't noticed until now. But have you ever seen him eat? He doesn't. He can't. And if he doesn't get out before the cold hits proper, he'd going to starve to death. He flies into a panic over the slightest thing. All he wants to do is sleep. He has . . . I'd hesitate to call them seizures, but at times of stress he has muscular spasms, or fainting spells, or . . . call it what you will. He's not right. He's not trustworthy. They won't take him back."

One, two, three seconds passed me by.

Then I felt myself open my mouth, and heard someone say in my voice, "He had a gun when he came. Captain Horrocks took the gun off him. The gun he had."

"Hayek emptied his rifle and revolver. He was given permission to shoot him dead if he started acting out again."

My blood went cold.

I swallowed, twice, taking out all of the moisture. I tried moving my tongue around my mouth to dampen it. Bannatyne was still looking at me. The fact that he might expect me to speak slotted into my head.

"Right," I said.

"I'm sorry to have upset you," he said, sounding consummately professional. "But I'm glad that you know. I've heard all of this first hand from Hayek, of course. The major and Captain Horrocks both know too. Do you understand?"

I nodded again.

"Good," he said. "Will you excuse me? I'm trying to go to my room. I don't want anyone else to try and talk to me while I'm standing in the open."

I let him past.

Then I turned on my heel and headed to my and Sasha's room, picking at the skin of my thumb with a fingernail.

My fugue state took me as far as the entrance hall, where it sat me down on one of the chairs near the cloakroom and left me. I tried to digest Bannatyne's words, but they refused to sink in, like excess ink sitting on top of paper. Those moments before it sinks in and you can never get it out again.

I thought back on Sasha. His words. His propensity towards sleep. He had slept a lot, but I'd put it down to sheer exhaustion.

Days, weeks of walking, and weeks, months of being out in the field. He *was* just tired. That bone-deep, soaking heavy tiredness you get when you feel removed, submerged, cut out. Tired of life.

I remembered those last few months of my life at home. Had I ever been in danger of that then? I'd had morbid attacks sometimes, moments of complete incapability; I'd looked back on myself and thought, *Why was I so useless? Surely it wasn't that bad. Surely I could have done something.* They seemed so childish now, so young and melodramatic. Maybe I had been self-indulgent, after all. That sheer, knap-edged hopelessness hadn't quite anchored, not become some deep-seated, soul-dredging growth that would find a home nestled in the soft cells of my veins and never leave. Not like it had in him.

I thought about how he moved. How he favoured one leg but only sometimes. How he'd been supporting that dying man on his left, bad shoulder. Had Hayek said he'd had trouble walking? Had that trouble been from pain, or from his apparent inability or unwillingness to eat? Had it been to legitimise his sudden weakness? After all, a solider that doesn't eat needs to get a hold of himself. A soldier that can't walk can't walk.

I remembered him, so small and pale and wan in the corner of the cattle carriage, his pack and all his worldly belongings as his pillow. Then I thought, with a sudden hot rush, about last night. Had I hurt him? Had I leant on him too hard, bent him the wrong way? He hadn't said a word. Hadn't drawn my attention to a single thing.

And the stress. Himself, his sexuality. It had taken a toll on me, and I'd been more fortunate than most. Did anyone know he was a homosexual? Had that played any part in getting him sent away? Or had concealing it maybe—

I sat, my hands locked together resting on top of my knees, for so long I could almost feel the dust start to settle on me. Hayek, his corporal. Permission to shoot him dead.

Had that been the reason (part of the reason) his travelling as a private? Had it been his idea, as I had assumed, or not? Nobody would question if Hayek pulled rank all of a sudden; no one would stop him from leaving Sasha out in that freezing, ghastly tundra.

I suddenly had to be with Sasha.

In my pocket I felt for my watch. In a silly, sentimental way I didn't want to put it on, for fear of it getting lost or broken. He'd only given me a battery. But it was something he'd held in his hand. Something he'd seen and touched and thought of me. Something that had resided, skin-warmed, in his palm for me to keep and to treasure. A little part of him to take with me, when he was eventually taken from me for good.

At least he wouldn't be yet.

He was asleep—of course—by the time I reached our room. The lights off and his back facing my bed. I had a brief moment of panic, my mind trying to ascribe meaning to that position.

Had he regretted it, last night? Us? Did he want to shut me out? Even in the depths of his unconscious, did he not want to see me? Me to see him? Me to wrap myself around him and keep him warm? I'd stay away, if he asked. Anything to keep him safe.

I bit the inside of my mouth. I never had been sensible about overthinking. If I had spent less time worrying about what he thought of me, I might have been able to put together who he was. Who he wasn't. If he'd ever have told me. If he thought it was better a liar than a suicide. Than a strange and pitiable man.

Who cries for the suicides?

CHAPTER ELEVEN

I sat on the side of his bed as gently as I could. His face was still scrubbed raw from the wind. Healing to the point of scabbage.

He'd shaved at some point in the day, welts gooey from where he'd nicked the scabs. Some of the dampness tenderly held fragments of bread from the dinner I'd pushed him to eat. It should have marred him, this built-up of entropy on his face, but it hadn't. He was still lovely. Still real. I stroked one of the locks of his pretty hair behind his ear, then let my hand rest a while on his cheek. I was as light as I could let myself be, trying my best not to disturb him. On some level, hoping I would.

He stirred sleepily, and I withdrew in panic. He moved his hand, following mine, until they both came to rest on the rough fabric of my hip. Then his hand relaxed and he sighed. It was a moment of such heartbreakingly simple tenderness. Something inside me trembled and cracked entirely.

As carefully as I could, I took my boots off, unlacing them clumsily with one hand. Journey's end. How many days like this, identical nights to this, did we have? How many were left for us? *People like us are rarely lucky.*

I kept one hand covering his, shrugging out of my greatcoat and trying not to dislodge him. My coat over his. The blankets provided to the overnight room weren't as thick as the ones they reserved for the cadets, and I didn't want him to be cold.

Then I slid in beside him and drew my arms around his tight, bony waist. His hip bones dug into my forearms. I pulled him closer, buried my nose in his hair, and heaved in a deep breath that felt like the beginning of a sob. It almost wasn't, until my breath caught in a single dyspeptic hiccough. It was quiet enough, I hoped, not to wake him. I tried to keep my throat clamped down against other stray noises but couldn't stop the tears. They came: one, two, then three, following the track of the first, and they fell into the dark wilderness of his hair. I kissed the back of his head, then the side, then that sensitive spot under his ear. He stirred again, made a sleepy huff. It would be hard to fall asleep.

If anyone came in, I'd tell them I was cold.

It might well have been a lie to explain away my sleeping with Sasha, but when the knock came in the morning, it had developed into a real truth. The front of me, pressed up against him, was deliciously warm to the point of being overbearingly so. My back, which had been left exposed to the seal-less window, was so cold that in those first few moments of consciousness, it seemed like all my muscle fibres had frozen into place.

I moved against Sasha and kissed his neck. He stirred and chuckled drowsily, so I did it again. In his squirming, he grazed against my full cock. I hissed. "Stop it, we don't have time."

"Mmmh."

He rolled over onto his back, and then onto his other side to cup my face and gaze at me. He smiled. My hypnagogic lover.

"You stayed."

"I was cold."

"Mmmh." He rubbed a stray lock of hair out of my eye. If I had time today, I would see the barber. "What time is it?"

"About ten past five."

He gave me a soft, comforting kiss. "Is there drill?"

"Yes." *What will happen to him?* I wondered with a lurch. Would he be expected to attend?

He kissed me again, one of his toes playing with the hem of my sock. I relaxed into the kiss, toying with running my hands through his hair, and then tore myself away. If I didn't do it suddenly, I wouldn't do it at all.

Getting out of bed was never easy, and it wasn't easier when the room was below freezing and there was a gorgeous man in the bed, all loose-limbed and inviting. I ached to give him one last kiss. When would I get to kiss him again? Instead I sat, heavily and pointedly, on my own bed and started lacing up a boot. He'd slept in his uniform as well, and I hoped that wasn't as obvious on either of us as it seemed. There wasn't a man in this building that hadn't—I was sure—but I was paranoid that someone would notice the same pattern on us and make the unrealistic jump to buggery.

I finished lacing and watched him dress. He'd placed his boots at the end of his bed last night, and crawled down now to get them in a gesture I found effortlessly charming. I don't know what I said or did to show this, or if he simply sensed it somehow, but he glanced up and gave me a small, knowing smile before lacing them. His sleep-tousled hair hung over his face. I pulled him across for another, final kiss, hoping it would sustain me through the long hours until I got to kiss him again.

"Did you see the Major last night?" I asked, unable not to push. It was like worrying at a tooth.

There was a beat of silence, hesitation as confirmation.

"I saw him at dinner," I continued breezily. "Perhaps you met before?"

"You know I didn't see him," he told me gently.

I bit the inside of my cheek. "Oh?"

I went to strap my watch back on, then hesitated.

I heard him stand, the covers fall away.

"I was at the RAP," he said quietly.

"Again?" My watch, my watch with his battery in, was still in my hand. It wasn't much, but it was mine.

"Again," he confirmed grimly. "They wanted confirmation I was fit to travel. They've already got it but— I didn't want you to worry."

Didn't want me to worry. "I wouldn't have if you'd told me straight off the bat." I rubbed my leather watch strap between my thumb and forefinger.

He concealed a bark of laughter, badly. "Of course you bloody would. That's why I didn't *say*. Look— I'm fine. I'm not due in with you lot today, so I'll spend this time on R and R, insomuch as I can. If that will put your mind at ease."

"My mind *is* at ease," I said quickly.

"All right. I promise not to drop dead between now and tomorrow. Now put that damn thing on your wrist before you worry through the buckle.

Putting my watch in the pocket of my uniform, which would be processed with dozens of identical others, didn't seem worth the risk. I slipped it into my pack instead, underneath where my books usually lay. The blanket got unstrapped for louse treatment.

He must have sensed my mood.

"When will I have you back?" He touched his mouth, trying inexpertly to hide a smirk. "Properly."

"I don't know," I answered, trying to supress the urge to kiss him again by getting to my hands and knees and scrabbling around for my rifle. Great, fluffy clumps of dust came with it from under the bed. The cold felt like it would split my fingertips, my kneecaps. "Chita, maybe. Or Harbin." I threw a look behind me. It would be such a long time. "Come on, we'll be late."

He picked a piece of dust off my coat sleeve, then pulled me to him.

After that, we joined the steady trickle of men from the stairs, to the mess, and out to the parade ground. My penultimate memory of the parade ground at Irkutsk, a great, flat square of a place that funnelled wind at you from whichever direction you were standing, it had been full of its titular cadets, none of whom had looked old enough to shave. They'd gone now.

Drill itself is a mind-numbing affair. Muscle memory helped me through, my mind wandering from belt buckles and about turns. The majority of the actual manoeuvres fell to my sergeant. Thank God for Brown. A good NCO will carry you further in a war than any number of young subalterns. I occasionally glanced aside at my platoon with a little thrill of pride. I had felt the same the first time they'd been able to march around the ground at home without marching through another platoon. We hadn't been keeping up with drill as much as we should. Barclay must live in fear of our fitness levels depleting in the weeks of sedentary wastage we had in the back of a rail van. My rifle had been cleaned more than it had been fired and was probably in better condition now than it was when I got it.

By the time drill finished, we were at the nadir of time where the weather just about reached freezing, before plummeting back down again at night. The blood in my legs seemed to stand still. It would be twenty, maybe fifteen minutes until we were dismissed. That time would be spent evaluating how well we could stand.

On the far side of the ground, a swarm of men busied around what looked like a rapidly erected circus tent: the fabled delousing station.

We dragged ourselves back for breakfast, most like myself still yawning and dreaming of coffee. Sasha hadn't come. Not that I'd expected him to. I'd caught a glimpse of him on my way into the academy, talking low and urgent with Barclay.

He didn't see me.

I insinuated myself into breakfast and snagged lukewarm coffee off one of the serving trays. A man I knew by sight as a logistician brushed by me, apparently harried. Our train must be getting ready.

I was hovering about, searching for somewhere to sit when a *clack*ing of quick heels announced the arrival of Martin, the major's batman.

"Sir." He bobbed his head. "Major wants to see you outside."

"Now?" I asked redundantly.

"Yes."

I swallowed the last of my ostensible coffee and followed him, placing my cup on a ledge where I hoped it would be seen and cleared up. Major Barclay was standing almost where I'd left him, with the notable omission of Jandáček.

I saluted.

The major nodded at me curtly. "Lieutenant."

"What can I do for you, sir?"

"You've doubtless heard that the Czech detachment wish us to keep their captain on with us."

It wasn't a question.

I wondered what would have happened if I hadn't had that conversation with Bannatyne last night. I'd still have answered, "I have, sir."

"They're sending their corporal back to the front. They need every man they can spare, and while Captain Jandáček is . . . regrettably indisposed, Corporal Hayek has requested that the man be placed with someone to keep an eye on him. Someone they both can trust." His eye met mine. "By all accounts, Jandáček has come to trust you, Lieutenant."

My heart thudded.

"We've got about a fortnight's travel, not including the voyage home. If we can't get him passage, we should be able to leave him in Vlady until the rest of his regiment turn up. What do you say?"

Two weeks with him, and then Canada. I thought of that sudden future—the Pacific to Vancouver, over to Halifax, across to Southampton. And then where, for him?

"Will he know?" I asked. "That I've been told to watch him."

"He'll guess."

Yes, I supposed he would.

"And you'd like me to keep an eye on him . . . how?" I asked, barely daring to believe it.

"It's a train, Ransome, there's limited scope to lose him. Look out for any irregular or erratic behaviour. The corporal was most insistent on monitoring his diet. He won't eat unless coaxed or reminded—" He coughed. "I'm sorry to have to do this to you, Ransome. I know you probably won't relish acting as a glorified childminder. But it's for the safety of your men as much as anything. You're in the quietest car in the train. You already have a relationship with him"—something tightened in me, almost-humour—"and it's embarrassing the amount that the bloody Czechs have managed that we can't. I told them we'd be able to manage this, at least."

"Yes, sir," I said.

"Won't be long, now. I want to press on as far as we can today. We have two more disembarkation stops. We shan't be stopping at Verkhneudinsk."

"Yes, sir."

He looked at me carefully. "Do you understand what I am asking you to do with regards to Jandáček?"

"Yes, sir."

"Good. He's not to be left unsupervised and not to be given a weapon. If the worst comes to the worst and we come under attack, you'll have to leave him. Are you clear?"

And if it comes to worse than that, said the subtext, *you'll have to put a bullet through his head.*

"Yes, sir" came out of my mouth. As if I was an automaton, only good to point and press, and expect the damage to be done.

Hot, childish fear ran under my skin.

"Good. You're being deloused in ten minutes."

And with that, he dismissed me and left.

The delousing station at Irkutsk was a rapidly shacked affair: one of those old-fashioned types where you had to strip and go through at the same time as your uniform. The coal-fire generator thrummed and the steaming machines kicked into life as I peeled out of that second skin. All around me there was life; free to do as it pleased, to come and go. Life without arbiter.

Toby had shuffled into place behind my back, humorously grim in just his thermals, and muttered, "Morning."

I put on a show of restraining a little laugh that my heart wasn't in. Appearances need to be kept up though, or what's the point of them?

They'd laid out a tarpaulin across the still-frosted ground, which I should probably have been thankful for.

It was not any warmer under the tent. The man ahead of me heaved himself up the ladder and disappeared with a bathetic splash. Then I stripped to my underwear resolutely and followed suit.

"Oh, Jesus Christ!"

I surfaced and met eyes with the man who'd gone in before me, who seemed equally as panicked. Presumably the water was somewhat warm, but in contrast with the air, it felt as cold and clear as the Lethe. It bit into all my little cuts so precisely it felt like they were opening more, like I was a scurvy-ridden Georgian sailor. I dipped down to my knees and covered myself, rubbing water through my hair. Fortunately, my undershirt and vest covered the worst of my skin and any of the less easy-to-explain scars. I didn't think anyone would be examining my upper arms too closely, but Toby's remark last night had put the wind up. Toby entered with an ungraceful flail behind me.

The water was, at best, knee deep, and it was meant for all of us. We had to follow each other, like prisoners on exercise. I trudged through, heavy-footed, then heaved myself out over the ladder, my skin suddenly shrinking in contact with the air.

As soon as my feet met the tarpaulined floor, which someone had had the good grace to put a towel over, another industrial towel met me, followed by a coat that didn't seem like my own. I shuffled over, drying myself the best I could, to a small pile of boots in an untidy line and picked my way over to mine, sliding my feet in still damp and unsocked.

Someone said "T.L. Ransome?" in my ear. I turned, nodding in bewilderment, and a man with yellow hair pressed my coat to me, and took the other out of my hands. All's well that ends well, I supposed. I shrugged mine on and discarded the towel into a pile for washing. At least the coat covered my arms.

Beside me, Toby was pulling on his own coat. When he was done, he set his shoulders with his hands in his pockets and said under his breath, "I'll never see my balls again."

"Ah, well. Every cloud and all that." I stamped my feet to try to get warm and shot jolts of pain up my shins.

"Don't do that," he told me. "Tell me something to distract myself from the fact I'm not wearing clothes."

With only boots and no clothes on underneath, we must have looked stupid.

"No one else is, either," I said, aching to ask him about what he'd said to me yesterday afternoon. But this wasn't the place, so I settled for "Hasn't that man got skinny legs?"

"Francis, stop pratting about."

"You're being very negative towards me today."

"Yes, well. I won't get the chance to be again until at least this time next week, so enjoy it while you can."

"You can always come up and visit me."

"I'm not going all the way to the arse end of a bloody rail convoy to call you an idiot, Ransome."

"I'm not coming to visit you. I might see the quartermaster."

Toby sucked in air through his teeth. "Yes, well," he said again.

"Maybe the Trots will finally blow up the train and we'll end up in a mass grave together."

"Maybe they'll burn us all on a pyre like Vikings." Then he frowned. "Something's certainly got the wind up Barclay. He's not even chancing a stop in Verkhneudinsk."

"Yet he'll stop in Chita with mad bloody Semianoff. We can have some fun there."

Toby pulled a face. "Hm. Maybe. Anyway, Your hair's getting too long."

"I know. I haven't been able to find a barber yet."

"Cut it yourself. That's going to break your mask seal if you leave it any longer."

"He's right," some other bloke chimed in. He clapped Toby on the back. "Where the hell have you been, Harris?"

"Missed me?" smiled Toby. "I wouldn't have noticed."

The man guffawed and clapped Toby's back again. He seemed like the type whose interactions were made up mostly of those two functions.

"You'd never have crossed my mind had the whites of your legs not almost taken my eye out. Who's this?" he asked, raising an eyebrow in my direction.

Toby glanced at me, clearly uncomfortable. "Francis. Teddy Napier. He's here with Battalion HQ. Teddy, Francis Ransome."

Teddy held out an overlarge hand to me. "Pleasure."

I took it gingerly. "All mine." His handshake was exactly what I'd expect from a grown man who went by Teddy.

There was a long, distinguished line of Napiers somewhere in the military. I wondered if he was one, or an offshoot, or a chancer with the same name who wasn't about to correct anyone's assumptions.

My name had obviously caused a similar train of thought in him. He squinted at me. "Ransome? Not any relation to that journalist, are you?"

"Who?" I asked good-naturedly.

"Author chap who writes for the *Daily News*. Wrote a book about a bloke who discovers the elixir of life and turned out to be a Trot. Ransome, that is." He smiled. "Not the chap in the book."

I smiled tightly back at him. "I'm no relation to any famous Ransomes."

"Come now, 'famous' is generous, I think. Wrote on Wilde and was supported by that godawful Robbie Ross. Wife trouble as well, so I hear," he added, knowingly.

I tried my best to feel confident and not ridiculous in my oversized coat. "Is that so?"

Napier gave me a look that was probably meant to signal a bond of heterosexual fraternity. After an awkward beat between all three of us, he did some final handshaking and strode off, doubtlessly looking for someone else's shoulder to clap.

"Of course," said Toby, after he'd gone. "He's not a real Napier. He just likes people to think he is."

"Like I'm not a real Ransome?"

"Don't let him get to you. It's blokes like him that give the rest of us a bad name. He was on my staircase at Corpus. It was an endless, cock-headed parade of Teddies."

"You're making my Bloomsbury background feel positively *dishabille*. Has it been twenty minutes yet? I left my watch in my pack."

He held up his bare wrist to me. "And you think I brought mine into the bath? I've got no idea, but there's no harm in checking back there for them now. Anyway, that was the chap that was ahead of you, wasn't it? The one whose legs you laughed at?"

I had no idea, but I followed him anyway.

The threshing of the steam machines was, surprisingly, louder outside. I hadn't thought waxed tarpaulin would be able to keep much sound out at all. The generator looked suspiciously like a locomotive that had been dragged over the bridge and inland. The capricious wind drove a thicket of smoke toward us, and I covered my face with my sleeve. The thick, matchy smell was so familiar that it was only now that I realised it had been absent in the past thirty-six hours.

We joined a coppice of other subalterns, all patiently waiting by the steps of one of the huge-bellied machines. A man at the top of the ladder was struggling to undo its hatch, his red face suggesting he was either too cold from the weather or too hot from the steam. After a minute, the door swung open, belching out dampness. That hit my face as well. It was more welcome than the smoke.

I'd wrapped all of my uniform loosely inside my blanket—perhaps unwisely, as there was no real way of keeping the bundle fastened—and put it underneath my hat, which were prominently marked with my name on the outside (of the blanket) and the inside (of the hat). It had cost an arm and a bloody leg enough to get myself kitted out before I arrived, and I didn't want to run the risk of any errant sartorial roaming.

My clothes had stayed together and were handed to me by a man whose request for directions to "Ransome" had promptly ended in "that one with the red hair there." Everything was present, with the exception of my socks, which were typically and inevitably errant.

I started pulling on my underwear.

If watching grown, combat-ready men paddling in a garden-bucket-shaped tub is absurd, watching the same ones clad in nothing but coats and shoes pouring over metres of identical cloth is the other side of that bizarre coin. If I were to argue the case that the armed forces remain inefficient, it would be that image on a postcard.

As I was tugging my tunic back on, Toby hopped up to me with one sock and hissed, "Some other bugger's got my trousers."

"Are you going to ask?" I replied, fishing around in my pocket for my tie.

"Of course not."

"Maybe you should get dysentery. That will show him."

"Thank you, Francis. Maybe I will."

"If it helps, my socks have gone."

"Well, then I hope you get awful frostbite and lose both feet. I'm going to hang back and see what I can scrounge from the leftovers."

This was an old trick, which seldom worked because everyone else was wise to it. I decided to wait with him, anyway.

"It's hard not to notice those scars," he said to me suddenly.

I twitched as if he were a livewire. "I know."

He nodded. "Thought you did. I just wanted to make sure."

"Thank you."

It seemed like he'd leave it well enough alone, until he said, "Look, Francis, I don't care what it was. It could have been a bloody enormous cat for all I care. But . . . watch out, all right? The last thing I want is for you to get bloody gangrene or something."

"I'll do my best to stick to frostbite."

"Take care of yourself. We don't want you ending up like that poor sodding Czech."

That was all Sasha was to him—a cautionary tale. That was why he shouldn't have been told. It struck me like a betrayal. No, not a *betrayal*—that wasn't the right word. A subversion of confidence. No one was supposed to understand him except for me, the other Bedlamite.

I pulled my coat tighter. "You've been told?"

He drew in a deep sigh. "Not a lot. But word gets around. I talked to his corporal, for a bit. He came up to see us all, talk to Horrocks and Barclay. Nice enough stick. One of those salt-of-the-earth types, you know? Anyway, I found out what I needed to know from him. Not that the gaps took much filling. Francis, it's a mess."

"Sasha's not bad," I said, quietly.

"I know he's not. Jesus, mate, I was on the bloody Salient. I don't think one of us came back sane. I'm not saying he's . . . dangerous or malingering or—whatever else he could be accused of. And I'm not saying he'd deliberately put anyone in harm's way. But his idea of harm is probably . . . different to yours or mine.

That's all I'm saying. Just . . . don't let your guard down around him."

"That's what you meant the other night, isn't it? When you said, 'Be careful.'"

And so quickly, his tone became hurt, almost angry. "Yes, Francis, it is. You're too trusting. You're the type to get flustered when you have the wrong fare on the 'bus. You're a pal, but you drive me mad at times. Please. I'd hate for anything to happen to you."

That admission tightened around my heart, restricting it to one, short, painful beat. Toby. I did love him so much. He wore his duty over his shoulders, shrugging it on in the morning and going about the day with it wrapped around him, shielding him from the cold and for all to see. I carried mine in my arms like a dying child, concerned for it, worried about dropping it. Silently hoping someone would come and take the burden off me. He belonged to war in a way that I did not, never would, and never wanted to.

"We're both still here, aren't we?" I asked him.

He gave me a tight smile. "Yes."

"Then we'll be all right. Both of us. I'm not as bad as all that."

"No, Francis, you aren't," he admitted. "You just inspire a sort of paternal instinct in me. It must be because you're twenty-five years old and still look like a schoolgirl."

I hit him with the loose sleeve of my coat. "Come on. Crowd's thinning. Let's go and find you some trousers."

I picked five socks up off the ground in the end, none of them belonging to me. An heir pair, a spare, and one for luck. Toby and another man—who'd also been waiting around and looking patiently inconvenienced as only a subaltern can—had swapped trousers, but neither had ended up with the right fit. They didn't want to go through the rigmarole again, though.

"You don't think those're waiting for their moment to split on you?" I asked.

"No," Toby said, his lips pressed tightly together. "But I'm going to try not to sit down much."

"Good luck with that, Tobes." We were making our way up to barracks. "People used to get bayonetted in the back for wearing trousers with the wrong fastening. Go out for a piss, trews take a while to undo, and before you know it, you're dead in a cesspit."

"You are really helpful to have around, you know that?"

"You keep me," I reminded him.

Our uniforms were still damp, and they'd dry sticking to our bodies with the potential for mould. Always a moist, foetid breeding ground for the unsavoury. Mine didn't yet have that louse-itch, but it would. The delousing never sorts them out for long. I had already caught sight of a few blind, beigey eggs sitting fatly in a seam and earmarked them to take care of later.

The wool carried with it the ghost of the smell of naphthalene, which I wasn't convinced could be used in the steaming process. Maybe they'd just thrown the smell in to make us feel better. It was strong but not unpleasant; reassuringly chemical.

We went our separate ways, packed, and got ready to entrain.

I found Horrocks, looking freshly scrubbed, and did my best to stay close. Our men would be back in a bit, and according to the major, we were expected to get them back to the station as soon as possible, in order to still have daylight to get over the bridge and start going around the lake tonight. Being on the banks shut off one flank of attack, logistically. And it was quite comforting. So close to such a large body of water made you feel like the land wasn't so big. Like one wasn't so nightmarishly far from the sea.

One by one, my platoon appeared. Nevis first of all, giving us both a small smile. Other men filed out after him. Names and faces I knew to joke with, to converse with. Jacobs was the last, loping into view. I thought, with a pang, of that little room with Sasha. Our little corner of the world together. I couldn't immediately see him. When I did catch sight of him, standing wraithlike behind the bulk of my carriage mates, he didn't meet my eye.

Horrocks did.

Roll, a cursory parade inspection by Bannatyne. Then we led out, down the wide, neo-Grecian streets of Irkutsk. Above us, wires crackled and popped. They looked like they were just being stored there, a temporary measure awaiting better organisation. I wondered if they'd ever be finished.

We went up, along the street that housed the post office, past the junction Sasha had led me down on our first night together. I tried to glance back at him, but he was too far behind me.

"All right?" asked the man next to me, evidently puzzled.

"Yes," I replied shortly. "Just don't know when we'll next be here."

Down the road with the police station at the end of it and across the pontoon bridge, where the railway station lay in its green-and-gold Christmassy splendour. Our train was something that was never meant to see the light of day: steam-belching and Rabelaisian.

The smell hit me again, and I couldn't believe that I'd forgotten it. Like returning to another person's house after an absence.

I ensconced myself on my old bunk, rolling out my newly-deloused blanket and sleeping bag and rummaging about for the furs I'd stored towards the back of the carriage, perhaps unwisely. I didn't know about lice habits on dead fur. I doled them out to my men, who grunted thanks, and to Jandáček, who was wearing a new hat.

I blinked at it.

"I didn't want to put it on before. It wasn't cold enough. I didn't want to get myself used to the cold if it was going to get colder."

"It looks very warm."

It did. It was one of those ones I'd seen on intermittent Russians and Slavs; I thought the Canadians had had a few stores of them. Cold weather countries. I'd even seen one on Mitya. It was a tall, fleecy affair, which contrasted with his curls and made them look darker while his hat looked lighter. I saw Owen do a double take at it.

"Begging your pardon, sir, but why haven't we got a kit like that?"

"They're with the mosquito nets, I'm sure," I answered, feeling a quick bite of bitterness at our army's doleful logistics corps.

The whole affair with the mosquito nets was something that we so often almost forgot and then remembered as we were listing things to get angry about. There was very little that could bring people together like a good, cathartic complain. Siberian mosquitos were huge, angry bastards that lurked in the wetlands around Ussurie and moved about with a thick, wet buzzing. Any bites from them raised your skin half an inch bright red and thin, fit to burst and straining. There'd been deaths. We didn't have any nets for them, of course, because Siberia was so synonymous with the cold that the concept of flying insects had been laughable. The army didn't think mosquitoes existed in Siberia. So we'd lain there, vibrating with lice and dreading that slow, oily hum until we'd put the wetlands far behind us. The Czechs had hats with nets built on.

"Well, fuck," sighed Gallehawk. I assumed he was talking about the hats, until he looked around and said, "It's good to be back."

"Christ, you cannot mean that," said Owen.

"I sleep better in my own bed. What's so surprising?"

"He's only saying that because he's never had a night in anyone else's," said Jacobs. The carriage gave a lurch and shivered into life. "Now, here we go. It's like we've never been away."

The air had that still quality I associated with old classrooms, the sort of atmosphere that didn't seem to have been breathed for a while. That would soon change, I was sure. Horrocks wasn't here, having been called upon to stay up with the major instead of risk his dashing about various carriages under cover of dark. Even with the addition of new, mysterious crates behind us, the train felt far emptier. I would be down here for good, now. On my guard duty.

"Where's your friend?" Jacobs asked Jandáček, unlacing his boot. He squeezed the toes of an improperly steamed sock and then crammed it back into his boot hurriedly.

"Gone back" was Sasha's quiet reply.

"Really? Christ. That's a way and a half. Where did you say you were before?"

"West of Tayshet. Took half my sodding kit with him."

"West? Good luck to him."

I waited, my heart in my mouth, for Jacobs to say something else, but he didn't. Instead, he turned to Gallehawk and started talking lowly about the quality of stitching on his bootwear, how merry hell was playing with it in the cold.

I exchanged a glance with Sasha.

The last of the cityscape scrolled by us, and the last of stone buildings for a while. The bridge that led out of Irkutsk was barely more than a pontoon itself. I had been so sure it was going to collapse when we'd first crossed it. We'd sat in silent, internalised, white hot panic. Our platoon was just in from Hong Kong, twenty of us already buried.

It had held, of course. It still held now.

And beyond? A period of flat, arable land that looked like it had once been claimed for farming, in the process of being reclaimed by the forest. My reaction to Russian forests had dulled since, but at the time they still struck me dumb. They were the deep, dark green of a fairy tale. Beside the tracks, little tributaries, big splashing rivers, and tiny capillaries of streams started coming together. Then they joined into a torrent. Then they opened out.

As we crossed it a second time, I felt that awe. That childlike wonder. Would I come back here, one day? Once all this was over? I'd love to see the lake again, in peacetime.

Lake Baikal is anything other than a lake. It surpassed even an inland sea. Had I not seen it—twice, now—I didn't think I'd have believed in it.

The watchman, Jacobs, kicked the wood to rouse us. Here it was: our last proper landmark.

Apparently, there was always ice, jewel-bright freshwater, and blue. It was so cold, I was told, that bodies didn't decay. It was so old that the gods formed it themselves. It was so deep, that if you fell in, it would take you over a day to fall to the bottom. Falling all of those miles.

You could look across Baikal and see horsemen in the fog. There were animals, grasses, waters, winds found here that didn't have a hope of surviving anywhere but this strange, semimythic place.

I could hear the water, restlessly hushing against the sand of the shore, beginning to get clunky with ice. By this point, the day had begun to break down into the pre-twilight blueness— nautical twilight—and the last of the sun was coming in from the undulating hummocks to the west. Eclipsed by it was a little cowshed railway station, situated so close to the shore I worried for it.

And there the lake stretched.

"That's us," said Jacobs, hopping down from his crate. "We're done for the night."

"Christ," said Gallehawk, standing and stretching. "That took no time at all. Hope I'm not getting used to it. How far, sir?" he asked me.

I started myself back into the present. "How far have we come, or how far do we have to go?"

"Come. I don't want to think about the future at present, sir."

"Far enough," I answered, trying to conceal my lack of real knowledge. "We've had to cut a swathe of forest to get here so quickly. Possible we've stopped because the shortcut spooked the drivers."

Possibly not in my professional interests to say that to them, but I couldn't be bothered with decorum right now. They were all thinking it, anyway.

East, back into the fighting. Back where we'd started; where the track rolled and curved in front of us for a who-knew-how-long distance.

Unbidden, a passage came to me. A phrase Helena had been fond of quoting at mundane partings, such was her sense of humour. *"No, stay here, in charge of what is yours and do not go wandering the unharvestable sea."* She had said it to me as I'd gone to school. Hadn't said it as I'd left with my regiment.

There was something comforting in knowing the lake was there. I liked it.

Which was fortunate, as there was precious other comfort once the sun began to die. We were past socialising. *"Hollow fires burn out to black, and lights are guttering low."*

I drew my furs closer up around me, keeping my fingers in underneath out of the cold. Sasha, on the swapped bed opposite me, had hunkered down under his coat, blanket, and downy, patchy fur that had belonged to Evans. He looked—in that moment—just like a native: all dark hair and quick, bright eyes. In the day's last light, we could have been anywhere, at any point. I could have been with him at the beginning of the world.

CHAPTER TWELVE

W e all slept fitfully, and I awoke with a thin layer of frost on my eyelashes. I blinked it away and sat up, the sound making Owen and Nevis stir. They were curled around each other like children.

There was more frost on my furs. The condensed breath of everyone in here, living together.

Sasha was folded in on himself, and I touched his cheek. It was cold, but not frigid. I traced his cheekbone, allowing myself that one small intimacy.

According to my newly repaired watch, it was about half past five in the morning. I unhatched and slid the door to, as quietly as I could, and slipped out onto the ground below. Several others were already outside, including a small knot at the far end of the train. The sentry detail, perhaps. The sun had started to rise.

We were beside a wrecked pier, which stretched out in pieces into the lake.

The stars had all but gone except for one, which hung over us like a jewel suspended. It stood out with the icy brilliance of the air on Baikal. The sky seemed to have frozen itself clear of any impurities or imperfections that could have been found anywhere else. The last time I'd seen the lake had been in semi-darkness, as we'd hurried across it and down the Angara to the safety of the town. It lay completely glasslike now, the mountains that hemmed it in on all sides were replicated perfectly. The dawn burst, from a deep, planetary blue to purple to a sugary pink, then white. The Pole Star hung there through it all.

I had never felt more like an astronomer than at that moment.

Being up at dawn always gave the day a freshness that I begrudge sharing with others. I didn't like people taking an equal share in it when I was the one who had witnessed it being born, when it was mine. There was a small nibbling of this same childlike feeling in me as I turned back to the car, the front of the train alive with unfolding action under the supermarine blue.

Sasha was sitting with his legs dangling over the side of the carriage. He saw me and seemed to think for a moment, before pushing himself off and making his way towards me. With his huge coat and fluffy hat, he looked like a mediaeval king. *"I shall know him by his face,"* I thought. *"By his Godlike front and grace."* The poets always said it better than I could.

"Don't want to let the cold air in," he said as soon as he was in speaking distance.

"Did I wake you?" I whispered.

He smiled at me beatifically. "It's not a problem. I'm sorry I missed it."

"There'll be another," I said, smiling back.

He came and stood beside me, his elbow touching mine. We looked no different to any other pair or three of men, standing out and watching the day dawn. He nodded towards the pier. "Do you know that story?"

"Some of it," I said, distantly remembering a debrief from some time ago. It had gone like they all had when we'd first arrived. The Trots, the Czecho-Slovaks, and the Railway Line. "I seem to recall Bolshie shot themselves in the foot by bombing out all the tunnels."

He smiled and worried a foot at the ground. "They've certainly done cleverer things. The whole affair was a bit of a blunder on their part." He reached into his greatcoat pocket and took out his cigarette case, then wordlessly offered one to me. I leant in as he cupped his hand around the flame of his lighter. It took four clicks.

"Feeling rather empty," he said apologetically, shaking the lighter. "Hope it lasts the journey."

"I'm happy to stand you for a new one," I said, frowning slightly. "Why does it jump up like that?"

"Must have knocked it," he said, slipping it back into his pocket. "All of my belongings are on their last legs."

He drew his scarf closer to his face, manoeuvring to smoke around it. I caught myself gazing at his profile and desperately tried to find something else to focus on.

"So fill me in," I said. "What's all this business with the pier?"

"The ferry pier?" He exhaled into the clear air. "There's a ferry under it. Gajda didn't like that all the shipping on the lake was Bolshevist. Managed to find himself two steamships from God knows where and stuck some howitzer shells on them. This was last year, by the way, after they'd just fallen back from Irkutsk."

"Thank you for the timestamp," I said, smiling.

"And you were . . .?"

"Still in Hong Kong," I admitted. "Anyway. Carry on."

He grinned. "They kept blowing up tunnels, and we kept trying to stop them, and this had all been going on for weeks. By the time we had them on three sides, Gajda had his ships and sailed them across the lake with a battalion approaching them from the east and another from the west, behind the armoured train."

"The train was a nice touch."

"Yes," he said, glancing back at ours humourlessly. "I rather imagine it was, at the time."

"You still haven't told me about the ship."

He took another drag of his cigarette. "I don't know if our ships were heading here or further along the coast, but they were allowed to get far too close. By the time the Trots realised they were hostile, it was too late. Burnt the pier, sank their ship and blew the harbour to buggery."

"Considerate of you to relay the tracks."

He exhaled and cast his gaze to the floor at his feet. "You're welcome."

His face was hidden and slightly red from the cold, but I recognised his demeanour for what it was.

"You're proud."

"What?" He glanced up at me.

"You're proud."

He met my eyes and looked away. "I don't like Gajda. I think he's a sabre-rattler and I don't think his dismissal could have happened to a better person. I'd much rather we stayed out of this and got to fuck off home."

"But?"

"But." He exhaled. "Novak was there, and I feel like I owe it to him to be proud."

The name was familiar, but I couldn't quite place it.

My cigarette was burning itself down to my fingers. I took a drag before it could go out. "Novak?"

"One of my fellow evacuees." He took a final pull on his own cigarette before treading on it. "No reason you should know the name. I didn't know him at all, until we were both offloaded."

"And after?"

"There isn't much you don't know about a man when you're together for days on end. That's how me and Hayek ended up the way we were."

"Do you miss Hayek?" I asked, thinking about the corporal. About where he might be now.

"I do, sometimes," said Sasha, apparently considering this. From his tone, the revelation seemed to surprise him. "Not all the time, he could be a cantankerous old bugger. But that was part of the appeal."

"What happened to Novak?" I switched. Now we were on the subject of his absent friends, it seemed we might as well discuss the fucking tank in the room.

"He shot himself." Sasha exhaled smoke into the clear air. "Not that long before we stumbled across you."

There were two things I wanted to say, and both of them caught in my throat. I wanted to apologise to him, knowing more about suicide than most. But then, in a far more immediate way, so did he.

"I know." His voice was low and full. He glanced from the ground up to my eyes. "I know."

I clenched my hand, trying to clamp down the urge to take his. We were about three hundred kilometres out of Irkutsk now. It seemed strange, a world away but just seven hours' rail travel. This time yesterday I'd been waking up, wrapped around him in a bed.

"Prurient decision of your major to stop here."

"He wants to get around the lake," I said. "There was a wood depot here, once upon a time. I imagine that's why we still stop here." After the comfort of Irkutsk, the relative normality of a town, I felt exposed in the open like this. "I, certainly, will feel far more relaxed when we're the other side of Chita."

Someone knelt down by the shore and stuck their head in.

"Oh, for God's sake."

Sasha flashed me a grin. "Rather him than me."

"They've just had a sodding bath. I don't know why they now have to use a wild lake. They'll bloody freeze."

"The first fresh water they'll get for a day? It takes all sorts, Francis."

I gave him a scowl, although something inside me flickered at the use of my first name.

"It's getting late," I said. "I'm going to head back in."

Sasha smiled at me. "That isn't a bad idea."

We walked back to the carriage, the door opening to reveal the rest of my men stirring about. Nevis dropped quietly to the ground with a shaving mirror in one hand and a tatty looking sheaf of paper, which had been sketched on and rubbed out, then sketched on again. Inspired, I went through my pack while Sasha curled back up on his cot. I'd get him up again for good when we got going. I'd managed to coax some bread into him yesterday, but I didn't want him to forgo breakfast. *Soup*, I thought. Clear soup. Full of nutrition, but not too rich. That's what I'd feed him, if I could.

I could see Gallehawk and Jacobs larking about with some other men from my platoon who were stored in a different carriage. I paid them a flying visit on my way up to Brown.

"All right up here, sir," Brown told me, smiling his avuncular smile.

"Good," I said, absently. "Stevens's belongings, Sergeant. Where are they?"

"On his bunk, sir."

And they'd stay there, I imagined. The bunk was still his.

"I'll write a letter," I told him. "When we next get somewhere to post. Do you know anyone who'd like to enclose something?"

"Church," said Brown. "Off the top of my head. I'll ask him to leave a letter with the . . . things."

I bit the inside of my cheek. *In all the endless road you tread, there's nothing but the night.*

"Thank you," I said. "Good morning, Sergeant."

The morning had a loose, unstructured feeling to it. I spent a few minutes down by the lake, just me and it, carefully shaving into a tin mirror and trying to gently strop away at the overlong ends of my hair. I stopped before I began to feel too silly.

There was an abundance of fresh water, so there was tea. I drank some from a tin mug that conducted heat up through my gloves at odds with the skin-cracking cold around it. I filled my flask. I watched men half in and half out of the train, and enjoyed the contrast between the air and my tea. It made me feel fresh in a way I hadn't before.

Despite the cold, the lake's placidity and the men around its shore gave me a strange impression of the beach. It didn't seem possible this was the same lake we had come around before, all beating water and twenty-foot waves.

Barely a month and a half after this happened—after Irkutsk had fallen and Kolchak had lounged in his cell—a general called Kappel would lead his men across this same route we'd come. He was half Swedish and had just been awarded the Order of St. George, with highest military honours. He brought upwards of thirty thousand with him: his men, their wives, their children and anyone who could pass as either. All of them trying to get away from the front line.

He walked them towards Chita, across the mountains and the grassland and the solid frozen water. Occasionally a quick and bloody skirmish would thin them out. When they reached the lake's empty surface at last, there was nothing to keep the winds off them. All those winds blew unobstructed across the lake: winds from the mountains, winds from the Arctic, winds that all have their individual names and stories, like fairy-tale demons. *Don't go out alone at night, the Sarma will get you.*

And it did. They froze, still walking, bending in on themselves against the cold. Mothers curling around their children, sons holding their father's hands. They stayed, in tableau, until the spring. Then the armies, their families and all of their worldly possessions began to fall into the lake's unfathomable depths, where they would never rot. Kappel died days later.

This hadn't happened yet, as I watched my men by the shore of the lake.

After washing out my mug with fresh water, I tried to get Sasha to eat something. I fetched him what passed for hot brown tea. It was lukewarm, a silty colour and was only palatable with some of the fresher bread: a heavy, dark rye-style that felt moist under my fingertips. Waggers the Quarter had managed to swindle tinned pilchards in exchange for a few spare loaves from the cadet college. The loaves and the fishes. They'd made a welcome break from the corned beef.

I swung myself back onto the carriage and presented pilchards on bread to Sasha wordlessly. He looked back up at me, equally silent but somehow more forceful about it.

"It's this or I leave you outside."

"I suppose you've got permission to shoot me as well?"

Cold dripped down my spinal cord. I glanced around the carriage, hot.

"Sasha." My heart was beating almost too fast inside my tongue for me to speak. "Listen. You need the strength."

I thought back to what he'd said by the side of the lake this morning. *"I know. I know."*

"I'd rather you had them."

"I don't like pilchard much. Besides, I have a cat called Pilchard and that's not something I put out of mind easily," I said, hauling a joke out into the air between us. "Come on, they're leaking on my tin."

He picked the slice up, rolling it at the edges to keep the brine from doing any more damage. "Pilchard the cat?"

"And his sister, Mackerel."

He looked at me, clearly amused. "I don't need to be taken care of, Francis. It was a moment of madness. The last thing I want is to be followed round, a one-man bloody Penza Agreement."

"Do they teach you to be this obstinate at boarding school? Harris is exactly the same."

"Everyone at boarding school is exactly the same, but that's beside the point. I don't need to be waited on."

I braved ungloving a finger to skim it around the rim of my tin, picking up crumbs and pilchard juices. "Think of me as your batman."

"Francis, you're barely important enough to have your *own* batman. What makes you think I would be?" From anyone else, that would have been vicious. "Besides," he said, grinning into my silence. "I'm rank and file."

"I don't need you to like it, I just need you to follow through," I pressed. "If you won't think of me as a military escort, then consider it age hierarchy."

"I'm older than you."

I looked at him, his big grey eyes and his boyish curls. "I find that hard to believe."

"I'm twenty-seven."

"You're not," I said, more out of surprise than anything else.

"Twenty-seven in January," he clarified. "Would you like to see my papers?"

"As long as they'll tell me when to put a card in the post" slipped out somewhat bizarrely before I could take him up on his offer. It was beginning to dawn on me exactly how little I knew about him. "But I'm not going to relent on this."

"What'll you do, have me pinned down and force fed?"

"Are you going to make me?"

There was a defiant glint in his eye. After a measured pause, he said, "Perhaps."

"Then make your mind up about it and let me know as soon as you can. In the meantime, eat your sodding bread."

Before he could say anything more, I tossed a can of jam at him. He caught it thanks to what I was sure was nothing but sheer reflex. He managed to keep hold of it in his gloves.

"You're welcome," I said, and began rolling up my bed.

After everyone and myself had eaten, I latched the door and awaited the whistle. It was a slow, empty sound, coming mournfully over the hills. It was the sort of noise I'd heard as a child from my bedroom window, after the owls were still. It had followed me all my life.

The train lurched, and then began to move off. Horrocks had instructed me to set a watch, so I did, and Nevis volunteered to go first.

I liked Nevis. He was quiet and had an artist's attention to detail that was well suited to the watch.

After making such good time yesterday, we should end the day just this side of Verkhneudinsk—different, although barely, from Nizhneudinsk, which lay on another river with an identical name about three days to the back of us. When this railway had arrived less than twenty years ago, it brought with it a fatty explosion of population, gooey and unsupported by any form of infrastructure. There were too many people in Verkhneudinsk, too many we didn't know for Barclay to feel comfortable stopping there.

"Your new uniform looks nice," said Sasha, nodding at my dark sheepskin. "I don't know whether you're going to read me the Last Rites or tell me my sons will be king of Scotland."

"I feel like a bear cub."

"That's the boots."

Our coats were long and black, but they couldn't cover us completely. Our boots attempted to make up for the shortfall by being too big in every way. I couldn't cross my legs in them, As I brought my knees up to my chest instead, Sasha eyed me sympathetically. "No luck getting winter uniforms?"

"These are our winter uniforms," I said darkly.

"You're joking."

I glanced across at him, trying to convey, *No, I absolutely am not*, silently.

"It doesn't look especially warm."

"I'd much rather have your hat."

"At least you won't have such a battle on your hands keeping it clean."

The colouring did hide some of the more major sins against cleanliness. It was impossible to keep something free from soot on a train, and our carriages were all insulated with ash. They didn't show up the dirt, but they did show up in the snow.

"The snow won't be here for a while yet," said Sasha, hopefully.

"I'd love for you to be right."

"Be hell for the tracks if it arrives in the next few weeks." He spared my uniform a wry look. "Still. At least you won't show up at night?"

"Oh, I'm reliably assured that we do. And that's before we start to frost over."

It wasn't cold enough for that, but it would be soon. And it was doubtful we'd be in Vladivostok by the time it started to properly chill.

The sight that greeted me as I looked around wouldn't survive it. Men, ruddy-faced and caught all over with frost, in huge black coats and one or two bizarre hats. And one in white.

Siberia scrolled by in all its aching monotony, the vast yellow landscape pitted with the occasional trickly stream or stagnant, malarial lake. I tried to read my book, still only ten pages away from where I'd started in Omsk, but the hypnogogia of the train forced me to give up after eleven. The omniscient onwards motion appeared to rock Sasha to sleep, like that old Akers Allen poem. And many more old ones besides. *In all the endless road you tread, there's nothing but the night.*

That night, out of boredom, I got out my lucifer and began burning along the edges of my coat. The lice eggs that had taken residence in the seams screeched and popped. I never dared do this with my sheepskin, but my uniform coat bore faint singe-lines from where I'd got a bit too close. For sheeps, you just had to sit and pick the eggs off.

One of the letters Dickie had written to my parents had described the lice in France, in fleeting detail. The image of lice had so permeated the public consciousness at that point that I don't think there was any way he couldn't pay lip service to them. Maybe he thought it would help persuade my mother to stop trying to post him socks. He got cross with her for doing that once, always sending them in the middle of the midsummer heat to keep him warm. It had seemed blackly humorous then. Looking back on it, I knew she was just trying to look after him in the only way she could.

The French lice had multiple fabled colours, Dickie said, but his were always a pale faun. Mine were black.

Mitya, in one of his strange twists of humour, had come and sat by me once while I went through the seaming ritual and had said in a grave voice, "Either the lice will defeat Socialism, or Socialism will defeat the lice."

I'd looked at him. "Pardon?"

He'd smiled at me, which was an event so rare that it hadn't helped convince me that I hadn't hallucinated the conversation.

Confirmation came in some little railside town just outside Omsk. Plastered across the station walls—among other things— was a melodramatic picture of an enormous louse hand in hand with a skeleton. The Trots had started defaming lice.

"Do the lice need the bad press?" I'd asked Mitya, nodding to the poster in front of us. Since he was our liaison officer, I often directed my mundane questions about the Russian mentality to him. "Isn't the biting enough?"

"Bolshie always have to have an enemy. Lenin declared lice an enemy of Socialism."

"Do they have a particularly strong sense of class consciousness?" I'm not sure he knew if I was joking. It was hard to tell with Mitya.

Enemies of Socialism or not, we could all agree with Lenin on that one. The one on the poster had borne a particular resemblance to the ones I kept finding in my clothes.

Another clutch of eggs exploded in my seam.

We ate, and then slept. Either at an unknown behest or with mutual unspoken agreement, we had started to double up at night. I hadn't had to ask them to do it, which was good because I'd dreaded giving that order. Perhaps they had started for fear that I would. No one liked being ordered to share with another man, especially when they couldn't choose who, to take the edge off.

All the beds were tight, which meant risking spilling out onto the floor if we didn't get in close enough. I curled around Sasha. The monotony of the day, the sleep that generated more sleep, caught up with me as soon as I was close to him. His warmth seeped into me. We lay together, me with my hands frozen to my sides, not daring to embrace him. With him, inside my bag, underneath my greatcoat and my furs. My pack rolled in a blanket as a pillow. It was hard, uncomfortable. I only relaxed where my body met his. Did he feel the same? I wished I was brave enough to kiss the side of his neck.

CHAPTER THIRTEEN

The next day: up, drill, eat, entrain. Sit and be cradled. Watch the view until the train came to its familiar grinding halt. Out of habit, I glanced at my newly working watch to see how much time we had made. It said two in the afternoon.

It was too early to have stopped, especially with all that daylight behind us. We were, or should be, spending the night in Chita, after two long pushes to try to get there in the best time possible. We shouldn't have stopped.

We all felt it begin to happen, and all looked from one to the other in a mutual, unvocalised conversation. The breaks locked beneath us, and it carried forward by force of its own momentum. It carried on, incrementally, to what could pass as a walking pace. Then the alarm went off.

It was a single, long, baleful sound. Like the metal was in pain, and when it faded away in a guttering sob, it was as if it had decided to curl in and die on itself. Either I had somehow given out the order for my men to take their prearranged positions or we had all acted on instinct. I remember looking at unarmed Sasha, wide eyed, furious, and hissing, "Do not, for the love of God, make me tie you down."

We tumbled out into the undefended air. A shot cracked through it. Someone else replied to it or joined in. Then it was quiet.

I checked my bayonet was fixed tight and waited.

Above the platform, I caught sight of what must have halted us. On top of the station roof, a ragged red flag. It meant stop or it meant Bolsheviks.

The middle of the train moved, where the major came forward like Moses on the Red Sea. Where the crowd thinned, I could make out a cluster of figures standing on the line, half dressed and half out of goatskin. There was another scuffle, and three members of my platoon came jogging quietly down the side of the train.

"Where the hell were you?" I hissed.

"Sorry, sir," Anthony Church whispered. "Tangled up with another carriage. Tried—"

I waved him away. "It doesn't matter! Just get in position."

They trotted off around the back of the train and out of sight.

I tried to train my eyes on the track beyond. Of course it would come, the inevitable conflict. But we all rather hoped that we'd managed to let it slip by us.

A liquidy spiral of silty rivers curled away in all directions from the embankment where I was standing, doing my best to keep my footing. They fell away into a bed of flat marshland. Not easy, nor welcome, cover for us, but it was unwelcome cover for them as well. I knocked my bayonet a final time with my thumb to make sure it was properly fixed.

I thought of bayonet training, both what I had been given and what I had given out. How I'd been chastised for taking my eyes off the weapon while parrying. For parrying too wide with no forward thrust. How a bayonet should be used under fire, darkness, or the cover of surprise. How we had none of the above at present.

No bother—my assault practice had all been carried out with a trench in mind. That made it worse than useless here.

There had been no other shots fired. There seemed to be a conversation taking place, aided, I have no doubt, by Mitya and dead-faced hand gestures.

"Thrust to the stomach and you can't go wrong. Less for your weapon to get caught on."

As whatever negotiation they were having unfolded, another shot cracked out and the figure furthest from the major fell backwards.

I didn't expect to find—and I hope that I'm not the only one—that sometimes death can be so bathetic. A man shot in the head, carried backward by the momentum, doesn't crumple, doesn't put his hands out. He just falls, like a man might fall heavily into bed after a long and tiring day. So much leads up to this last moment, and when you get there, it's banal and bathetic. Is that irony?

The men that were with the killed man—three of them, I saw now—had reactions that each differed completely from each other. One went for his gun—or his breadknife, or his carbine, or his handkerchief—and was swiftly dispatched by Mitya. He held his Webley with a confident arm, barely flinching with the recoil. He looked like an executioner.

One of the men went for the riverlands. I shouldered my rifle, but he, too, was shot before I had the chance to act further. He tumbled down the embankment and landed in the slurry to the side of it. In his haste not to sink, he tried to claw his way back up the embankment, before apparently having a change of heart and pulling himself along to the side. His face was in the marsh.

Lift your head, I found myself hissing to him, in my mind. *Lift your fucking head*. Imagine dying such a pathetic death. It made me red-hot with anger.

Lift your goddamn, fucking head.

I watched him until he went still. He drowned, I supposed. In less than six inches of water.

I wanted to feel something other than a curious emptiness, but nothing came. All my anger went cold watching that gelid water still around him. All I could do was watch, in camera.

The other man I didn't see. Some furious fire—*crack, crack, crack*—to the other side of the train, out of my sight, told me either he was a runner or there were more of them. I ducked around to see which it was, almost colliding with Church, and glimpsed the dark flurry of a coat leaving the station.

Shit.

For the first time in my life, I was glad for protocol. I knew better than any other officer in the world that all my men had clean rifles, clean cartridges, and a shovel to every third person. The nature of travel had done away with a lot of the need for carrying parties, and the iron rations in our packs would account for any errant time away from the makeshift quarters.

I hauled myself onto the platform, following six or seven others and helping up an eighth. The station comprised of a waiting room, a platform, and an office with a small telegraph machine. It was barely worth making it secure, but we did anyway.

Haddock was detailed to stay behind with the fifty-odd of his platoon and their team of Lewis gunners. Toby's platoon was to lead, with Warren and—once upon a time—Evans coming up in support. I came in with the moppers-up.

I cast my mind back to Sasha, who was alone. Hoped fiercely he wouldn't catch the attention of any men in the trees. *Or worse, the wrong kind of attention from our own.*

I bit the inside of my cheek and watched Toby's scouts and first wave. We knew, without having to move from our post, that there would not be much to find. The place was barely more than a hamlet, where two or three of those strange, mud brown roads ran into a dusty pool outside the station forecourt. I could see the last house, and Toby's men beyond that. It was doubtful they'd do much more than secure the perimeter.

Ten minutes later, Toby's second wave left, the rifle bombers and the Lewis gun team. It was silent out there.

After a few minutes, an unfamiliar voice climbed into my ear. "I'm going for a recce," said Warren. I think it was the first thing he'd ever said to me. "Station-side wall of that last house by the courtyard. Don't keep us waiting."

I waited, my platoon behind him. Usually you were meant to be undercover, but there were limits to how undercover one could be in the wetlands.

There was a burst of gunfire from beyond the forecourt. Warren dashed back, whisper-shouting "right flank, right flank" to his section commanders. "Riflemen!"

I held up my hand to mine. Exposed flank or not, it would only add to the confusion mixing in another platoon when we'd yet to be engaged.

There was a hollow *bang* of a grenade. Dust rose.

Warren glanced back at me, his mouth opening. Whatever he'd been going to say, he didn't. He turned around and slipped out with his second line.

I knelt down beside Brown. The moppers-up are rarely used in open warfare. I expected that was why they put me in charge of them.

"Sergeant," I said. "I'll know more after I liaise with Lieutenant Warren, but be prepared to swap places with the rifles. He's taken his men up the right flank, and I want to know why."

"Of course, sir."

I told my bombing commander the same thing. I debated talking to the Lewis gunners, telling them they might be more use at the train. Decided against it.

My watch said it was time to go, and I dashed out with my men through the courtyard to the station-side wall and stood with my back up against it, Webley in hand. If it hadn't been tied to my neck, I might have dropped it.

I didn't see Warren, but he must have known broadly where I was since we collided in his haste to get behind the wall, and I put a hand out to steady him.

"Harris has fucked it."

"What?" I said.

Warren exhaled frantically. It seemed at odds with how placid the place was. How empty.

This wasn't battle-panic.

"His Lewis gunners opened fire, and I think they've shot a civilian," he said, words tripping out over his tongue. "And now he's bombed the place to high heaven. If they weren't already hostile towards us, they sure as fuck will be now."

"Where do you need me?" my mouth asked on my behalf. I couldn't stop to think about what he was telling me. "My men are ready to go."

"Well, there's no endearing ourselves now, is there?" He ground his teeth. "Look, Harris has gone into the woods. I'm meeting him there shortly and I might need my platoon with me.

Take yours and round up anyone still here for the major. And for the love of screaming blue Christ, keep your grenadiers in check."

"Yes," I said. "Anything else?"

"If I'm not back in ten minutes, I'm waiting for you by that outbuilding. The one with the washing line. The one next to it— Well. Have a look and tell me what you think."

I relayed this back to my men, still taking the rifles and bombers out first with me. The Lewis gunners and rifle bombers followed on. The place was so small there was almost two to a house.

The building next to the rendezvous point could, feasibly, have been a rural country school. We approached it gingerly. There was one window facing out toward the station, almost large enough for me to see inside. Then something exploded, in a whirl of black feathers.

I jumped back and opened fire.

The movement stopped.

It was on me to go in first.

My heart was curiously regular, like clockwork—that automaton feeling back again as I stepped in. The room was full of letters. The blast had taken out the table and the chair in the middle, and the ruined corpse of a man lay slumped where he had been thrown.

His coat still billowed around him. One arm stretched towards the open window, catching what little there was of the wind. That's what I'd seen from outside. I'd shot at a dead man's clothes.

There were no identifying symbols on him: no armband or sash. Either he hadn't wanted them, or he hadn't had them.

I didn't want to pick him up, so I took his thick black cap instead. It had been blasted clear, and left lying at the other side of the room. Which was well, as he only had the back half of his head now.

It was soft, rough. It looked homemade.

I left, walked towards the cluster of buildings and outhouses on the other side of the station forecourt. My sergeant was coming the other way, shaking his head.

"Seven houses out there, sir. Eight of them including a privy. Live civvies—some women and three children that I saw."

"Four from me," added a man called White, whose skin had gone blotchy in the cold.

"Did they say anything?" I asked, desperate for all not to be lost.

"They said plenty sir, but none of it I could make head nor tail of."

The station didn't have a door; I could see straight through to the platform. I sent Brown to relay this to the major, but it turned out I needn't have bothered. A few seconds after my own arrival, I heard his boots on the ground as he and Mitya strode over to us. The latter slid over to the single road with the houses, followed silently by my searching party.

"What's happened, Ransome?" asked Barclay.

"One dead, sir," I told him. And then, "I'm not sure they're militiamen."

His check twitched. "I'd be surprised if they weren't."

I tossed my eyes back to the station, to the flag. There was no way of knowing who'd set it. The soldiers in their earnestness or the stationmaster in an act of final warning. Either way, it had the same message.

We hadn't come across the stationmaster yet.

I glanced at my watch. "Sir, Harris is in the trees and Warren has gone to recce with him. I need to meet him for a debrief."

"Of course," said Barclay.

I glanced back to the rendezvous point, to the bombed room. Everything in my head told me he was a partisan. The way the train had been stopped, the flag. But I couldn't get over that lack of identification. I knew a lot of them didn't fall into uniforms, but you had to have something to make sure you weren't shot by your own side.

Warren was waiting. "I need your Lewis gunners," he said, before I'd had a chance to stop. "Someone needs to clear down the left flank. You stay and tie up any loose ends. I'll wait for them here."

"Of course," I said. "Section commander's name is Corporal Kent."

"I know him," Warren said.

Of course he did. I'd inherited Kent from Evans.

I sent Kent and his men off and turned back to the station.

The other officers had left for the ticket office into an interview room, the major asking questions to those my men had rounded up. James dutifully transcribed. Mitya translated everything, and translated it back. He was a well-oiled conversation piece. It was as if there were no third man in the room. My men stood around the perimeter and occasionally rotated. There was the odd spit of Lewis gun fire from the trees, once or twice with an answering *crack*. I thought about the man who had run from the train.

Toby's party were first back. "Whoever they were, they've gone now. They'll either come back here or die out there."

"Any casualties?" James asked, glancing up from his paper.

"Two dead," said Toby. "Not ours. And we found the stationmaster. Someone hanged him about a day ago."

I wished I had a reaction to that other than *Sounds about right.*

James's mouth twisted. "They knew the forest?"

"At least well enough to plan their route."

"Thank you," said Barclay. "You can take over Ransome's role here. Cool your heels for a bit. Ransome." He looked at me, as if remembering I was in the room as well. "Take your men and find Haddock. Tell him to take a detail ahead of us to check for any fouled track."

"Warren has my Lewis gunners, sir," I told him.

"Have mine," said Toby. "Yours can fall in when they come back. They won't be long."

He smiled at me, and I forced myself to return it. The image of the man with half a head came back to me.

Haddock wasn't pleased when I told him to assign a work detail, but he did it anyway. He sent his Lewis gunners off for cover, and I installed Toby's where they'd been. It seemed far more logical to just ask Toby's team to accompany him, but I didn't mention it. It wasn't my place.

I checked in with my men, with Toby's. It had gone half past four. We'd lost the rest of the day and—depending on the state of the track—tomorrow as well. I thought of Sasha, to what extent I could check in on him. How far I could stretch the excuse of checking the stores.

Our rifles were installed to have a field of fire from all angles. Even if I could see him, we wouldn't have any privacy.

There was a crunch of gravel as someone stepped over the couplings nearest me. I turned, expecting it to be Kent and my Lewis gun team. It was Mitya.

"Ransome," he said, pushing me gently out of earshot of a rifleman. "Here is what we know."

From what Mitya gleaned, they had been local boys. A group from up the road, some village sons and a defector from one of our cadet schools. They'd come down through the towns seeking support and gaining one, two, three members. They'd arrived here and made bread-and-roses promises they could never have fulfilled. Then they'd held up our train by threatening to shoot the driver. I didn't know what else we'd find of them, these people in the trees. Mitya didn't seem to really care.

"To their credit," said Mitya. "I don't think they knew what sort of train this was."

I swallowed. "Should you be telling me all this?"

"The major asked me to keep his men up-to-date. And now you are."

"I see."

He turned to go, but something in me stopped him.

"Mitya," I asked.

"Yes?"

"Not . . . everyone always has distinctive markers, do they? Even if they're a partisan?"

"You know that," he said pointedly.

"Good. Mitya—"

He turned again, this time looking incrementally more exasperated. "Yes?"

"Has anyone been reported missing? From the town? A civilian?"

"Not unless they fell in. Joined up," he added redundantly, when I didn't react quickly enough.

"Thank you." I didn't feel any better.

I gazed back down the train, half-trying to catch a glimpse of Sasha, and surprised myself by actually seeing him. He was standing platform-side with one of Toby's men, who he seemed to have cadged a fag off.

There was a short flurry of Lewis gun fire from the woods. Mitya glanced at it idly from his way back into the building. "Well, that settles that."

There was another round, longer this time. I tightened my hand on my revolver.

He saw me do it. "Don't."

"My men are out there, Mitya."

"And you are not. Stay here, in charge of what is yours."

Mitya could have stabbed me himself—it wouldn't have surprised me more than that did. He offered nothing when I blinked at him, perturbed, except, "The Greeks. I like them."

For fuck's sake, I couldn't deal with this as well.

Before I could dwell on what he'd meant by that, there was another burst of gunfire.

Warren—my Lewis team.

I almost dragged Sasha off the platform myself. It was always fun to bag an officer. We made good targets: the fatted calves at the feast.

Nobody knew about Sasha's rank, of course. And Warren came back eventually.

It was only Nevis who didn't.

Barclay gave an ultimatum that at six that next morning, all of the workers were to come to the station. If they came, Barclay said, we'd give them breakfast. If they didn't, they'd be shot. I found out weeks later from a demobbed friend who'd been behind us that that had been what the "revolutionaries" had told them too.

Nevis wasn't the first man I'd lost. I hoped—although I didn't believe—that he would be the last.

I found out later how devastatingly useless that hope was.

Nobody, not even the men who had been with him, could offer a satisfactory explanation as to what happened. One minute he'd been there, Kent said, and the next he hadn't been. It was likely that he'd caught one in the back or the front and gone down in the water. To hear it told, it was like he'd simply vanished.

At six o'clock, the station workers came. It wasn't clear what would happen to them now, with the stationmaster dead. They wouldn't have killed him themselves and then not taken up arms.

What can I say? What do I know? Shortly after that, we left, and it wasn't our problem anymore.

CHAPTER FOURTEEN

As we slept, I thought of the man we'd left with half a head. The ground had been too hard to bury him.

I tried to put it out of my mind, reaching around Sasha and trying to hide behind him. There was something about having him sleeping next to me, so wholesome and so trusting. The way I could feel each single pulse of his heart. The comfort of just being close together.

Had he had this, the man who'd lain ruined in that pitiful wreck? I found myself hoping he'd had this simple pleasure before the end. He must have been so scared.

Sasha stirred in his sleep.

As soon as my boots hit the platform, Horrocks came to join me.

"Francis," he said. Then, "I'm sorry."

"What are you sorry about, sir?"

"It's never easy. To lose a man."

"No," I said. And right on the tail of Kim Stevens. "It isn't."

"I'll write the letter. You shouldn't have to be in that position. It ought to come from me, anyway."

"If you say, sir." The letters. They weren't difficult to write and that made them worse. A pro forma to follow, a few trite words to say. You could write a dozen out at once and only change the names at the top. And then send them and never have to see the damage you were doing. It was like throwing a grenade.

"And Stevens—I had Owen collect his belongings yesterday. It makes sense to send them all together."

I nodded at him, tartly. He wouldn't know what to say to a coal miner's wife.

Chita was broad and half-familiar, half-American in its layout. The wide straight lines of its roads lay from west to east. The area around the cakelike station was a riot of language, quick staccato Japanese punctuated with the lower guttural rasp of Russian or Mongol. We were hustled from our carriage by an ambassador from the quarter's cadre, who wanted us out as quickly as possible so he could do something incredibly important. There was a commotion around the boxes that had been loaded on at Irkutsk, which hadn't been packed well enough. After that was sorted, we were given our new billets. A new place to dig in. The major took Horrocks to debrief while Warren and I went to list Harry Nevis as Missing, Presumed Dead. We were accompanied by Sasha and Mitya, who seemed to be amusing themselves by comparing words in their native languages. Warren had two more men to list than me. We hadn't got away as cleanly as we'd thought.

Even now, a trail of bodies.

"I'm sorry," he said to me, awkwardly on the way back. We were walking slightly ahead of Sasha and Mitya, their laughing coming up behind us.

"Don't be," I said. "It isn't your fault."

"I know. But I am."

Lost for words, I surprised myself by squeezing his shoulder. I expected him to flinch away. Instead, he smiled.

We had made the shift into November a matter of days ago, and the weather was veering from moderate to bitterly, bitterly cold. Any temperature above minus ten made one feel as if they could undo their coat. Shivering, we were glad to cross the open parade square and duck into our building, where we had the pleasure of finding a manned desk and assigned rooms. Mitya was visibly relieved. Our rooming list seemed to have started at the beginning of the roll and descended, hitting "Jandáček" before it hit "Ransome." Someone had evidently informed them that we had to be kept together, because my space was shoehorned in around Sasha. It allowed me the negligible pleasure of having both Harris and Haddock in the room. We were also, it seemed, sharing with three Japanese officers, whose hospital-cornered beds were fronted with boots and sabres.

There was a clatter of boots on stone, and Toby appeared.

"Am I with you?" He cast a glance around the room and his eyebrows almost hit his hairline when he caught sight of the swords. "Christ. I thought the Japanese were all massing on the border in Irkutsk. What's all this about?"

I shrugged and sat down heavily on a bed. "Leave it, Tobes. They're garrisoned here."

"Must be nice," he half spat. For a moment he looked stony. It was to be expected. Aside from their unforgivably pro-German stance in the war, the Japanese in their famous administrative chaos had not given—or at the very least, not given the impression of—intending to aid the strategic or military organisation of Russia in any way. There was a rumour they hadn't forgiven the Russians for the kick-off in 1905 and were promoting disorder to make it easier to annexe their "parts" of Russia when the time came. I didn't know about that. But I hadn't seen anything that convinced me otherwise.

"As long as none of them snore," said Toby tersely. "And that spare bed better not be for Haddock."

I let a beat of uncomfortable silence pass rather than say anything inflammatory. If he'd come up here without taking a moment to read the lists, he obviously wasn't in the mood for discussion.

Sasha stretched out languidly on his bed. "I rather thought I'd find lunch, but I don't think I can sit up."

"Yes, you can," I told him, as Toby looked askance. "Don't snooze at midday. You'll never get rid of the headache."

Sasha laughed and, to my surprise, Toby smiled too.

I thought I knew him so well—I *did* know him well. It didn't matter what Warren said, I knew Toby. Warren was worn out, taking it out on him.

And yet, I couldn't stop that traitorous little silkworm of doubt. I could understand the Lewis fire, which Toby might not even have directed—occasionally someone did see "movement" and think "gun." But the grenade—he must have either let that happen or made it happen.

In front of me, he stood, stretching. "I am going to the post office and then to find a café. I invite either of you to join me."

"Respectfully declined, Lieutenant Harris," Sasha said from the bed.

"Ah, well," he said. "Another time. Maybe we'll take you back to Blighty with us. Ta-ra."

I waited for a beat, then followed him out of the door.

"I would," I said hurriedly.

Toby turned and blinked at me. "Pardon?"

"I would. Come with you."

"I . . . wasn't suggesting that you wouldn't, Francis."

"I know. It's just I have to . . . stay with him."

"I'm aware." He shrugged. "Would you like me to bring you back anything?"

"From whatever café you find? No, thank you, I think I'll manage. I'm going to try and cadge something from the kitchen in a minute."

"Rather you than me. See you at dinner?"

I nodded and turned back into the room. Sasha was still sprawled out on the bed he'd claimed, by the window in the worst of the draft. In a glance, I knew I'd lied to Toby. There was no way I'd have gone with him. Not with Sasha here, all sleepy and warm.

I weighed up the idea of lying down beside him. Instead, I sat lightly on the end of his bed—that was easily justified— and allowed myself the minor pleasure of threading my fingers through his hair.

He covered my hand with his and squeezed it gently.

I grew soft, warm. The inside of my body purring like a cat on a blanket.

"We haven't got too far to go now," I told him, somewhat redundantly. We were less than a hundred kilometres from the River Onon, and in less than five hundred would break through into northern Manchuria. We could do it in a day, maybe. Then not come back into Russia until it was time to go home. Until we were in sight of Vladivostok.

I wanted to touch him again.

Through Chita and out. Out into the world on the other side.

For days we'd passed through nothing but marshes and wet flatland, now frosted over for the year. All the rivers seemed to reach their peak on the Mongolian border. One of those rivers was the Ussurie. Another, the eastern branch of the Shilka, was the Onon, the birthplace of Genghis Khan. Allegedly. This corner of the planet was a world of allegedlys.

Before the war had ended in Europe, back before the Far Eastern policy had existed, the whole border had been a nest of Germans, Hungarians, and random bandit forces. The bandits had thrown in their lot with the Bolsheviks at first opportunity and with the Germans and their thinly veiled attempt at Teutonic expansionism across the East. Even if the Bosch faced total annihilation in the West, the potent mineral and matériel wealth of the then-tsarist dominions would place them in such an economic position that their loss would be almost irrelevant. Hence, ultimately, our presence in Siberia. Trying to take Russia from the East and West. All of us made into a vast, vast pincer.

The Hungarians were all but gone now. I didn't like to think too hard on what must have happened to the Germans.

Somewhere within the disconsolately flat waste wilderness of Manchuria and Mongolia we arrived at Manchulli. It was a mandated stop for coal, but I wished we would just push through.

Manchulli was characterised chiefly in my memory as home to a disgruntled Chinese general who had just been forced out of his own barracks by a contingent of Japanese troops. There was no sign of him now. And there was no sign of the Japanese division that had replaced him. This was ominous.

Shouting echoed further up the line. My hand went to my pistol, but a shout from Barclay down the line told us to hold.

A flock of logisticians moved across the platform, clearly trying their best to look serene and above the petty politics of diplomacy. They'd have bread to fetch.

They were about halfway down the platform when someone shot one of them.

He keeled over and rolled onto his back, clutching the fleshy part of his muscular thigh. A thick, deep scarlet wetness was beginning to spread. *Good*, I thought inanely. At least the bleeding wasn't fast.

"Jesus fucking Christ Almighty!" he said, with the stricken expression of a spin bowler. Everything seemed to have happened too quickly to be real.

I tossed a glance over in the shot's direction. It wasn't hard to tell who was responsible. One of the NCOs was lying on top of the man, whose arm was wrested behind his back like a paper twist. Mitya, always present at a scene of chaos, was squatted on the floor next to him, speaking rapid fire. What little of his voice carried was scarce heard above the major's incandescent shouting. The major brought himself down to Mitya's level, as if it would help comprehension between the two.

Mitya turned suddenly and called to us, "Stay!"

I extended my hands in a universal puzzled gesture. Then the logistics men and I exchanged glances, before two of them began attempting to roll the third's trousers up over his gunshot wound. It seemed like a graze, of all things.

There was more jagged Russian, and a selection of men had begun to gather round the far end of the platform. They were visibly unarmed but steely, like palace guards whose arms were hidden from the public. The man on the floor—who else but the stationmaster—was looking at them pointedly and shouting. So was the major.

Something squat fell out of a further carriage and began to make its red-faced way up the line towards us. It was Bannatyne, and it was one of the only times I'd been genuinely pleased to see him.

"Bannatyne, what the fuck is going on?" I asked, doing my best to fall into step with him. He blustered forwards importantly. I tried to keep up with him and caught my foot on a step.

"Pay attention to where you're going, Ransome, for God's sake," he said. "We don't need you out of action as well."

He drew level with the wounded man and crouched.

I glanced at Waggers the Quarter, the only one of the four not on the ground. His face was white.

After a minute, Bannatyne grunted and heaved himself back up. There clearly wasn't much he could do.

And then the major came along.

The shot man looked up at him as if he were an elder god. Barclay bent down until he was face-to-face with him. "Are you all right?"

There was a beat of silence before he answered, "Yes, sir."

"What's your name?"

"Baker, sir."

"Baker." The major turned to Bannatyne. "Get this chap back on the train."

The quartermaster loomed over, a frown crossing his features. It was one of the only times I'd seen him show anything but vague superiority. The major pulled him aside and exchanged a few terse words. In the meantime, the men at the end of the platform had moved forward.

Mitya appeared to be gathering subalterns.

I joined the ranks as quietly as I could, standing slightly off centre but with a clear view of the man who seemed to be the stationmaster. A coldly furious man, his semblance of a suit picked out in beige by steppe dust. Mitya paid him no attention.

"He apologises," he said to us. "It was an accident."

All four of us tried talking at once.

"Accident? You can't just shoot a bloody man by—"

"—the most basic fucking rule of—"

"—his gun out? Don't draw unless—"

"They think you're working for the Japanese," said Mitya, catching the tail end of that last question. "He had his gun out because they think you're working for the Japanese."

A wave of stunned silence hit us. Two simultaneous thoughts came into my head, and the vague hubbub of conversation expressed both on a sliding scale of concern. How dare we be colluding with anyone. Of course we were working with the Japanese.

I did not, nor did anyone, get the chance to ask Mitya to elaborate, because the major chose that moment to call him over. Mitya fixed his hard stare on the stationmaster and then jerked his head. The two crossed over to the other side of the platform together.

"Has someone checked that bloody man's all right?" asked Haddock in an undertone.

I realised he wanted someone to answer.

"It didn't seem . . . too bad," I supplied. There wasn't even a need for an implication. The implication was always there now. The subjectivity behind the phrase *too bad*. "It looks like it only grazed him."

"What damn fool thing was that trying to achieve?" It wasn't really a question.

Mitya had his gun out. That realisation soured down my entire spinal column. He held it in clasped hands, behind his back. Like a judge. Unprofessional and uncaring. Confident.

I watched him shadow a conglomerate group, our men and their men on the platform, down to the train. Major Barclay watched them go as well, his mouth thin and tight.

"Our friend the station commandant insists on searching the train before he lets us go any further. He's not happy with the fact we've stopped at Chita. Fugi turned up last year and threatened to annex the whole bastard lot of them. They're still not happy."

A muscle twitched in his jaw.

"I've given them permission to search, provided they're accompanied by Horrocks and an interpreter. Then he's going to give us our bread and we'll be on our way."

There wasn't much grain at all. God knew what was going in the bread.

There was someone standing on the edge of us. Some angel-eyed, tow-haired country boy who looked like he'd end up with his blood spread all over the steppe. He seemed to want to be noticed but not to speak. Warren caught a glance of him, and I had to stand still and pretend not to overhear them.

"What is it?" Warren asked, not unkindly.

"Is Baker all right, sir?"

"Yes, fine. I daresay he'll be back with you later."

Warren turned back to us. Barclay didn't seem happy, but he didn't say anything either.

"There isn't much news from further up the line as far as I can make out. I want you men to just . . . keep yourselves here, while you can. Don't leave the station. Make sure you've covered every angle of the train."

Always make sure you've covered every angle of the train. Front, back, both sides. An old formation. One so old I found my men almost in it out of habit by the time I got back and relayed to my section commanders what I'd been told.

"Do they know we're both on the same side, sir?" Jacobs said flatly when I got back to my own car. It was worth me upbraiding him, perhaps, but I didn't.

I cocked my head tiredly to the side. "I'm assured they do. And they know better than to make a hostage of a fully armoured troop train. Let's try and see the show through and hope we can get out as soon as possible."

There were just under two hundred of us. Ataman Dutov buried ten times that many still alive. And we were—nominally— on the same side.

The tiredness. I'd never known a tiredness so extreme. It went beyond feeling. All of my cells were turgid with it. The weather wasn't helping. It was windy because it always was; it scythed across the plains because there was nothing there to stop it, and it could. The story of this corner of the earth. Because it could. It could, it could.

The ragtag committee make its way down the train. They gave across this false air of officialdom, like children standing at the front of the class. There was a crispness to the atmosphere, a tinderbox being sized up by a match. The question sounded at the back of my mind: *When is a search not a search?*

I just hoped they didn't know how much power they had. Or more importantly, that they wouldn't conflate this power with the importance of their opinion. It would only take one wrong look, one snap decision that a rule had been violated. It didn't matter how few of them there were. Any damage to the track and we were dead out here.

Could we shoot the whole lot of them, and how far down the line would we get afterwards? We'd have to take the bodies with us. Who could replace the station commandant until the next station?

Who had I become, even considering these things?

They came closer. Then they were here.

Our end of the carriage would be of the most interest. That was why they'd left it until last. The door of my home caught slightly on the railings, like it always did. Three men I didn't know piled in. Then one of them drew his gun.

It was obvious who they'd seen. Perhaps Sasha had been asleep and they'd just woken him. Perhaps he'd been awake and listening. Perhaps—and I hoped to God he hadn't—he'd thought to defend himself.

It took one stupid beat of my heart to remember he was Czech.

Panic flashed behind Mitya's eyes as they met mine. The same thought seemed to strike us both, a coup de foudre, and it rooted me to the ground. Mitya's features—always so concealed, so effortlessly buttoned-down—schooled themselves so quickly it was like watching a slate being wiped clean. I heard a word from him—*shackter*—both unfamiliar and guttural. He stepped up into the carriage languorously, flanking one of the navvies. Said something else, pointed to me.

I caught a glimpse of Sasha, hemmed into the side of the wall. He was wrapped up, trying to keep off the worst of the cold. A sad, sheer tableau. If one wanted to, they could make a case that he was hiding.

He's not, I wanted to say. *He's just cold.*

Sasha didn't have his uniform anymore. Everything he owned were castoffs from our regiment headquarters, with the exception of his furs. He hadn't allowed himself to be separated from those.

"как вас зовут?"

Ludicrously, I realised I understood the navvy's question. The introductory utterance of every piece of schoolboy French or German or Greek. *Kak vas zavoot? What is your name?*

Mitya answered for him, almost bored. "Он не понимает." *He does not understand.* Almost nursery rhyme in its sound; *ony ponny myet.* Its sibling, *yany panny myu* had been one of the only gaggle of words in my repertoire for a long time. Mitya had told me my pronunciation was terrible.

My thoughts were on such a panicked string that I barely, barely caught the rest of Mitya's reply. "*He doesn't understand,*" he said. "*His name is Nevis.*"

One of the men, the stationmaster, knelt down to Sasha's face and said that word that Mitya had done, "*Shackter.*" Sasha gazed at him uncomprehendingly. The man said it again, and mimed digging. Sasha nodded and tried to crack a smile. The stationmaster said one last word to him, one that even I knew. "*Khorosho.*" Good.

He joined his detail in their method: checking through the bunks, looking underneath tarpaulins, rooting through open crates. Testing the seals on the closed ones. I could feel the quarter's cold anger coming off him like sweat.

After what must have been about quarter of an hour, they finally disembarked. That seemed it from them. There was nothing but the flatbeds behind us. I made eye contact with Sasha, briefly, just to make sure he was all right. His gaze was bewildered but not shaken. I returned to my duty of holding a gun and looking like a threat.

As soon as they were out of range—handshaking on the platform, all animosity forgotten—and the crates were being loaded, I caught up with Mitya.

"I—" I started. "Thank you. *Spasiba.* I mean, you didn't have to—"

He gave his contemptuous one-armed shrug. "Not a problem. I don't think he was in real danger."

"Even so. He was inside when the rest of us weren't." I flashed him a smile I didn't mean in order to shrug off some of my worry. "He could have been. We all could."

He fixed me with that stare I'd come to recognise—and disregard—as hostile. Mitya was cold but probably not malicious. "Perhaps. Your major threatened them all with a military tribunal."

"Is that what he was shouting about? It's a favourite of his. Don't know how much jurisdiction he'd have out here with the rail companies." Barclay was an idiot.

Mitya gave me a guarded look. "They don't all work on the railway."

"Oh?"

"They're not station men."

There was only one group of people with a vested interest in stopping us who weren't station men.

He let a beat of silence pass between us, and when I opened my mouth, he pre-empted me with, "I won't tell you here." Then, "You aren't in danger."

If they weren't station men, they were Trots. But then we would certainly be in danger. So who were they? Chancers? The stationmaster's friends? If that man was the stationmaster—but then he had to be acting in some official capacity to have access to our supplies. Perhaps the Trots stopped everyone. Like a tithe.

I was prevented from questioning Mitya further by Brown appearing at my side and advising me to entrain with the rest of my platoon. I cast Mitya one last, fleeting glance. He'd already turned his back and was making his way, conveniently, to the rough building that housed the station proper.

"Thank you, Sergeant," I said absently, casting an eye around for men of mine who'd strayed farther than they should. It seemed that Barclay's new order had not fallen on deaf ears, as the general milling crowd of human flesh that had furred the train had thinned out considerably. I did think that I should supervise, just to show myself doing so. Brown and I walked back towards the line, him offering me a hand to hop down off the platform, which I refused. Mitya's comments were needling at the back of my mind. I almost—almost—asked him what he'd heard. Then I didn't. I decided it was for the best.

It was all very well for Mitya to say *"You're not in danger,"* but the second-person pronoun only went so far in helping Sasha. There were few things worse in Russia than being discovered travelling on false papers. It was especially bad if you were Czech, and it was worse if you were an officer. If these non-railway men had realised Sasha's status, either element could have been enough to execute him.

Execute him. He'd have been shot by the side of the tracks.

Almost everyone I was responsible for had made their way back into their respective carriages now. I had to break up two conversations with the good-natured geniality of a schoolmaster to help speed us along. All a front, of course. It was probably the same for most schoolmasters.

By the time I reached my own car, the men I'd shared it with for all these weeks now were sat on the floor, like children, eagerly swapping half-heard rumours like currency. Gossip—the only thing that spreads faster in the Army is dysentery.

I gave them a quick smile as I came in behind them, hoping they didn't ask me to join.

"Anything you've picked up, sir?" Jacobs asked. There was a guffaw from Gallehawk, who I daresay had put him up to it.

"About what, Jacobs?" I answered, humouring them.

I could see him thinking over his answers in that clever blond head. "About the past few days."

Such a politician's response. He exchanged a glance with Gallehawk, who seemed to be congratulating a no-less-proud Jacobs on his diplomacy.

I replied, "Nothing out of the ordinary."

He nodded, clearly digesting my answer. "And where to next? Sir."

"Hazelar. That hasn't changed, as far as I've been told." These long, long weeks did eat away at your social etiquette.

"What's in Hazelar?" came an unexpected question from, of all places, a bright-eyed Sasha.

I blinked at him.

"Sir," he finished, with what we probably both wished was plausible absentmindedness.

"That I can't answer you, Jandáček." I hoped my addition of his name didn't sound too on the nose. "I'd be surprised if we reached there tonight."

And, indeed, we didn't. However, we did keep pressing on, further into the dark than we had before.

The nights here didn't fall quite as quickly in the winter as they did in England. We were that much more south. One thing that did pick up was the cold. The November air had had a feasible undercurrent in it since we'd left Omsk: a nibble of cold, a riptide. The train wasn't good protection. The slats on the cattle cart would never fit together snugly. Some attempt had been made in the past to wattle-and-daub the air gaps between them. Whatever had been used had flaked off now, leaving a black, tar-like substance in its wake. Leaky as the hull of an old ship.

CHAPTER FIFTEEN

We'd been billeted in an old farm house together again; once more not alone. All through my roamings the next day, I subconsciously searched for Mitya, but he seemed to have disappeared from the face of the earth. Toby was evading me too.

Sasha had clearly noticed my searching. On my fifth scan of the train's length, he caught my eye with that intelligent look of his. We were obviously in for a Conversation.

We were meant to be eating. I couldn't and Sasha, presumably, wouldn't. I thought of what had been said to me back in Irkutsk. If he didn't eat, in this cold he could starve to death here.

Maybe that was the point.

I had managed to pressure him into a bowl and a half of soup and some bread, though I wished there had been butter, some dripping to spread on toast. Nobody paid much attention to either of us at meals, as Sasha had gained a reputation for being a moody recluse and me for encouraging him.

"You're upset," he said as we left the immediate confines of the carriage.

It wasn't a question.

"I'm not, Sash."

"Something's wrong with you."

"Something more than the normal?"

"You're more withdrawn than you usually are." The *with me* was silent.

"I'm just mulling over a lot."

"Are you angry with me?"

I pulled up straight. "Am I what?"

"Angry," he said. "With me."

"No!" I said, and then in disbelief, added, "Sasha, why would I be?"

He shrugged his little shrug. "Because of Mitya. After what he said. On the train."

I tried to hone my memory. Mitya on the train. As if I hadn't been looking for Mitya on the train ever since Sasha and I had had our last proper exchange. When he'd been in danger.

As I rounded the corner up to our billet for the night, the memory fell into place.

"Do you mean . . ." Again, I glanced around. I couldn't help it. "Sasha—you don't mean your name?"

He nodded. My heart grew several sizes. I felt my compassion for him in my throat.

"Sash . . ."

He blinked at me.

There was so much I wished to convey. So much I wished he knew. How I felt. About him.

Recently, I'd been having daydreams. They were easy to fall into and it was a bad habit of mine. Something about that continuous, rocking motion seemed to induce it. I'd been the same way at school, as I travelled on the train twice a day. Everything out the window was fodder for the imagination. Now I imagined me and him. I imagined us, at home in Essex. My quasi-middle-class house.

He and I were there. Sometimes we were in the kitchen, me hanging over Hestia's shoulder like I was twelve again. We'd have honey and thick, full milk. Stews, right from the pot. Fresh shortbread, fish from the river. We'd go out traversing Sophie's wilderness and come back with armfuls of bramble fruit, baked into a crumble, and eaten with cream.

Sometimes we were in the garden, just the two of us, lying out flat on the lawn and staring up at the sky. We were climbing trees, seeing who could reach the highest. We were playing tennis, badminton, croquet. Sometimes my sisters were there, and others just one of them was. Sometimes they left us be. I never saw Dickie there, in my head. I played chess with Sasha in the conservatory; we sat in the cosy living room, both of us reading. We'd retire to bed together. I brought him towels in the en suite, thick and white. I stirred his bathwater with my finger while he pretended to be embarrassed and splashed me. In my head, he was so safe. I'd never let any harm come to him. He was here, in my mind. He was mine to look after.

I could not, of course, say any of this, cold and amid the tides of men ebbing in the corridors around us. "I would never be angry with you, Sash."

He sat on his bed and gave a wry, downcast smile, one that wasn't directed at me. After a while, he said, "It's very difficult to lose a man."

He stretched his leg out, clearly trying to free a path into the depths of his tunic pocket. He drew out a cigarette case and tapped two on the silver.

"I wouldn't want to lose you."

He met my eye and smiled again, this time, more sadly. This time, in my direction. I watched as he put the cigarettes between his lips, his errant lucifer spitting the flame too high again. He drew on both ends and then handed one to me.

I held it between two fingers. "Sasha. I don't want to lose you. Mitya was trying to keep you safe."

He drew in deeply, then exhaled. "I was never in real danger."

"You don't know that."

"I can take an educated guess, Ransome. You saw those men."

"They weren't railway," I said, in the way I had often repeated Greek or Latin at school. A catechism. He nodded. Sensing an unwanted lull, I put my cigarette in my mouth at last.

"Matters have progressed. There are far worse things on the line than a few rogue Czech."

"That doesn't matter, Sasha. What matters is—"

He stopped me. "You *saw* those men. They didn't even take food. They didn't take anything off the trains, and they could have had everything. They could have taken up the line. All they were was desperate." He took a drag and exhaled. "Desperate and stupid."

"They aren't mutually exclusive, Sasha."

"Yes," he said. "They are."

I bit my tongue and waited for a second. Then I said, "And they let you be."

"They did. And you did. All I can assume is that we're no longer the priority to be strung from the rooftops. God help everyone who doesn't look like us."

I did wonder, then, if that was a fluke of translation or an act of extraordinary insight on his part. It could have been both. It could have been either. I thought of all the faces we'd seen at the parade the last time we'd passed through Hazelar. Chinese. Mongol. Tatar. Bashkir. *God help everyone who doesn't look like us.*

On the fringes of Hazelar was sand, gathered into duney outcrops that gave me an unexpected pang of homesickness. All of that sand and scrub, though it was strange to see it without the sea. It cast my mind, unwillingly, into thinking on the thousands upon thousands of years that would precipitate those hills being there. All those winds: hurricanes, gales, breezes. Those seeds landing exactly where they did.

And even now the landscape wasn't sturdy. When the wind, the wind of a thousand years, gets up, the sand whorls and eddies and folds in on itself and then out, carried to and fro and to again and ending up hundreds of feet from where it started. Or sometimes within spitting distance. And those piles aren't without destruction in their own right. For every grain of sand that's disturbed, one disturbs some other delicate balance in the ecosystem. Whole trees, pines and the ubiquitous silver birch, are choked up and killed. Sometimes the sand can take down hundreds. All the trees at eye level. Entire woods, entire forests.

Through our journey along this endless sandscape of land, we never did once see water. I became light-headed, suffering vertigo from the sheer thought of so many kilometres and uninhabited kilometres. All of this land, stretching into oblivion. And across it all, the railway, this tiny line. The men that must have built it.

Some benevolent God must have taken pity on my—and all of our—minds. The sand's formations, firm and conical, gave the impression of a campsite or a desert settlement. The impression of humanity, of life within shouting distance. Every night at sunset when the view became less discernible, we could look out and pretend there were other people with us. Sitting beside us as we gazed without end onto that enormity.

Anything could be hidden in the valleys. Anything could be buried.

Growing up by the sea, or as near to it as I could get, I had harboured a healthy respect for open space. But even I had no point of reference here. This vast, unforgiving antithesis of the sea could drown you just as easily. It would dehydrate you and starve you.

That relentless sense monotony was broken up only by a spattering of trees. From where they found their sustenance, I couldn't possibly guess. They marked each stopping-place, along with the stern-looking wooden-framed winter dwellings, which were built right into the earth and swallowed by almost two feet of it. They were flat-roofed and contained only one room, like somewhere a mediaeval apothecary would live. When the snow froze, the whole thing was impossible to see unless you trained your eye on the patches of hot, dark air. The smoke escaped through the eaves, built gappily for this very purpose. I supposed the heat kept the eaves clear of snow as well.

Tiny lanterns were visible at night, like ships on the unharvestable sea.

There was an endless, endless nature to the plain. Such an unforgiving, Godlike landscape. This place was like the surface of the moon must be.

We were almost set to come into Harbin. There was a gorgeous bridge in, over the river Sungary. It was a deep, fertile land. There was so much history there in the farming. So many cultures that dovetail at that junction of the world.

And it was so cold. We slept, all of us, huddled together like children.

Sasha was so kissable. He lay against me, warm and loose-limbed. I made a habit of engineering my cuffs so that they left my wrists half-bare in the morning chill. The vulnerability of their thin skin frightened me, but it meant I could touch my skin to his. Feel him—just barely warmer than I was. His heat suffused into mine, sustaining me. Warming me from the outside in. I felt him in my throat, under my rib cage. Deep in my groin. I kindled near him. I lit up like tissue paper.

I curled around his warm form at night, hyperaware of how we should be lying. His soft breath hit my cheek and ruffled my hair ticklishly across my nose. I buried my hands in his long blue scarf and tried to disguise how I held him as sleepy anchoring only. He fit so snugly against the curve of my body, like cats in a basket, like nested eggs. I'd do anything for the comfort of being near him.

I rested my left hand between his layers, trying to get closer and closer to his skin. Never quite reached it, but I grazed his underlayers, the grimy underclothes and base shirts stiff and rich with a film of sweat and body grease. I held his thigh sometimes, when I was positive no one could see me, when it was dark. Sometimes he'd cover my hand with his and press it to him.

One singular time, I felt him go to his fly and rub himself. Slowly and deliberately. He pushed himself up against me, and I pressed against him as best as I could, my heartbeat in my throat. *This is happening. This is really happening.* But I could only listen to his hand, his breathing hitch and then stop and then sigh out. Then, he reached down again and squeezed my hand gently as the muscles in his thigh tensed and spasmed.

I hid my face in his hair, my teeth clenched tight.

Harbin seemed to consist of a collection of houses thrown together towards the junction of the Chinese-Eastern railway against the laws of diminishing returns. The buildings themselves were a watercolour rendition of Chinese houses. Pretty, but I just couldn't take them in. Perhaps I had been travelling too long, or perhaps I had reached the maximum saturation of things my eyes could see. There was too much jammed into my head already, swirling about. Too much about where we all were and what our little future could hold.

It was these thoughts of small mortality that prompted me to search for Mitya again and finally find him. I'd known I had to, in the vague way you know you have to visit the bank or post a letter, but now I went to him with the hope I could unpack some of these thoughts for him to hold.

"Mitya," I started.

He looked at me. "Lieutenant Ransome. Our last talk got cut short, did it not?"

"The station. Does the major know?" I assumed he'd be able to fill in the blanks.

To his credit, he didn't feign ignorance. The answer came straight away: "Yes. The men at the station were common soldiers. Little more than bandits."

"Bandits?"

"No," he said archly. "Although little more than."

"They were scared of us."

He shrugged again. "Maybe."

"They could have blown up the line."

"And risk not getting supplies through themselves?"

I knew that I couldn't get much more out of him. He wasn't under my command. As far as he was concerned, he probably wasn't under anybody's. He dipped and dovetailed as he saw fit.

He caught my eye and drew in a breath, like a swimmer up for air.

"Mitya," I preempted, trying a different tack. "I want to thank you."

He waited in silence. It was his best weapon.

"As you know, Jandáček is my charge. Your thinking may well have saved his life. Thank you."

He waited, still in silence.

"That's your lot, Mitya," I told him. "You're not getting any more."

He cracked a smile, then. "You're welcome, Lieutenant. I liaised ahead to Harbin back in Chita."

"You're a miracle worker."

"Not at all," he said, shifting. Then, turning away from me a little, he asked, "You and he . . . you are his guardian, are you not?"

So he wasn't going to let this go. I glared at him. He'd done well, tying me up like this. I couldn't answer no, couldn't answer yes. Instead I looked at him sternly. "I believe you're aware of the situation."

He took a moment too long to answer. "Yes."

A lot passed between us then. Unspoken subtext, tacit acknowledgement, a transaction of truth that I'd always been dreading but somehow, now it was here, I welcomed. There was, looking back on the conversation, no implication of threat. I couldn't know, at the time, how profound that omission was.

"Mitya . . ." I began.

He glanced at me with the same impassive face as always. "It's no trouble," he said. "You have to take care of him."

"Mitya—"

"It's not a problem."

I allowed the desperate beat of silence to pass between us, a tight little bundle of nerves. What a perfect trifecta of an answer. Mitya. What a politician.

A corner of his mouth twitched. "I'll see you in the morning."

I could have strangled him. With my heart in my soft palate, I wheeled around in search of Sasha. My pack was gone, presumably carried up to my room. I couldn't see him, though. I had a brief conversation with a man in what passed for a uniform in what passed for English. He told me to go up the stairs and turn, gesturing to the right. His right and my left, I assumed. I could feel my heartbeat in my tongue.

I climbed the stairs and turned to the left, absentmindedly counting doors. Needn't have, because ours was open, and Sasha was there. The sun broke in his face when he saw me.

"Sash," I said, pulling the door to and throwing the lock as I came in. He was with me when I turned around, one hand in my hair and another on my waist. He'd just brushed his teeth, and I could feel the dry residue powder on his lips. I breathed him in and my diaphragm dropped. I held his hip bones in my hands. It wasn't a hungry kiss. It was a kiss of welcome, of homecoming. A transaction of feeling. *I'm glad to see you*, it said. I was glad to see him as well.

I pushed him away.

"Sasha," I said, "Mitya knows."

My revelation seemed to do nothing to him. He looked at me, without a nerve twitching in his face. "I know."

"You—"

He smiled and squeezed my hip. "I know. He's already propositioned me."

The floor came out from underneath my feet. "He's *what?*" I asked, not sure if I was more surprised or indignant.

Sasha grinned. "Don't worry. I didn't accept."

"Sasha, this is . . ." *dangerous*. "Sasha, this is absurd. What will you do if he says anything?"

He shrugged, one shouldered. "What could he say? And why?"

"But if he *does*, what can you do? What can *we* do? If you say he has an interest in you, that makes you look like you're being vindictive because you're forced into a corner. We've got no insurance on him."

"Mitya won't."

"Mitya . . ." I let the name leave my mouth, with nothing to follow it with. Who could say what Mitya would do? I doubted even he knew himself well. Times had been hard to him. He'd grown like a plant without sunlight, all pale and twisted. All etiolated and wrong.

"Why would he do anything, Francis?" Sasha asked me. I loved that he said my whole name. I couldn't abide it shortened. He touched my face. "Why?"

"Why wouldn't he?" I countered.

He kissed the bridge of my nose, right between my eyes. The hand in my hair cupped my jaw. I closed my eyes.

"We homosexuals need to stay together. We're the only friends we have."

"Very profound." I smiled, opening my eyes again and looking at him. He gazed back. He had that expression on his face that he got as that cruel, sublime landscape scrolled by. It looked as if he were watching the sea. Then he smiled back, and then he kissed me.

As a student, I had thrown myself into the trappings of homosexuality. Many of the men I'd been with had gone on to live perfectly normal lives. Wives, children. I didn't know if it had been a sacrifice for them or if they'd known they were capable of enjoying it. I didn't know how many had wanted to simply give the dishabille lifestyle a whirl at university and get it out of their system. The ultimate taboo, the ultimate rebellion. Like being a socialist before graduating and becoming a banker. Some had lived like me. Thrown out into the wide world with no frame of reference for how to navigate it as creatures like us. Those who enjoyed each other's bodies and each other's company. Being with people like us. Knowing that they'd know what you were attempting to say.

I had reluctantly come to realise that this life was part of my personality; it was sewn in. I wished it didn't have to be.

I leant into his kiss, pushing him further into the room, until the backs of his knees were pressed up against the ridge of the mattress. I glanced anxiously towards the door.

"Francis," he said, stroking my cheekbone. "Relax. It's all right."

It was all right. I looked at him like the sun. Him sitting, gazing into my face; it was such a perfect picture. The white sheets behind his face. How could I not kiss him?

He spread his hand out into my hair—overlong, salty from sweat and grit—and pulled me onto him. I fell blissfully. He enveloped my body in his, his legs met around my hips, and one hand anchored firmly in the small of my back, as if I might leave him. As if I ever could. As if I ever could.

I loved everything about him, and him like this particularly. The adored and simple leisure of his body. Of stroking his skin, of feeling his hair. That thrill of seeing a new part, some little nick or imperfection that I had overlooked before. A freckle, a scar. I wondered who else in the world could know about them. I wondered if even he knew they were there.

Up close, I could see his individual lashes. The beginnings of growth where he'd neglected to shave this morning. His throat.

I'd heard descriptions like "the long white column of his throat" in so many books and poems. I had never understood that comparison, thought it rather trite. The cold and stately, the noble sentiment projected by that phrase was hardly synonymous with something as warm and comforting as a lover. And yet that phrase came to me with Sasha who was not cold, yet had a nobility I could take in my mouth. A long column of throat to wrap myself around. To anchor to.

He lay below me, eyes closed and unaware of how he looked. How he was outside, and all that was in him: a seething mass of blood and nerves and muscle; tubing and cartilage. I loved it all. I kissed his neck, so lightly. Felt his pulse butterfly underneath, his life close enough for me to lick.

He let out a breathy sigh. "Francis, I want you to fuck me."

I pulled back. He blinked, gazing up with that beatific face. A mediaeval saint.

"Are . . . you sure?" were the words that left my mouth.

He propped himself up on his elbows, taking hold of the back of my head and kissing me through a smile. "Francis. I've always been sure."

I returned his kiss. He leant into me with the warm contentment of a housecat. I wanted him so much.

"Please," he said.

Without moving away from his mouth, I placed my hand on his chest. He had done away with his overcoat and goatskin and heavy dark jacket. His sweat still soaked through the stiff cloth, cooling in the winter air. I slipped a finger between his buttons. His skin was so hot.

I undid the buttons with my thumb, making my way down as slowly as I could. I grazed the tender skin of his stomach with my little finger. I loved it there, that silken expanse of skin that nobody else was allowed to touch. The shy, dark, downy hair, the pallor from the lack of light, the gently rolling elevations of his hip bones. I held them both, feeling that skin beneath the rough skin of my hands. Underneath, all of his soft, undefended insides worked with relentless monotony to keep him alive. That he could trust anyone here, in his most vulnerable of places—I kissed him, right under his navel.

He sighed and leant his head back on the pillows. "Do that again, Francis."

How could I resist? I did it again. Then I did it again, and again. I kept kissing him, letting my tongue trail over his pelvis, indulgently and unhurried. I had to fight not to squeeze and let everyone know I'd been there as heat bubbled in my throat, under my skin. But I did allow myself to trace an ur-pattern on his flesh while I worked on snapping open the buttons of his trousers. Heat in my veins and under my nails. Both of my hands rubbed the rough musculature of his legs to peel off the uniform and thermals. He was hot, his heart beating close to the surface. I could feel it in his blood vessels. I could feel it on my tongue. Could this desire really be for me?

I pulled his underwear down with my teeth, then buried myself in the twitching skin of his thighs.

I love this part of a man, so much. Those smooth, hairless patches worn to a tonsure by years of fabric abrasion. With my face between his legs, I dragged my lips up from just above his knee to the crease where his legs met and licked into it. He tightened around me, a visible tremor like a cello string being plucked. I could become an anchorite in his skin.

There was a minute tang of blood from where a seam had worn its way into his skin like a river. Did it hurt, or had he stopped noticing? If it hurt now, would he tell me? I kissed it, just in case. Made my way to his other leg, never taking my mouth off him. Never wanting to. Not again, not ever again. My hands held his thighs apart, stroked his inner skin with the barest of touches

as I sought my way into him with my tongue. I heard a moan—
felt it—from within, a breathy keen. I smiled, then took one of his
balls into my mouth.

He jolted. To reassure him, I pressed my palms to his legs,
working my thumbs in circles against his smooth thighs. He
groaned from deep in his throat, and I grinned around him and
then lifted my mouth.

"Sash?"

His breath hitched and he gasped.

"Is this . . . all right?"

He didn't make a noise to the contrary. I sucked on him,
very slightly; he made a noise opposite of contrary. Such a man.
A beautiful, beautiful man. One whom I adored. Who I hoped
adored me.

I carried on, licking and stroking and covering every inch of
what should be covered by my mouth.

I couldn't keep my lips off him. If I tried to separate us, my
heart might stop. I lowered my mouth, laving at any part of him
I could. He had that taste, the flavour that all men have there. I
loved everything about him: the coarseness of his hair against my
cheeks and mouth; the expanse of skin between my nose and lips,
already chapped from the cold.

His hand fluttered down to meet me, laying itself ever so
gently and tentatively on my head. I tried to press against it, letting
him know that it was all right. I had been treated far rougher than
this. He didn't need to worry as I could tell that he was. I tried
to slow my mouth to get my point across more clearly. His hand
came down tighter, trying to bite into my head. He was holding
back. It was always obvious with him. Those tendons in his wrist
carried the weight of the world.

I licked the silk skin of his inner thigh, gently and slowly. He
gasped; it seemed to travel through his bones. I carried on, over
his soft, shy ball sack to the proud head of his cock. I glanced at
him.

He had his eyes closed; his teeth clenched. His cheekbones
stood out from his skin like sentinels. I sucked down, taking him
further, and a muscle in his jaw twitched. A sudden, reckless need

to make him moan seized me out of nowhere, unbeholden to common sense. It became my mission to get him to know how much I loved him, to want him to see and to hear it.

I braced my hands in the junction of his thighs. I rubbed them rhythmically in time with my head, gently massaging the tight, sensitive skin. So roughly used by months on the road. Months and months in freezing, chafing wool. I loved this being done to me.

How long had I longed to do this? Have him like this, spread before me happy and warm and safe. Since I'd seen him, laughing in the snow, all dark hair and eyes? Seeing him curled up on himself inside all the layers he could manage? Seeing him in his goatskin, like an exiled Ruritanian prince? Or the first time we'd met, both of us barely standing and half mad with the cold? All of those moments flashed through my closed eyes. All of those moments, leading to this. His taste on my tongue. The closest I could ever, ever get to him.

I pressed my thumb inside my fist—an old university trick—and took him farther, as far as I was able to go. It was a habit now. His hand tightened in my hair.

My hand left his leg, wrapping around his wrist. I squeezed, rubbing a firm circle around that juncture of skin. Just enough to let him know I was here. Thinking of him. He caught my hand and squeezed back.

He tensed then, and I felt that tell-tale swelling coming closer and closer to my mouth. I sucked again, hard and luxurious. His resolve finally cracked, and he made the most wonderful, drawn-out whine, clamped behind his teeth. As soon as he made it, I wanted him to do it again.

I took my mouth off him and moved lower. He gasped at the loss and a small illicit thrill went through me that he could miss me that much. I buried myself in him, kissing all of him I could reach. Right through his skin, through his body wall and into him for ever. For good.

"Is this all right?" I asked him.

He tugged my hair yes.

"Shall I keep going?"

Another tug.

I smiled, then licked his cooling skin, pressing a myriad of small, imagined kisses up and down his shaft. He pulsed, leaking. Could he feel everything I wanted to say to him? I couldn't ever vocalise it all.

I moved further down. The contrast of texture here, the subtly different tastes—here was what I loved.

He seemed to realise where I was going, because he sat up all of a sudden.

"Francis."

I raised my head. "Are you all right?"

"Yes, I—" He was propped up on his hands, his stomach muscles tense. I wanted so much to reach out and stroke one of them. I wanted to touch every part of him. His gaze never left my face. "I— You don't have to."

I couldn't resist seeing how far he'd go. "Don't have to do what?"

"Do . . . that," he said, breaking off. "If you don't want to."

"What makes you think I don't want to?"

He opened his mouth but didn't speak. His tongue came out and wet his lips.

I lowered my mouth and licked the crease of skin behind his balls. "Do you want to?" I asked him. "We don't have to. One word and I'll stop."

I knew how it felt. I remembered the first time someone had done it to me. The mixture of repressed thrill with the abject terror of someone going there, on you. The embarrassment. The fear of humiliation or rejection. Or worse, the fear that they'd remember and be able to hold it over you. That they had done that. How they must think of you. The instant power imbalance that became apparent as soon as it had happened. All of these thoughts had teemed around my head until he had put his mouth on me.

Sasha obviously didn't know this. How could he? Or if he did, he only knew the half of it. The half that came before. I had no idea how different it might be for him. Leaning on my elbows, I watched his face. If I were closer, I'd have run my fingers over his cheekbones, cupped them in my hands. Let him know that it was all right to want it; it was all right to not.

He didn't break my gaze, and swallowed, wetting his lips again. He nodded, once, his eyes still wide.

I understood.

I moved his legs up my shoulders and lowered my mouth, seeking him out. I licked over him once, gently, and he tensed underneath. It was a reflex or embarrassment or something in between. He was clearly sensitive. I kissed him, keeping my tongue all but still, moving it in the smallest circles. He should get used to this movement, relax into it. To know I was here for his pleasure and nothing else.

He pressed against me so gently that I doubted he knew he was doing it. I pushed further into him, almost breaching that ring of muscle, and waited, pulsing my tongue and teasing. He was so tense—that was all right; there was no rush. I could go on like this for hours. I stroked him more, gently urging him on, urging him open. Finally, he seemed to relax. With a small sigh, he shuddered and sank back a little. I kept myself anchored, gave him something to hold on to. Something to steady himself with. I pushed in by degrees. Pressing slightly, pulling back, licking his skin, kissing where my tongue had been; starting all over again. He grew loose-limbed, rocking against me gently. A brief worry about the headboard flitted across my thoughts, but then he balled his hand in the sheets and it was forgotten. Washed away in a warm sea of desire. If I could, I would have reached up and covered that hand with mine.

"Francis," he gasped.

I stopped and smiled at him. He was all tightened muscle against those sheets, and he looked back at me with huge eyes.

"Francis," he said again. "Fuck me."

"Are you sure?"

He huffed breathlessly. "If you ask me that one more time, I'm going to pull rank and have you court-martialled."

"I'd hate for that to happen. Sir."

He grinned. "Fuck you."

I kissed him. I could feel him smiling still.

Pulling away reluctantly, I gazed down at his face. Some of his thick hair, damp from sweat, had fallen in front of his eyes. I pushed it away fondly. "As you wish."

I kissed his forehead, his brow, had to pull back. If I started, I'd never stop. And then, with an unwelcome throb of reluctance, I realised that to go any further, I'd have to do the unthinkable—leave the bed.

"Are you all right, Francis?"

Evidently I'd telegraphed my worry more than I'd meant to.

"I'm fine, love," I said, kissing him again. "I've got to get up."

"Are you sure?"

"Things will get very uncomfortable for you if I don't."

He smiled and nuzzled against my chest. "I can manage."

"No, you can't." I turned my head towards the door, gauging the distance I'd have to launch myself into that burning cold. "Don't go anywhere."

He snickered as I threw myself across the room. The sweat on my body cooled like a morning mist—I hadn't realised exactly how much heat we'd generated. Not able to face rooting through my pack, I grabbed the whole thing and brought it back to bed with me. Sasha was sitting up on his elbows, beaming.

"Be quiet," I told him pre-emptively, and burrowed under the blanket. I put my cold feet on his legs to warm them up. He yelped but didn't push me away.

I arranged the blanket so it covered the most of us and propped myself up, methodically going through my pack. Sasha did not attempt to make himself useful, instead opting to lie with his head on my neck, a hand draped across my abdomen. I dropped a kiss onto his hair absently and felt him sigh.

"I love the way you smell," he said, then returned the kiss to the sensitive part of my neck, behind my ear.

"You're getting incredibly soppy, Sasha."

He huffed out a beat of laughter against my skin. "I must be thawing out."

"Do you fancy not being an incumbrance?"

"No."

"Good." I balanced my shaving kit on his head. "Hold that, will you?"

He shook his head and it fell off immediately. I knew he'd do that. Still, he held it and the book that followed. I dug into the side of the pack—the tin was there somewhere.

There was a false alarm when I pulled out some forgotten mints, but finally I managed to locate it: another castoff from the Canadians before us—hopefully the contents would remain usable. If they could survive the Arctic, surely they could survive northern Manchuria. Sasha made a vain attempt to help repack my bag, which I sabotaged by pushing everything to the floor, almost taking half the blanket with it in my excitement.

"We should have got the cover from the other bed," said Sasha absently, helping me pull it back.

"Are you volunteering?"

"Oh God, no."

We sank into another kiss. I had never fully appreciated it before, the simple closeness, the communication. For the first time, kissing had become a conversation. A continuation of talking by other means. I stroked an erstwhile lock of his hair between two fingers, shuddering in delight as he rubbed his face to my hand. He took my bottom lip between his teeth and held it there, gently. I kissed him around it. I kissed him and kissed him and kissed him.

Through an amount of digital acrobatics, I managed to get the lid off the Vaseline. Unable to face waiting for it to thaw, I pressed a finger in and made sure it was coated with a generous amount. I worked my way down his back until I reached his crease, which was still slightly damp with saliva. Good. My one spare, dry finger parted the cheeks and started to rub slowly, careful not to lose any of the jelly to spillage or erstwhile overuse. He pressed against me, wrapped around me, made a noise that could be a gasp or a yelp. The jelly was probably cold.

"Sorry," I whispered.

"Don't be."

I carried on massaging, dividing my attention equally between his mouth and my hands. After a minute he relaxed into me, as if boneless. When he seemed ready, I pulled back to face him. "This is going to feel strange."

"I know."

"I want you to be aware—"

"Francis, I *am* aware. Please. Just do what you must."

I cupped his jaw and kissed him hard, working my middle finger up into his entrance. Took my time rolling my fingertip in a mirror of what I'd done with my tongue, giving him a chance to back out if he wanted to. But he only pressed against me, so I pushed into him, meeting a resistance that held tight for a few seconds. Then, with a suddenness that never failed to surprise me, it gave way, and I felt both the inside and the outside of him for the first time.

"Are you all right?"

"Yes," he said. "You're right. It feels . . . bizarre."

"Give it a moment."

He smiled. "I will."

He buried his face into my neck as I rocked my fingertip gently inside him, working those tense muscles loose. I used my other hand to stroke his side, from his rib cage down to the small of his back; the occasional teasing glance against his hardness, which strained proud and damp next to my own. *The things I could do with that.* I bit my tongue to force myself not to rock against him—that would spell the end for me and possibly both of us.

I worked him open enough to delve in up to my first knuckle, then pulled out and circled my finger with my thumb to make sure it was properly coated. I pushed up further, brushing against that little bundle I knew so well.

He seized up and gasped against my throat. "Jesus Christ, Francis, what the hell was that?"

Confusion stabbed me in the ribs. "You don't know?"

"No, I don't."

I pressed my face into his hair and nipped his earlobe. "That," I whispered, "is going to be your closest friend."

I curled my finger again, allowing myself to delight in the groan of pure pleasure that left his mouth. He was so unspoilt, so new. There was so much he could learn. God, I was looking forward to discovering it with him. He rocked back on my finger, starting slowly and then growing in confidence, breathing raggedly through his mouth. I lined up a second finger and pressed it parallel to the first, working them up together. His wetness was dribbling onto my abdomen. That tight knot in me grew, threatening to tie me up completely. I bit his shoulder to keep myself from making too loud a noise, and he jolted against me and guttered out a hum. Neither of us were going to last long through this.

I kissed his mouth a last time and began my descent down the lovely expanse of his chest. His skin was calloused and dry, too abused by the rough, dry air to have anything like the lustre it might have. I didn't care. He was here, in the here and now. If it weren't for this place, he wouldn't be. I wouldn't know him.

Taking care not to remove my fingers, I tongued up from his navel, then down, taking his head briefly into my mouth again and punctuating it with a curl of my fingers.

He all but leapt off the bed. "Francis!"

"All right?" I licked a jewel of fluid off his crown.

"You're a bastard." His voice was an octave higher than usual.

I answered by taking his head into my mouth, slowly massaging the glans with my tongue in time to my fingers on his prostate. I didn't want him to spend too soon. He crossed his legs behind my head and moved his pelvis to my thrusts, making a small litany of little subvocal grunts in his throat. I was so close. I dug a fingernail into my thumb to distract myself. How was he was holding on? When I glanced up to check, he had one hand on the headboard and another screwed up in his mouth. It was the most erotic sight I had ever seen.

Either he felt my gaze or noticed the absence of my mouth, because he opened his eyes and gazed down at me. It seemed the spell should be broken now he knew I was watching, but it was the opposite. God knew what I looked like, between his long legs with swollen lips and a damp mouth. He groaned and his thighs tightened around me.

"Turn over," I whispered, my throat raw.

He met my eyes and bit his lip. "No."

"Sasha . . ."

"I want to see you," he said, and my heart broke.

I left the little nest I'd made for myself between his legs and pressed my mouth to his. "You will," I murmured, stroking his cheek. "I'll make sure. But I'm not running the risk of hurting you."

"You won't."

"Not as long as you do as I tell you."

His hand cupped my jaw.

I was in love with him—it hit me with a thud. I could barely, barely stand to hold his gaze. It was like looking too long at a star. Looking too long at the sun.

"Turn over," I said, hoarsely.

He let his thumb linger, stroking over my cheekbone. Then he did as I asked, hugging a pillow to his chest. My heart gave a single, painful beat.

I squeezed the base of my cock to ward off what was becoming inevitable. Then I fetched his pillow, forgotten over the side of the bed, and crudely balled it up so that it fit under his hips. Touching his pelvis, looking at him like that—I could hardly bear it.

"Are you . . . comfortable?" I asked, desperate to say something. He nodded.

I lowered my mouth once more, pressing into the core of him. His moan was muffled by the pillow, and he rocked his hips forward.

I traced my thumb along his crease, dipped into his hole. He had tightened slightly since my fingers had left him, and I spent a minute or so gently persuading him to open out. A fine sweat had broken out across his shoulders and back. It seemed to be taking a Sisyphean effort to keep himself still. Every now and again his hips rocked forward, as if shocked with static.

He jolted, and the almost-empty Vaseline tin was nearly lost to the floor. I caught it and used the last of it to lubricate myself, only thirty seconds or so from finishing the job by hand. God only knew how I would last inside him. Squeezing my shaft again, willing myself to think of anything but him, I lined myself up.

I introduced myself into him slowly. But, as anyone who is familiar with the practice will know, there comes a point where there is nothing for it but to push. I warned him with a quick press of the hip, pushing through that initial tight resistance just as I had done with my fingers. I stopped my hips dead as soon as I burst forth, out of necessity for both of us. Just being surrounded by him, by that heat was almost enough to do for me. As soon as I thought with any depth about being inside him, all would be lost.

His shoulders were tight. I stroked them, all the way down his spine and back. "Take your time," I whispered. "Tell me when you want me to move."

I waited, biting my tongue and the inside of my cheek. The smooth muscles I was rubbing against pulsed. I was so engrossed by their slick hold that I almost went into shock when he pressed up against me. Pushed onto me, or me further into him. Holding him steady with one hand and still stroking his spine with my other, I took a deep breath. "All right?"

He canted his hips towards me in answer.

I rocked forward, as slowly as I could manage, and felt myself sinking through him, into his warmth, straight into his core and the beating heart of him. A long, slick moan was dragged from the depths of me. I pulled back, then moved forward, reliving that sensation again and again. Each time, wallowing in the decadent joy of it, the slow heat. Each time I edged slightly further, until I was as far as I could go. I savoured the moment of being so deep. Such a part of him.

With one hand still on his pelvis, I enclosed the other between him and the duvet. The wet heat of his cock was thick against me, swollen and neglected and gorgeous. He was gorgeous. Everything about him was gorgeous. I nearly felt it physically. I worked a hand around his cock, squeezing it up against the cotton. He made a lung-deep hum and angled his hips up toward me. *Yes, yes.* I pulled him up further with my supporting hand, rubbing him slowly in time with my thrusts. He started to leak over my hand.

I shifted my position on the mattress, pressing into him from a slightly harder angle. His groan when I pushed home told me that my guess had been correct—the new angle worked better. He said something that I couldn't hear, too muffled by the pillow and the blood in my ears.

Neither of us could hold out.

Lost in the sensation of him against me, the need for my own release, I thrusted, first shallowly and then deeper. My hand wasn't working. Neither was my mind, which was throwing out sparks left and right. My thoughts were on him and only on him. *He's so close—I'm going to push him over that edge. Be the first man to do that for him.*

How often had he fantasised about this? Was I matching up?

I was doing my best to keep up with him, but I kept falling out of rhythm. His breathing was ragged as his hand joined mine, brushing up against my wrist. His fingers folded over mine to work him towards his climax. I wanted him to know I was there. I wanted him to *feel* me every moment I was there.

Then, every fibre in his body seemed to knot up. With a slight whimpered warning, a squeeze of his hand on mine, he released all over us both.

Desperate to hold on for a few more seconds, I bit my lip, hoping the pain would ward off the inevitable. It worked for four, maybe five more beats of my heart. Then that gorgeous spasming did for me as it had done for him. I tried to keep the moan in my throat but it managed to spill over and out through my teeth as I lost myself in him, coming so hard I saw white.

After a boneless moment, I removed my damp hand out from underneath him and placed it on his back, taking a steadying breath, and then another. Steeling myself. Then I began my slow withdrawal, pulling out incrementally, not wanting to hurt him. He was almost completely still, occasional twitches of muscle rippling his skin. When I was completely out, I gently tugged the duvet from under him and covered the both of us the best I could.

"Sash?" I stroked his hair.

He turned to me, his eyes large and shining. "Yes?"

There was a bead of blood on his chin. I stared at it, aghast, and moved to rub it away with my thumb. He smiled and caught my hand, kissing my wrist with his eyes closed.

"Was that all right?" I asked him.

He lay there, silent. Then he pressed his mouth to mine in a long, deep answer. He rested his head against my throat. "Is it always like that?"

"No," I answered, honestly. The full answer was no, not for me. Not ever. I had never been made to feel so a part of someone else, so acutely involved in and devoted to another person. I elected not to say that, though. He didn't need that pressure.

He hummed and moved warmly against me. "Jesus, I'm all sticky."

"I can help with that." I skimmed his abdomen with the hand that wasn't buried in his hair. He was so beautiful. I imagined him coming, watching his face, watching his cock erupt over that tight stomach. I imagined the hums he would make, if we were alone.

I gathered some of his release on my fingers and licked it off. He had chosen that moment to open his eyes and look at me.

"Francis!"

"What?" I asked him. "Don't tell me it's scandalous."

He chuckled, and I kissed the top of his head. I could feel him becoming all loose-limbed and heavy, that peculiar sleepiness that struck after one has spent. He hooked a leg around mine and I whispered, "I love you," into his hair.

It happened twice more that night, and once in the early morning.

When the sunlight finally started to creep through the curtains, he came to in my arms, stirring sleepily. I kept my eyes closed, not wanting to face the day yet. Hoping to keep these last moments. His thumb traced, butterfly-light, across my cheekbones, my eyebrow. I almost made a joke of it—snapped at him or licked his hand—but the tenderness of the moment held with a single painful beat that I had succumbed to. He did it again, and again. Then he gently kissed my brow.

I opened my eyes.

"Hello," he said, smiling his wide smile. His thumb was still stroking my face "Did I wake you?"

"No." I caught hold of his hand, kissed his wrist. "No, you didn't."

I kissed him. His lips, the slow movement of his limbs—they were such wonders, such dreamy bits of heaven He uncurled and came awake, like a bloom in the sun. I kept my lips to his, sure that if I were to leave, my heart would break. He huffed out a breath through his nose, tickling my cheek, ruffling the hair across my forehead. I pressed my lips to his harder.

"How long do we have?" I whispered.

He had to leave me to roll over and check the time on his watch. In those few seconds, I missed him.

But he came back to me, smiling. "About thirty minutes. We've got time."

His smile. I could die for it. I could kill.

I imagined meeting him in peacetime. Him at a party, the last one leaving. Throwing a smile over his back at the host. I loved him. I loved him.

I kissed him, fusing ourselves in a way that seemed inevitable. Us, forever. When our mouths met, it was always the same and I hoped it always would be. Sasha. He'd be the death of me.

One thing led to another. Soon I was on top of him, for the first time since the first. We rubbed together, my hand snaking down the sweat slick front of both of us. The noises he made; how could I ever forget? I didn't ever expect that I would. He, he, and only he. My body and his. Mine and his. Us, and us, and us. I could kiss him and kiss him and kiss him. I felt my heart would melt through my fingers into his. Christ alive, I really was in love with him.

His little groan hitched and coagulated in my ear, and then they spilled over, I felt him, kettle hot, on the delicate skin of my abdomen. My Sasha. I spilt on him, matching his speed. I spilt all over him, for the fourth time those few hours. His hot hiss of breath caught the sensitive skin of my ear. I wanted to communicate something meaningful to him, something that only I could say. Something never said before.

But running through my mind was only: *Was I all right for you? Did you like it? What didn't you like? How could it be better next time?* Of course I didn't have the words. The only thing I could do was kiss his mouth. He kissed mine.

We lay together.

He asked, "So?"

"Yes," I agreed. "So."

He pressed his face against my hair. *Oh god, my Sasha.* I felt him with each painful beat of my heart.

After a minute, his breathing evened out, deep and low. I kissed him again one last time and one last time he responded sleepily. Eventually, we came up for air. Neither of us could breathe in each other.

Just one last kiss, again. Just he and I. With each painful beat of my heart.

CHAPTER SIXTEEN

We were awakened, rudely, by a brief and abrupt knock dead on half past six. I leapt. Sasha did not. Nervous, I transferred myself to my supposed bed. Five minutes later, he shook me gently awake. When I stirred, I hope enough of me had been left behind to fool those who could think in corkscrews the way we did. Looking back, I realise how daft that was. Us, in a bed together? To anyone else, the cold would explain it. Just us two, in the cold together. Huddled for warmth, like we had been.

Being in love with a man is such a sensual experience. You do it with your whole body. I felt his breath on me, on the tip of my ear. The ends of my hair. I felt him everywhere, but there specifically. His hot breath, warmed by his cells, his cilia, the moist inside of his alveoli.

That I couldn't kiss every part of him was a genuine source of sadness. His sclera, his anchorite vertebrae, the nerves deeply embedded in the socket of his thigh? There were some parts of him that I would never, could never touch. I don't know how to express that feeling. The wish to dissolve into him? I suppose that was most accurate. Each particle of him bonding with a particle of me. Us, together. Unsustainable. What would have changed? At least they could bury us together. A hideous collection of flesh.

Our quiet, peaceful moments together would have lasted so well had Barclay not had his face knocked off.

It happened in early November. Stupidly, *stupidly*, we had it in our heads that we were home, almost. We hadn't considered—as an officer, *I* hadn't considered—the things that could still go wrong. And we were so close. We were within breathing distance of Ussurie.

I shouldn't have been surprised, therefore, when the conflict came to us.

Of course, my superiors wanted me to protect everyone but Sasha.

The turning point came two days later. Out of Harbin and into the woods. Brits aren't good at judging depth or severity of a forest. If you walk far enough in one direction in the UK, you're bound to find a pub.

It was the middle of the night, but someone was missing and I was recklessly leading us into what would prove to be an unnavigable thicket of pure, dense, prehistoric evergreen. Then what should I see? A body—an older man. The body of an older man half stripped and on a pike. The Orilux torch picked it out in such unforgiving detail that I turned it off. And then I had to turn it on again to flag the rest of the party over. I didn't look at it again, but I didn't need to. I saw it most weeks after.

Before I'd been dragged out of bed that night, I'd laid curled around him. I hadn't been sleeping but lying in some hypnagogic panic I couldn't escape. My heart beat so fast I wished it would stop and put me out of my misery. Who was left at home to care?

But suicide, even passively accomplished, wasn't an option. Not because suicides go to hell—I'd been raised well enough not to believe in such things. Not in the ontological sense, at least. But there was still the question of dull necessities I'd leave behind. I had men. They might not have loved me. They might not have liked me, but I was theirs. If Gallehawk, or Jacobs or Owen had woken up to me with a gun in my mouth, they would have had to carry that. That would be their cross to bear and not mine. And who would take my place? Who could? We were low enough on junior officers as it was.

Evans's blood was still on my uniform. I'd put a gun in my mouth all over again than wish that on them.

CHAPTER SEVENTEEN

S asha and I had read a lot of the same things as children. Every child educated in England read a lot of the same things, and some were more excited about them than others. I should know, because I had to put up with a great deal of quotation from my elder sister, one of the most enthusiastic of the bunch.

I remember when Helena had returned home from Egypt, solidified in her state as both a failed digger and the other woman. The schoolroom poetry had found its way back to the forefront not long after she'd let her suitcase fall to the floor, looked up at the ceiling, and said, slowly and decisively, "Fuck." After several nocturnal glasses of port, curled up in the conservatory, she'd told me what it had been like out there. She'd used to gaze up into the warm night at the stars, which were the same, but subtly different to our own. The lighting out in the desert had made them so much brighter.

"Of course," she'd said, "I've no idea what the stars in England look like when I'm not looking directly at them. It's not the sort of thing one commits to memory, unless they're you."

She'd broken off for a draught of port. "But it reminded me of that poem. I suppose everything has to remind you of a poem, when you're in a place with that much history. Plus, I felt I had to intellectually prove myself. You know the one? 'And why uprose to nightly view/Strange stars amid the gloam.'"

I remembered the beginning of that poem. *"They throw in Drummer Hodge, to rest/ Uncoffined — just as found . . ./And foreign constellations west/Each night above his mound."*

I had thought of her, of that conversation when we'd first arrived in Ussurie. I had smelt it in the air. Ussurie—even that word sounds hostile, as if it promises bears. Promises men dragged out of windows. Men taking shelter in cabins, screaming. Nailmarks on the deep dark wooden frames. And fingermarks, the bloody fingermarks in the ice.

We'd skimmed past the worst of the fighting last time we came through. Because it hadn't happened to us, we'd forgotten that the people who *had* been fighting were either still here or had fled from something worse. Semenov, in this case.

Was the fight coming for us? How would it change us?

I thought of Toby, overseeing that boy's death so casually. His quarry had been in civilian clothes. It disturbed me, to think of a man so full of merriment as that cold-blooded adjudicator.

I can't forgive what he did next, but I can understand it: wanting to take back that little bit of power.

They took the major first.

We had just arrived back in Russia—to our feeble cheering, trying to keep the spit in our mouths to speak. We were forty kilometres out of Vladivostok. A hair's breadth away.

We had slept on the train, two nights in a row. This was not unusual; unless there was a reason to disembark, we tried not to in rural areas. It would mean leaving the train undefended. In the cities or the smaller towns there was often either a militia or too few people to ever worry about. Although things were different out in the wild.

I didn't know how they got the major. Presumably he was outside for some biological function. Gone too far past the sentries. The first I knew was a frantic hammering at the door of my carriage. I still had not moved up to the officers' car. There was so little time now it hardly seemed worthwhile.

Jacobs stirred after me, sitting up sleepily. I had, in some recess of my brain, a bizarre sense of déjà vu, perhaps a reminder of the night we found Sasha. We had thought we were almost there then, as well.

My name was hissed, and the thumping came again. It was bizarre, as though whoever was on the other side wanted to be heard and yet also to be quiet. I scrambled up, over a dozy Sasha and the chaos of the bags. The plan of a well-regimented car had decayed long ago.

I took down the paraffin lantern from the ceiling and cracked open the door. The lung-scorching cold hit me instantly. Horrocks was there, with a lantern of his own, wrapped in an overcoat like it was a dressing gown. He didn't have a hat on.

"Francis," he said.

A pair of boots arrived beside me. Sasha. I smiled at him, but all I could see were his wide eyes in the dark. I jumped out into the snow.

Horrocks didn't say anything. He just turned on his heel and walked off in long, loping strides like he was trying his hardest not to break into a run. Up ahead there was a small knot of people, each distinguishable from the other by paraffin lamp. It was our fellow subalterns.

Horrocks didn't waste any time making his words palatable. "The major's gone."

We stood, blinking and uncomprehending. Waiting for the second part of his sentence. Where had the major gone? Why? When would he be back?

A question was volunteered by Warren: "*Where* has he gone, sir?"

James looked like he was going to bite through his own tongue.

"I don't know," he said tightly. "We don't know. Sentries say they haven't seen him for half an hour."

The first ripple of disquiet began to spread through us all then.

"When did we find this out?" my voice said without a conscious effort on my part.

James sucked in his cheeks. He'd done that just after Evans had been hit when he'd realised what it meant for him. "Half an hour ago," he said. "I've checked all the cars."

There was, of course, an official policy for if someone went missing. It read like it had been drafted for finding schoolboys after house silent. The lining of my spine went sour.

"Our next port of call is to make sure the local area is searched." James clearly didn't want to say what came next. He glanced at me. "You'll go left. Warren, right and Harris up the centre. Haddock on defence. Get your men up and armed."

I nodded, pursing my lips. The few of us against that big wide plain.

I swapped my lantern for an Orilux, then banged on the door that contained Church. I trusted him enough to select men himself.

There had to be enough of us so that if someone got hurt, a few could stay with them while the rest carried on. Five? Six, per party? That would mean nearly thirty out at once: too many. We'd make do with three. I bit the inside of my cheek to stop my lip from quivering.

It was punishingly cold, so we couldn't go far. If we found him too much of a way away, we might not be able to retrieve him. And if we didn't find him within our half-kilometre search radius, we would *never* find him. If anything went wrong, we'd never return ourselves.

This was at the back of my mind, as we headed out, and judging from everyone's expressions, it was in theirs too.

I had the compass and was directing Church and his two mates. Their faces were familiar, though I couldn't put a name to them. I kept taking my eyes off the compass to watch them and the trees ahead. Recklessly, perhaps.

Then we found the major.

I vomited. I hate to admit it, but it would make its way into the record anyway. So did the others who saw him. Because a sharpened cattle horn was stuck up through his throat. It had gone through his soft palate, come out through his mouth long before we'd realised he was missing.

I doubt I will ever get the image out of my mind. And Barclay—I couldn't help but wonder. I will always wonder. Did he know what that horn was for?

I'd heard stories from men who were farther north than us, of teeth exploding in the icy air, blood freezing as it poured from the mouth. That sort of cold is another thing us Brits don't fully grasp; what effect a continent can have on your temperature.

Barclay's blood was merely sluggish, like honey. Not only warmish—it was still liquid. I know because I carried part of the body.

I have a lot of problems with what was said by others regarding the incident. I daresay it's clear this is not the first time I have objected strongly to something. But what went on official record was an "opportune killing"; what we found was a tableau. Whatever had happened, had happened recently—within those twenty minutes of our arrival.

His blood was almost warm. The scene seemed to have been abandoned mid-act.

They must have still been in the area when we discovered him. They stopped because they heard us coming.

And why not strike out? They had nothing to lose. Our forces had secured the area, almost. It would have been suicide to attack us head-on. And—most likely—suicide for them to wreck the track. Was this a single token seized where they could take it? Or had it been more than that—a threat? One last kick of a hanged man?

So they must have waited until someone came down into the woods and happened to get phenomenally lucky.

His body was slumped beside the pike. The horn itself wasn't that big. God knew what the original plan for it was.

Once we'd screwed the head free, Tony Church—by accident or design—put it in the body's lap.

Even if suicide didn't run in my family, I'd have put a pistol in my mouth there and then if I'd been alone.

CHAPTER EIGHTEEN

They got James next.

Despite the fact he'd ended up as my senior, I felt protective towards James. The martial field never was for him. He'd been sent out by government order, and he'd had to live with it. And now his mother and father had to live with it too.

We took the major's head, and only the head, back to the train. Perversely, this felt almost the best-case scenario to me. Body found and the whole detail back unharmed. Fantastic. James—Horrocks—tightened his jaw in the way I knew he would. He had been expecting this.

I put the head down by the tracks.

"And?" he asked, white and tight-lipped.

"*And?*" Blood on my face. Just like when we'd found Sasha, all those nights ago.

His expression changed to one of almost anguished pity before he made his next request.

The head had come back. The body had to follow.

At least I didn't carry his spine. But the weight of his wet life—his blood, his breath, his nerves—there was so much there. I had seen too much of it already. I hadn't known that bones were wet. I had not thought about it. They were wet until, maybe, they were not. I don't remember the whole time we spent repatriating his two constituent parts back to the cars.

The ground was like iron. It was too hard to dig. It was too hard to try. We scraped together what debris we could find by the trackside—branches, leaves, stones—and did our best to construct a cairn for the major. We could still see him on all sides afterwards. His head was there too, but not sewn up in anything.

I couldn't say I liked to think of it, leaking alone. Uncoffined, just as found.

We stood in silence around the gravesite.

In the scheme of things, we had not lost many. Evans, Nevis, and Kim Stevens, true. The three men of Warren's. Other units had been wiped out entirely. But to have this blow catch us from below set our teeth on edge in a new way. Our head had been cut off. Our most senior officer.

And those who did it must have been beside the train, the sentry detail not seeing a thing. How close could they have been? How long had they been there?

Nobody wanted to consider this, so we pretended that none of us thought it. We had a funeral. We encairned him near the tracks though we knew his graveside wouldn't last, and we left before we could see what became of it.

Along we went, until.

Nikolsk is almost next to Vladivostok. Touching distance to our gateway out. It's closer to Vladivostok than it is to the Manchurian border, which we had crossed but twelve hours ago. I could feel the sea. So almost-close that it broke my heart.

After the major's death, command had fallen to James. Would it all have happened the way it did if the major had still been there? I wonder about that, and the journey through Ussurie a lot. There is no point to it—it will never change the way things went. We all should have known better. There should have been more safeguards around leadership, communication.

At least that whole affair wasn't an individual failing of my own.

It started in a bivouac camp.

Ussurie—to our minds—was a convergence of the Russian and Chinese branches of the line. When we had first been launched into Russia, it had been pitifully defended by us, through either hubris or bad map reading. Knowing the Army, it was literally impossible to guess which. The prevailing opinion that personnel were wasted here, in this brackish corner. The position was hopeless.

Coming back through, with our senior officer dead by the tracks, it seemed odd that we'd felt so pessimistic then. What right had we had?

But back then, we'd all been ill-fed, ill-fated, and ill-equipped and more than ready to believe the worst of wherever we were flung. After the company of Czechs ahead of us had retired behind the river at Khamerovka, we'd spent a fortnight in the septic swamp of the Ussurie plain. That fetid, infested water sheltered from the scouring wind by a pitiful covering of marsh grass. Our skin grew thick and waterlogged, broke apart at the slightest pressure like a peach. It crawled. There wasn't an opening in my body without an insect in it. Thousands of little black flies buried their heads beneath the waterline of my eyelids. The mosquitoes, huge ugly house-spider sized, attaching to my forehead beneath my cap. Sometimes we couldn't wear caps at all. Then the heat would beat down on us like we were copper and the bites would swell. God, how they would swell. At Hong Kong, the matter of tents had been raised and rejected by HQ, either because there were none to be had or because they were considered a frivolity. The equipment shortage didn't stop with the tents either: nets, ordnance, proper transport. Maps.

And then there was the matter of the fighting, and who we were fighting.

The latter was always a thorny question.

At home, the Bolsheviks are thought to be democratic idealists: people's heroes. The men for the working class. I had thought myself as somewhat sympathetic to that group in London, but I wonder what any of the home front would think if they saw what this war had done to those supposed heroes.

All war makes a mockery of what it proposes to fight for, I suppose. But this was the first time I'd seen it. This war was, for better or worse, mine.

We'd been shown photographs, almost the moment we arrived, of what could happen if the Reds got us. The men pictured had all been Czechs or Slovaks. Legion soldiers who had fallen into the maw of the Bolshevik engine. The Bolsheviks had done to them what an engine would do. Some had been recognisable as people. Some were not. Killing them could only have been a mercy.

They had deployed a hundred bloody Marines to protect the embassy alone once upon a time.

All of these happy memories came back to me as we came in low through the fetid waters agglutinated into gelatinous ice. *We must be a first-line service battalion now.* All this work, and for what? For how many lives?

On what was meant to be our last full day of travel, the day after we found the major, a red flag stopped us at a station.

The station seemed to be abandoned. They only get more threatening when they're abandoned.

We pulled to an uncertain stop.

"Arms up, boys," I told my men, as though they hadn't been on guard the past twelve hours.

We watched through the slat in the carriage, all of us balancing on the balls of our feet like we were trying to spy on a dinner party. Outside, there was no movement.

And then there was. Every last wisp of breath left me. I tightened my hand on my pistol. My Enfield was over my shoulder.

The man approaching wore a generic greeny-brown uniform that I couldn't instantly recognise. From this distance, he seemed both imperious and incredibly well-kempt. Clearly an officer.

I allowed my hand to relax, marginally.

James's voice started up. "You are approaching a troop train. Who goes there?"

The man shouted back, "Major Barclay?"

"No. Who goes there?"

Christ, it was like a bloody pantomime.

"Lieutenant-Colonel Eto of the Imperial Japanese Army 12th. Where is Major Barclay?"

"Is there anyone with you?"

"Yes. Where is Major Barclay?"

Jesus, James. Just let him on the bloody train.

The familiar sound of a door on its tired runners. Someone was getting out.

I turned to my men. "We're expected."

"D'you reckon that's a good thing, sir?" Owen asked me, wincing as he stretched a leg. We were sitting so much recently that it was a wonder we didn't all atrophy.

"I suppose we'll find out, Owen," I said noncommittally. I did hope so. If another battalion was expecting us, they must have a field telephone. Or a telegraph. I wanted to find out what news we'd missed. We had to file Barclay's death, still.

A minute later we emerged, joints cracking and muscles stretching waxily. Eto and his men had managed to scramble together a vague camp. It revealed itself gradually: Tents, at first. Small fires, smelling earthy.

The Japanese tents were hoary with frost and stiff enough to break with your fist. The men around the camp were wrapped up in fur, layers and layers of it. They weren't so far from home. Perhaps they were used to dressing for the weather.

We heard the low, indistinct chatter in a language none of us could make out. Eto had arranged for food to be put by for our men in what had once been the station waiting room. God knew how the higher-ups thought everyone would fit.

Parting with the men at the waiting room meant parting with Sasha. I caught his eye and tried to farewell him. He gave me a slight smile and followed Jacobs in.

We, the officers, were led to what must have been the stationmaster's office once upon a time. The maps and timetables still hung there; a clock too, stopped. There were papers on the desk—these were Eto's.

I could hear a low conversation coming from the wall behind us, followed by a roar of laughter and a clink. The Japanese officers, presumably.

Eto sat down. We stood. There were just about enough of us to fit around the table without feeling like sardines.

James took the only other seat opposite him. "Barclay's dead, sir," he opened. "We buried him this morning."

Eto nodded once, sharply. "I see."

"I am James Horrocks, the new acting CO of the battalion. On behalf of Lieutenant-Colonel Moore."

"You are the A Company Hertfordshires?"

"What's left of them, sir."

Eto nodded again. "Omsk has gone."

The bottom dropped out of my rib cage. Shock swept through the whole room.

It crossed James's face.

"How—" But he broke off and just stared at Eto. I filled in the rest of that sentence any number of ways. *How had it happened? How long ago? How will this affect us? Christ—do HQ want us back?*

How long do we have?

He cleared his throat and tried again. "How long ago? Sir?"

"Days," said Eto. "Two, three."

"Kolchak?"

"Capitulated."

James's shoulders dropped to his sides.

So. That was that. If Omsk had been taken, we'd better hope like hell the rest of the Hertfordshires were as close as they said they were. They'd been three days behind us in Irkutsk.

Eto went on to detail what would happen next: Kolchak's forces had fallen back to Irkutsk. They would hold the front line there. The Japanese held this little corner of the land fast. The Czechs were still out with Kolchak, but Eto gave them weeks, if not days.

"And you're departing from Vladivostok, I believe?" he said.

I held my breath.

"Yes," said James, carefully. "We are."

"With the rest of your battalion? They were at Harbin, last I heard."

"When was that?"

"Yesterday."

Yesterday! They'd made even better time than I'd thought. They were catching us up, and we would all go home together.

The Canadians had already gone. The French, the Americans—God, the Japanese hated the Americans. They'd been squaring off over the South Pacific since the Americans had taken the Philippines from Spain, back in my dad's time. Eto must have been glad to see the back of them. And here we were, the last of the foreigners to mop up.

"You have a Czech officer with you?" Eto asked.

"We do." James glanced at me. "He's Lieutenant Ransome's charge."

Eto eyed me. "The Czechs don't want him back."

I nodded, a small dam of relief starting to crack.

"I assume there will be space for him on the *Wessex*?"

"There will." James shifted at the mention of our ship. She was waiting to take us home. The rest of the Hertfordshires.

And she'd be taking Sasha too.

The talking carried on, but I didn't listen. The only thing that registered with me was the gleeful sound of the accordion as we left, coming from the central circle of tents. Uproarious singing about where to find the lance-jack. Why didn't Haddock play his mouth organ anymore? Perhaps he was saving it for home.

The officers were billeted in a rough one-bedroom cottage. It probably belonged to a tenant or a housekeeper of the stationmaster, if stationmasters had such a thing. The Japanese were lodged in the house proper, which was only marginally larger. Sasha, regrettably, was not with me. I spent a cold night sandwiched between two of our lieutenants, one of whom snored and one of whom wriggled. I was glad. If I had slept too deeply, I might have forgotten myself. Who was next to me.

I thought of Sasha, alone in the cold night.

Of course, he probably wasn't alone. He would be cosied up with familiar men, on a floor that wasn't saturated with effluvia of the people who'd been living there for months. He'd have blankets and a sack to lay his head on. He had his furs. He would be all right. I lay awake and thought of him, and hoped he would be comfortable. I hoped he would be warm and safe.

That morning, I was startled awake by something I had not heard for weeks: the reveille. The frantic scramble to wakefulness of the two men around me told me they'd all but forgotten that morning call to arms too.

I didn't bother to dress. The only item of clothing I had not slept in was my cap, which I fixed as I walked out the door into another morning.

If there was any silence or stillness, it had long since been cracked by the bustle and noise. God, the noise. I had forgotten that too—what it was like to be in a camp.

I found Haddock, who was awake, and Horrocks, who was beside him. James gave me his usual friendly grin. Today was the day. We were going home today. We were getting into Vladivostok. Today.

Eto had assured us of that yesterday at dinner. The recent "developments," as he had couched it, would not affect our orders. We would go home. He was to stop us, debrief us, and feed us and then send us on our way.

The men seemed alive in a manner they hadn't for a long time. Boots were being shone. Faces, so used to being encrusted with grime and railway dust, were being scrubbed in the snow between tough gloves. I felt a deep, warm pull of love for everyone around me, for this old routine.

I lit a cigarette, and we entrained.

It isn't far, from Ussurie to Vlady. Less so if you weren't crawling through God knew what behind a lookout hill. Hence our fatal mistake.

Because a few kilometres out from the camp, there was a stray car on the line.

Now, a stray car could mean two things. That there was a train somewhere with one-too-few carriages, or that it was a bomb. Our train was as armoured as we could make it, but she was also coaled, full of fire. The chance wasn't worth taking. Not this close to the end. So James dispatched a detail to investigate.

"What're your thoughts?" I asked him, stamping my feet against the cold as we waited.

"It's old," he said, tersely. "Been here at least a month. Almost iced over—stuck on the rails."

He moved farther up the track. He didn't know how to be in command. To this day, I'm sure he was just putting on a show of looking.

If she wasn't a danger—anything explosive in her must have been frozen solid by now—she could be tipped off the tracks. It would be difficult, but she could be tipped.

The Japanese must have had supplies come in their way from Vlady. They would have warned us if there was something amiss.

The train guard hung on, spiderweb-tense.

After a few aching minutes, the detail came back.

The lead man shook his head. "Nothin'. Just a detached supply cart."

"Christ," someone murmured next to me. I didn't take my eyes off the track ahead to see who it was.

A tangle of voices, talking about moving it. The incompetence of the bloody Russians.

"Get it seen to."

"Get it off!"

". . . so bloody careless . . ."

"Didn't check the links properly after pulling away from Vlady."

"Bloody Russians, wouldn't know how many ducks makes one."

From my position by the middle of the carriages, I could just about see the speakers' movement from the corner of my eye. The small knot of committee deciding what to do, the same detail volunteering to move it. Another setting up to guard them as they did.

And then, only thirty feet away, James got shot.

The bullet caught his cheekbone and destroyed his right eye.

I didn't know where it came out. Or if it did.

I didn't see him after that, and no one would tell me whether he died quickly.

I hoped he wasn't scared.

My mind was nothing but screaming wind.

There was an urgent tug on my tunic sleeve before he'd even hit the ground. "Sir, Captain Horrocks—"

"Yes," I said.

He was still speaking. "—and it seems to be coming from the trees."

"The trees," I repeated stupidly. Everyone attacked from the trees.

"—and I can't—" the voice continued, but I didn't hear the rest. *The* trees, I remembered, from years ago. The trees.

Struggling for that thought was like turning out a light. Having to grasp your way through the same, half-remembered corridor from memory.

"A fold—" I broke off, as a crack of wood or shrapnel whipped past us. My voice seemed flat, even to me. "To the left. You see that fold in the ground? Just inside the forest."

The man I was talking to—familiar face, a name I couldn't recall at that moment—nodded. He looked like someone who had been cornered by a particularly boring acquaintance on the way to put out a fire. I wanted to shout at him, repeat what I was saying while I was saying it, tell him twice so the message would get through.

"There are too few of them. They're hammering too much— trying to make it look like there's more." I gripped his shoulder so tight I could feel his bones beneath the khaki. "They're hidden by the grass. It's like at the beginning—the beginning with the Czechs."

This tactic had proven fatal on many occasions, to all involved. Dig in to the enemy's projected left flank and give them hell. Take as many with you as you can, or—better case scenario—put the fear of God into them so quickly they fall back to whence they came.

Right here, right now, we were being squeezed with the same technique we'd used when there were barely enough of us to play five-a-side.

James was dead, and we were in an ambush.

Then the shelling started.

I felt, rather than heard, someone next to me say, "Oh *fuck*." I ducked, my hand on my cap to stop it coming off. Stupidly, as if this was a concern. Why were they *shelling*? Did they think we'd shell them back?

In front was the captain's position. There wasn't a captain there.

So I grabbed the man nearest to me and shouted at him to fall back behind the carriage. "Don't go down the embankment." I did this to another and another, had to shout to them individually. I didn't register names, barely registered if they were in my platoon. It was a bombardment, and we had nothing to reply with. The only thing that we could hope to do was wait it out. And we couldn't sit in the train if it was the target. We couldn't sit in the forest.

Seconds later, I had another man's coat in my hands. I was pulling him towards me to instruct him when the ground lifted. We were forced into a face-full of hot, unbreathable air.

A hand grabbed at me and I squeezed it once and firmly. I don't know whose it was, to this day.

I couldn't see Sasha, but he'd be close. He was sensible. He'd be close. Those shells fell so wide.

That betrayed two things. Inexperience and an abundance of ammunition.

There was a metallic scrabble, from the left.

It was a water bottle gone astray, falling down the scree of the embankment. But as soon as I turned to it, I knew where we were. Runovka. A hill. An Orthodox Church stands there.

My first, my immediate thought was that the situation couldn't have been more fitting. Destroyed, after all this time, by a gun from a church. I closed my eyes. The gunnery rumbled. There were two old Czech field guns up there. Repaired by the artificers from the *Suffolk*. The *Suffolk*, whose guns were currently roaming the Russian countryside on another train, without her and us.

If there had been more of them, they would have killed us all. Shelled one side; hit us with a Maxim gun on the other and have mown us down in our shelter. If they had a machine gun, they would have been using it.

There were at least two firing on us now, but they were feeble. Shells are unpredictable if you aren't used to them. They go wide. They don't go off. They don't aim correctly. I had heard it all, as a cadet, from Dickie.

Another gun joined. Another voice to the choir.

A voice in my ear. "That'll be Eto, won't it, sir?"

I opened my eyes.

Once, I'd heard a story. It was about a young Czech and a Bolshevik gunnery team—not my young Czech, although it did take place at Runovka. Years ago, shells were coming down from the church, an old Orthodox tower being used as an observation post. That was why one always knocks them out, before they can be developed into anything else.

A shell was planted, by that self-same Czech, right into that tower. It broke it to flames and then his team, working like packhorses, fired four shots so quickly that the Bolshevik gunnery team became convinced that they were facing four new guns. After almost two hours, they fell back with their two guns out of action. If those Bolshie guns had stayed, they would have protected troops coming in over the river. It would have been an all-out offensive; the gunners never knew.

That one Czech artillery officer and his one gun had done the impossible. And the impossible mentally occurred to me now: the sheer volume of those shells.

I found Owen and hissed in his ear. "Find H—" Not Horrocks. "Find Harris. Tell him they're firing too many shells. They can't last."

It was a show of strength.

The more common sense returned, the more I was aware that their shells weren't bursting as they should. Some were. Soil and roots and worms and rabbits and tree roots a thousand years old were raining everywhere. But many didn't. And those exploding consistently were from the Japanese in the distance.

Another burst from our left.

I had been able to locate two guns, both in the treeline. We probably weren't in their prime position, but if they hit the engine, we weren't going anywhere except Kingdom Come.

I was measuring the distance in my mind. Taking stock of how many men I would have to take. What I could do with them. Then a tug at my sleeve. Owen. "Sir."

He didn't have to say anything more, because he was followed by Harris, who bent and shouted in my ear, "What?"

I shouted back. "Too many shells. Not enough pause."

"I know," he said. "Where do you think the second gun is?"

"We're bloody under it, Toby!"

He nodded, tense. I had seen James pull that expression, so many times. Perhaps it was a rank tic. *Oh, James.* A pang at my heart, then he was Toby again. "Take six men."

Six. As many as he could spare in case we got knocked out. We were right under that gun, after all.

I took my three, at first: Gallehawk and Jacobs and Owen. And I took three others from my platoon: Anthony Church, his friend Dickerson. David Young. Over on the other side I could see Warren massing the same number. All my six I knew well.

I led them over the tracks and into the grass.

The wet soil hit me so hard I couldn't breathe. Like jumping into cold water. The temperature froze me so much my lungs forgot to hold onto air. I bit the inside of my cheek to lock my jaw and led us forward.

The crawl was like a kick to the gut. The undergrowth was thick and matted, and it was defended. I thought what I'd crawled over was simply throwaway material at first.

But they were metallic and sharp, jagged and fierce. They would tear your stomach open if you let them.

"Caltrops," I whispered to the men either side of me. "Pass it on. Don't crawl over one."

There hadn't been time to put my jerkin on to ease my slithering. My torso was bare and soft as a kitten's, and so were my men's. The grass and caggage from the ground snagged on my woollen tunic, waterlogging it. The undergrowth was dense enough to crawl over rather than through; solid enough to keep the ridge of the hill within eye's reach. Even the caltrops sat above. I never, in all my life, thought that I would be thankful for the advent of the Russian winter. It wasn't the view one would get from a horse. Barely enough to see from on the ground. But enough. I counted three, four figures on the brow of the hill. Around them, bits of twisted shell casing, bits of tin can. Shells filled with whatever they could find in the hope of taking us down. Killing us with what they could scramble together in the wrecks of their houses. We crawled.

Their field gun loomed, but she was so small that I almost felt sorry for them. There was a pile of shells to the side of her. They had a single row left.

And I had six men. On their team, I saw four.

I couldn't see any obvious arms. I couldn't see any obvious men in the distance. No second line.

A huff besides me drew my eyes from the battle for a moment. My men had drawn level. I had two on one side and five on the other. Not ideal. But better than nothing.

I whispered to Gallehawk, on my right side, "Get the gunner. Ask the man on your right to mark you. But wait until the field gun goes."

I whispered to Owen, on my left, "Get the chap feeding the shells. Ask the man on your left to mark you. But wait until the field gun goes."

They did.

The man beside the gun went down without a sound. I almost would have believed that he'd tripped. He was so silent and so gentle.

The shell-feeder took more time. The rifle shot caught him in the side of the head and he collapsed over the shells. He made a low noise, like a cow lowing. It was a noise you knew that a person wasn't making consciously. His head wasn't there anymore, but his body thought it was.

Young, covering Owen and I, fired the parting shot into what little of the man we could make out.

Before the other two could turn, before they could see what had happened under the din of the gun, we shot them too.

This wasn't a gunnery team.

They were partisans, opportunists. Trying to see what they could score from the trains going in and out of the port town. That's all they were. And this far east, they didn't have reserves. They didn't have any form that we couldn't match.

My heartbeat pounded in my tongue. The air around us solidified, dark and droning. Above us, a high whine. At first, I thought it was the shells, ringing with their metallic persistency.

It got louder. It got closer.

Instinctively, I covered my head. The men either side of me covered theirs too. The dead on the ground looked up with blank eyes.

And then, a plane.

CHAPTER NINETEEN

The plane flew low. Each shot parted the wood of our train as if it were paper.

What the hell have we just walked into? What had I led my men into?

The plane began to turn. Owen lay on his back and aimed his rifle in the air, but Church next to him grabbed his arm and hauled it down so sharply I was worried the gun would go off.

It did not. The plane circled.

I faced Owen. "Less of that, now," came out of my mouth. As if he had been throwing pencils rather than threatening our position.

Planes were such fragile things: all wood and canvas and nails. I'd heard from Dickie that a steel dart tossed from one could split a man on the ground in half.

Christ.

But nobody new came to the gunnery.

Toby must have sent out another party. He must have done. He wouldn't just leave us on our own. I tried to swallow my unease and focus on the matter at hand. If Warren's party had secured the other gun, could they angle it high enough to hit the plane? Could we secure the guns and the shells that were left? They'd simply mow us down from the air.

I started to crawl again. I signalled for us to move forward.

Us. That simple first-person pronoun. How much damage it can do.

There was little point in staying where we were, with the cold seeping in like a hot knife. Less so us lying there and waiting to be strafed.

"Whatever happens to *that*," I told them, gesturing vaguely at the sky, "is none of our business right now. Church, Dickerson, and Young, make sure no one gets near that gun. You lot," I said, turning to the men I'd shared a carriage with all this time, "are coming with me into the forest. Shoot anything that looks like a Trot."

I couldn't have known. But God, I wish I hadn't said it.

The forest was deep and thick as the sea. There is no way that you can comprehend the size of a forest like that until you have been in one. They subsume you. It's like the polar opposite of drowning.

We didn't have to go far in. Just enough to make sure there were no reinforcements, no supply dumps waiting. The support party Toby sent would be coming up behind us. It had to be. Brown and Kent and the Lewis gun.

I had met a defaced major when walking through a wood like this, once. A horn through his mouth. I had seen dead men in a forest like this. I had seen mutilated men.

This time, I saw movement.

He was exactly like I had imagined.

He was small. He was bony, and his eyes were huge. He held a gun at me. I held a gun at him.

He was a child. He was holding a gun at me.

There was a gunshot.

For one, awful second, I thought that it was me. That I had fired.

But then from behind me came the most awful sound I have ever heard.

It was wet and guttural. The boy glanced towards it, and I almost strained a muscle in my neck not glancing back.

Quickly as I dared, I took aim and shot the ground near his feet. One bullet, aimed to go wide. Then I spun toward the source of the noise.

I didn't look at him again. Couldn't check he wasn't hit. Not much I could do if he was.

The forest, like the sea, reflects sound well. So I hadn't waded in far before I came upon the clearing where Jacobs had shot Gallehawk.

CHAPTER TWENTY

I need not tell you he was dead.

A fine, syrupy arterial spray had misted everything within two feet, including Jacobs.

He was white. Catatonic.

Gallehawk was at his feet. He didn't have a jaw anymore.

I gaped at him, a hot pistol in my hand. I'd just shot at a boy, after all.

Jacobs's face didn't change. It was like he was marble, all marble. It was the only time I'd see him express any emotion but mirth.

"What happened?" I asked him, trying to keep my voice level. *Is there danger, still?*

He didn't seem about to talk. I opened my mouth to ask him a second time, and he said, "I shot at anything. Just like you told me."

He had his Enfield in his hand still. *I should take it off him. He's now a danger. To himself, and to others. I should disarm him.*

"Listen," I said. "It's all right."

"No." He turned at me, and his gun came too.

I think he'd already made up his mind to die.

I had my pistol out, still balanced on one knee. Other knee behind me. It was just like being behind a sandbag, back on Salisbury Plain. He had his rifle, his bayonet, and one less bullet than he'd had before. I don't know if he would ever have hurt me.

His rifle was too large to shoot himself with. He had to make me do it instead.

Afterwards.

I was standing by the deserted field gun. I didn't know how I got there. Another man was with me: Anthony Church. There were meant to be three, but two had gone. Church must have sent them somewhere.

A second man came. Owen. More and more and then there were four and we were all there. We had to stay by the gun.

I've come to understand that it was staid and thorough Reggie Owen who waded into the forest and pulled me out. After all, the ocean wasn't that deep.

I still couldn't breathe.

They came for the artillery gun, in the end. The Japanese.

Things were told to me. I didn't hear them. And then someone took pity on me and led me by the shoulder back to Sasha.

CHAPTER TWENTY-ONE

I came to in flashes along that long and terrible plain of wakefulness. Every time I woke, it was in Sasha's arms.

CHAPTER TWENTY-TWO

Sasha was so soft, so gentle with me.

I finally came to properly with his hand in my hair. His voice reverberating in his throat, through my skin and my skull. He'd shushed me and held me like a child. I turned into him, trying to block out all the world with him. His smell. That strong fresh tea-smell of his sweat. The mould of his uniform; the steady fast drumbeat of his heart. Him, and him, and him. I hung on to all of it. I listened to it. Up and down. I rose and fell on it like the sea. He stroked my hair like a child and I cried onto him.

I later found out, among other things, that it was Mitya who'd made sure I got to Sasha. When Owen had brought me back from the forest, loose and unseeing, it was he who had taken pity on my pathetic figure. Pried Warren's frantic hand from my sleeve as he'd talked at me, mud down his face. Then Mitya had led me back, into Sasha's anxiously waiting arms.

He'd had the rear car cleared for us. There had been room, then, for it to go back to being a supply car. He'd insisted that I needed space and quiet. Bannatyne had agreed. Owen had agreed. Mitya had enforced.

There were a lot of questions about what had happened that afternoon in the woods. We came, gradually, to understand. A group of partisans, left behind, had been trying their luck on a piece of track they'd come across—as we had surmised, from their guns. Their positions. As is the Army. Give them an inch and they'll take a mile. It will be a mile in the wrong direction, but they'll take it anyway. The group who'd got us had been going for the Japanese. They'd done the same on roads and the farm tracks. They'd had no idea, I am told, about the significance of the place. They'd apparently had no idea we were coming. I don't know how far I believe that.

The Japanese had panicked, as we all had done. The plane had been theirs.

It had been on manoeuvres when Eto had radioed the situation to his headquarters. The damage the train had taken was structural; the cars were riddled with holes. If we had been entrained at the time, we would have been trapped like animals. As it was, we had five dead and twelve casualties. At least there was a real hospital in Vlady.

As we left, the Japanese moved up from Svagena to Dukoveskoie. They seemed to push their right out as far as they could behind enemy positions. I gathered it was a theme with them.

In the early evening after our departure, they'd begun to envelop the area to their left. They had two heavy batteries, one of which had been supported with the two guns we'd captured that day: old and German make. They had been installed long before: 1918, 1917, perhaps. Relics of a larger war. The fact that they had been overlooked was both deplorable and typical.

Radiating out from that beautiful Orthodox church on the hill, the Japanese units were in position before sunset. We left them like that: watching and waiting. Alone and facing the land we left. I don't know what happened after. I won't, if I can help it. What good could ever come of what we left? A wiser man than me once said, *"Look not to left nor right:*

"In all the endless road you tread
"There's nothing but the night."

CHAPTER TWENTY-THREE

After all the time and effort I had spent imagining the journey back over that bridge to Vladivostok, I was barely there to witness it, folded as I was in Sasha's arms most of the time, unable to face the world. His scent was all that mattered to me—his smell.

Toby wasn't talking to me anymore, by that point. He must have finally guessed.

That day we crossed the bridge, I was warned that there might be an inquest into what had happened that day by the gun.

If there was, I've never heard of it. They buried James, Gallehawk, Jacobs, and a few others in the churchyard overlooking the sea that they'd spent all this time fighting towards. Uncoffined, just as found.

Later, in hospital, I could make out a little tapestry of noises from the men. They coagulated later on. No blame was ascribed by them, it seemed. And Toby hardly wanted to pursue the matter of Jacobs's and Gallehawk's deaths. Not in the least because the first thing Warren had done on landing had been to go straight to Regimental HQ and report him for gross negligence.

"He didn't phrase it in quite those terms," said Sasha. "But that was the upshot."

The six of us had been alone out there, trying to take that gun. Toby hadn't sent any support after us. He'd undercut Warren and gone after the second gun himself, leaving the train uncommanded. As the most senior lieutenant, he should have stayed back and made sure everyone got where they needed to be. Warren seemed to think if more men had been in support, then what happened to Jacobs and Gallehawk wouldn't have happened. Warren thought it was unforgiveable to neglect a duty like that in pursuit of vain glory. I couldn't find it in me to care.

Instead, I lay down and replayed shooting my friend in the head. Again and again and again.

Two days in Vlady and they still hadn't worked out what to do with me.

There'd been a frenzy of twenty-four hours and two-day passes issued on arrival to all the men that weren't needed for packing. All the freedom they hadn't had previously in one fell swoop. There are hotels in Vlady, bars and clubs. The company was put up at a hotel by the waterfront, awaiting the rest of the battalion.

I wasn't. I was still in hospital where there was always someone looking over me. They didn't need the beds, yet.

It was my last day there when Sasha kissed me gently on the side of the head and said, "I wish you knew me."

"I do," I said, gently bewildered. "Know you."

He smiled. "I hope you will."

I hope that Jacobs had wanted me to shoot him. I will never know.

I'd taken Mitya's hand just before they sent him back, and said the first words I'd said to anyone, apart from Sasha. "Good luck. I'll miss you."

He nodded, a warm and stoic brightness under his face. "You too."

We had left him behind, of course. He had been just as impassive as always, just as tall and imposing and sharp.

Would he be all right?

Jacobs could not have shot himself with that rifle. There had been no way forward for him, than to get me to shoot him. Pretending to aim at me. He would never actually have shot me. I'm sure.

I'm sure. I hope I'm sure.

God, I will never stop hoping that he wanted to die.

There was no way through the war. We'd have to go around. It was the sixteenth of November. I was standing on the deck of a ship called the *Wessex*, and she'd been sent to bring us back. Across the Pacific to Canada, across Canada to the Atlantic. Across the Atlantic to home.

The Czech headquarters had barely registered that Sasha was with us. Just as Eto had said, they hadn't seemed to care. An entire section had been wiped out, and all they'd got back was a half-mad captain. It would be a waste of resources to send him to the front now. So he was coming all the way to England with us. With me.

That was all the distance I could ever allow him again.

Sasha was with me. Or I was with him. Home would never be anywhere now, except with him.

I didn't know what he'd do when he left Russia.

He had told me of where he lived, far north in the mountains. I knew it as Reichenberg, but he called it Liberec.

We'd spoken of his home for a minute or two, before the conversation had lapsed. Now he said, "You should come and visit. You seem nice."

I kicked his foot.

He laughed and stood slightly closer to me. Our hands rested on the handrail together, as close as propriety would allow. "I'd like to."

There was a bustle of people behind us. There always was. So many people—there always were. Men I knew; men I had shared the past year with. Men I could navigate around in the dark.

"You'll come?" I asked him, for what must have been the fifth time. "You'll come to stay, when we land?"

Although I couldn't see his face, I could feel him smile. "I will."

I couldn't wait to have him in my house—with my sisters and my cats and a warm bed and stew. To be in the garden with him. When we were out of view of the place, I would kiss him so soundly it would take breathlessness to force us apart. And maybe one day, when all this was a dream, maybe we would talk.

I knew my demons. I could only imagine his.

Whatever I imagined, there was nothing that would dissuade me from him. I turned and he met my eyes. "You know I'll stay with you." He flashed a smile, and I got the briefest glance of him in mufti. A serial-smile flasher, a loveable rogue.

My heart beat. I held his gaze and tried to say everything I could without speaking it.

He already knew. He touched my hand, and we watched in silence as the engine throbbed beneath us. Until the land fell away, and there was nothing but sea.

Dear Reader,

Thank you for reading Ravella Ives's *Cold Comfort*!

We know your time is precious and you have many, many entertainment options, so it means a lot that you've chosen to spend your time reading. We really hope you enjoyed it.

We'd be honored if you'd consider posting a review—good or bad—on sites like **Amazon, Barnes & Noble, Kobo, Goodreads, Twitter, Facebook, Tumblr,** and your blog or website. We'd also be honored if you told your friends and family about this book. Word of mouth is a book's lifeblood!

For more information on upcoming releases, author interviews, blog tours, contests, giveaways, and more, please sign up for our weekly, spam-free newsletter and visit us around the web:

Newsletter: riptidepublishing.com/newsletter
Twitter: twitter.com/RiptideBooks
Facebook: facebook.com/RiptidePublishing
Goodreads: tinyurl.com/RiptideOnGoodreads
Tumblr: riptidepublishing.tumblr.com

Thank you so much for Reading the Rainbow!

RiptidePublishing.com

AUTHOR NOTES

Although the Royal Light Hertfordshires never existed, their journey and movements are based on that of the 1/9th (Cyclist) Battalion (Royal Hampshire) and the 25th Bn Middlesexes—or the *Die Hards*—who fought under Colonel John Ward during the Allied intervention in the Russian Civil War. Spelling of place names, such as 'Ussurie' and 'Sungary', reflect contemporary British spellings rather than contemporary or modern-day Russian usage.

In September 1919, an Allied offensive was launched against the Tobol front in a final attempt to change the course of the war in the East. In the narrative, this is the offensive in which Sasha is due to take part and which Hayek is sent back to. Its failure signalled the end of Allied intervention on the Eastern front, and by December the White Army in Siberia had effectively been disbanded altogether. The march across Lake Baikal that Francis describes in Chapter Twelve happened almost exactly as narrated, and is part of what has become known as the 'Great Siberian Ice March'.

On 14 November 1919, Omsk was captured by the Red Army. Admiral Kolchak resigned as head of the White Army forces in Siberia. He was arrested by the Czechoslovak Corps as he made his way to Irkutsk in the opening of 1920. He and his Prime Minister were executed in early February.

The 1/9th Cyclists left Vladivostok on 1 November 1919 and arrived back in Southampton on December 5th. Assuming the 6RLH take the same amount of time across Canada, Francis and Sasha would arrive back on 20 December 1919.

The other Ransome referred to by Teddy Napier is Arthur Ransome, children's author and journalist who spent much of the 1910s in Russia as a foreign correspondent and provided information to the Secret Intelligence Service (MI6). The "wife troubles" alluded to by Teddy—so far as we know—had nothing to do with his sexuality.

Confusingly, the phrase "public school" does not mean a school open to the public. British public schools are schools given independence from direct jurisdiction by the Public Schools Act 1868. Historically this refers to the original seven; Charterhouse, Eton College, Harrow, Rugby, Shrewsbury, Westminster, and Winchester College. The term is often used as a catchall—especially in a period context—for an elite all-male boarding school. Stonyhurst—Sasha's alma mater—was attended by Arthur Conan Doyle (Moriarty was named after a fellow pupil); Oscar Wilde's two sons; Evelyn Waugh, and Waugh's creation the Earl of Brideshead. Gerald Manley Hopkins was a Classics teacher and J.R.R. Tolkien wrote sections of *The Hobbit* while staying at the school with his son, who was also a teacher there.

Gerald Eversley's Friendship: A Study in Real Life (1895) is a novel by J.E.C. Welldon about the friendship between two public school boys. As with many novels of the time, it celebrates the cult of Victorian "manly love" while simultaneously hyperaware and particularly scornful of "indecent behaviour."

Other texts mentioned in *Cold Comfort* are mostly poems, aside from an allusion to *Macbeth* ('make assurance double sure') and H. G. Wells's *The Red Room*. Poems quoted include Bret Harte's "What the Bullet Sang" ("I shall know him by his face/By his godlike front and grace"); Homer's *The Iliad* ("Stay here in charge of what is yours/and do not go wandering the unharvestable sea"); Wilfred Owen's "Smile, Smile, Smile" ("not many anywhere now save under France,"); Thomas Hardy's "Drummer Hodge"; and A. E. Housman's "Now hollow fires burn out to black" and "On the idle hill of summer," both published in *A Shropshire Lad*.

Neither Owen's poetry nor this particular translation of Homer (which I first came across in Adam Nicholson's 2015 *Why Homer Matters*) were known at the time. However, I thought their particular elegiac tone suited Francis's particular elegiac mind, and so they stayed.

ACKNOWLEDGEMENTS

Cold Comfort originally started as a book about a woman living in the aftermath of the First World War and the Czech man who lived in her lighthouse. As I started writing, I found the narrative voice better suited to her brother and what he'd carried through the war. Eventually, I realised that if this story was going to take shape at all, I'd have to go back into his past rather than his stultifying present.

The book that became *Cold Comfort* started on a notepad in Holland and followed me from a Cambridge college attic to several flatshares and three continents. My life has changed almost unrecognisably since I first conceived of Sasha, Francis, and the Ransome family (who went through many surnames), but they were there through it all.

This book is much indebted to any number of sources, most notably Ian Hay's *The First Hundred Thousand* (from whom I borrowed Toby's monikers 'the Fairy Godmother Department' and the 'Department of Practical Jokes'); *With the Die Hards in Siberia* by John Ward; *Training for the Trenches* by Captain Leslie Vickers; *The Siberian Overland Route from Peking to Petersburg* by Alexander Michie; *North Russia Expedition Summer 1919: A Diary* by Mr R A Jowett; *The Allied Intervention in Russia, 1918-1920: The Diplomacy of Chaos* by Ian C. D. Moffat; *Interwar East Central Europe, 1918-1941: The Failure of Democracy-building, the Fate of Minorities*, ed. Sabrina Ramet; *The Military Writings of Leon Trotsky Volume 1, 1918: How the Revolution Armed—THE CIVIL WAR IN THE RSFSR IN 1918—THE CZECHOSLOVAK MUTINY*, transcribed for the Trotsky Internet Archive by David Walters; *The Literary Representation of the Czechoslovak "Legions" in Russia* by Robert B. Pynsent; *White Siberia: The Politics of*

Civil War by Norman G. O. Pereira; "The Allies and the Czech Revolt against the Bolsheviks in 1918" by J. F. N. Bradley (*The Slavonic and East European Review*); *A Well-Kept Secret: The Allied Invasion of North Russia, 1918-1919* by William Ward; and the wonderful OldMapsOnline.org. and rh1hamps.com, which provided invaluable info on the movements of the 1/9 Cyclists, who eventually became the Hertfordshires.

Cold Comfort would also not be in front of you right now—down to the title—were it not for the efforts of Caz, Grace, Alex, L.C., and the rest of the team at Riptide. Thank you so much for taking the chance, and thank you for your constant support.

And thank you, for picking this book up. I hope you enjoyed, and I hope we meet again.

ABOUT THE AUTHOR

Ravella Ives likes heavy metal and buying secondhand Doc Martens. When she isn't milling away at the day job, she spends her time directing and producing plays, thinking about her never-ending Ph.D. thesis and telling people how to spell her name.

Enjoy more stories like
Cold Comfort
at RiptidePublishing.com!

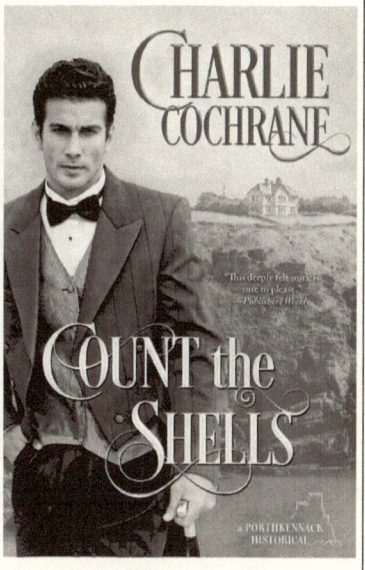

Dancing with the Lion:
Becoming

Two boys, one heroic bond,
and the molding of Greece's
greatest son.

ISBN: 978-1-62649-897-6

Count the Shells

Is he the answer to an old
soldier's prayers or the last straw
to break his back?

ISBN: 978-1-62649-655-2